DYING FOR MERCY

MARY JANE CLARK

DYING FOR MERCY

WILLIAM MORROW

An Imprint of HarperCollins*Publishers*

DYING FOR MERCY. Copyright © 2009 by Mary Jane Clark. All rights reserved. Printed in the United States of America. No part of this book may be used or reproduced in any manner whatsoever without written permission except in the case of brief quotations embodied in critical articles and reviews. For information address HarperCollins Publishers, 10 East 53rd Street, New York, NY 10022.

HarperCollins books may be purchased for educational, business, or sales promotional use. For information please write: Special Markets Department, HarperCollins Publishers, 10 East 53rd Street, New York, NY 10022.

FIRST EDITION

Library of Congress Cataloging-in-Publication Data

Clark, Mary Jane Behrends.
    Dying for Mercy / Mary Jane Clark. — 1st. ed.
        p. cm.
    ISBN 978-0-06-128611-7
    1. Women journalists—Fiction.   2. Rich people—Crimes against—Fiction.
    3. Tuxedo Park (N.Y.)—Fiction.   4. Serial murderers—Fiction.   I. Title.
    PS3553.L2873D95 2009
    813'.54—dc22   2009016272

09 10 11 12 13   OV/RRD   10 9 8 7 6 5 4 3 2 1

Once again, for Elizabeth and David.
And for Steve Simring, who helped me solve my own puzzle.

# PROLOGUE

A FEW HOURS FROM NOW . . .

The moonlight trickled through the glass roof. He pulled a large clay pot from the corner of the room and sat on the cold ground beside it. Then he removed his shoes and socks.

To be accurate, he would have had to use thick nails and a lance to make the wounds—but how would he be able to hammer the nails into both his hands or maneuver the long spear into his own side? The hunting knife would have to do.

He held the blade in his right hand first. He drew up his knees so that his feet would be as close to the rest of his body as possible. Leaning forward, he positioned the point of the knife over his foot. He closed his eyes and pushed.

He let out a long groan while pulling out the knife. Then he quickly repeated the motion on the other foot. He tried to block his mind from the searing pain, directing his thoughts instead to the greater good that would come from this act.

Turning his left palm upward, he held the back of his hand against the ground to steady it. The knife found its mark in the middle of his lifeline.

He must act quickly, not knowing how rapidly he would bleed out or if he would lose consciousness. He transferred the hunting knife to his left hand, opened his right hand, and stuck the blade into his palm. There was only one thing remaining to do.

SUNDAY
OCTOBER 4

CHAPTER 1

Y ou look pretty, Mom."

Facing the mirror, Eliza stared at the reflection of the child standing behind her in the middle of the bathroom floor. Janie was wearing her soccer uniform. One kneesock was bunched around her thin ankle, dirt smudged both her knees, and more wisps of brown hair sprang free from her ponytail than were caught up in it. Her cheeks were still slightly flushed from running up and down the school field. Turning, Eliza bent and kissed her seven-year-old daughter on the top of the head.

"Thank you, sweetheart." Eliza held herself back from gathering the child in her arms and holding her close. It was a familiar urge now, the desire to hang on to Janie and not let go. Almost three months since the kidnapping, and Eliza still woke up in a cold sweat many nights. How close she'd come to losing her only child, the daughter whose father had tragically died before she was even born, the little girl who was at the center of Eliza's world.

"I want to come with you," said Janie.

"I wish you could, honey, but it's a party for adults. There won't be any children there."

MARY JANE CLARK

"But Valentina and Innis would want me to come," insisted Janie, hands on hips. "They like me. When we went to their house that time, they said I could come again anytime I want."

Eliza turned back to the mirror and picked up a tube of mascara. "I know they did. And we will go there again. Remember I told you about the little house we've rented near the Wheelocks'? Our lease starts next week. I'm sure we'll be able to visit Valentina and Innis when we go up there on weekends."

Janie's expression brightened. "Can we go in the birdhouse?"

"It's called an aviary, Janie, and I think that can be arranged."

"You know, they have a bird in there that talks," said Janie.

"A parrot?"

"Uh-huh. Innis showed me. And it can tell you what it likes."

"Really?" asked Eliza as she put gloss on her lips.

"Yep. It says 'sun' and 'air' and 'grapes.' It likes to eat grapes."

"You'll have to show it to me," said Eliza.

Mollified, Janie followed her mother as she walked into the bedroom, went to the closet, and took the jewelry case from the wall safe.

"Which ones should I wear?" Eliza asked as they sat side by side on the bed. "The pearls or the garnets?"

Janie considered carefully before answering. "The dark red ones," she said decisively. "They're the color of your dress."

"Good choice," said Eliza, fastening the stones to her ears. She stood, slipped on her heels, and took a last look in the full-length mirror.

"What kind of party is it, Mom?" asked Janie as they left the bedroom and went down the stairs. "A birthday party?"

"Not exactly," Eliza answered. "It's a party to celebrate the feast day of St. Francis of Assisi."

"Are you bringing him a present?"

Eliza laughed. "No, sweetheart, he won't be there. St. Francis died a long time ago."

"Then why are they having a party for him?"

"Valentina and Innis want to celebrate his spirit. St. Francis was a very good and holy man who did many things to help many people and animals in his lifetime. He's the patron saint of Italy, and when Valentina and Innis lived there, they became very devoted to him."

"Did people give him parties when he was still alive?" asked Janie.

"I don't think so," said Eliza. "He taught repentance. Parties weren't on his agenda."

"That's too bad," said the child.

"I doubt that St. Francis thought so, Janie. He loved nature and animals and wanted the people who followed him to live simply and take care of other people. I suppose St. Francis would consider a party like this frivolous."

Janie cocked her head to the side. "What does 'frivolous' mean?" she asked.

"Silly, not really important."

Janie considered this. "I don't think my birthday party is silly. I think it's very important."

"Of course it is," said Eliza, "but as you get older, a birthday party, believe it or not, isn't always something you want. Besides, I bet St. Francis would rather see the money spent on his party go to feeding the poor."

While Janie thought about this, Eliza looked out the living-room window and saw yet another car driving slowly past her house. The place where they lived had become a tourist attraction since the kidnapping. Sightseers strained for a glimpse of the famous mother and the daughter who'd been the subject of a nationwide search.

Eliza hated the loss of privacy. Ordering tall evergreens to be planted along the front of the property might help shield them from prying eyes, but she knew the drive-bys would continue.

She'd hired a security company and it was reassuring to see the car parked out front. The guard inside was watching—and armed. The local police also patrolled the street more often these days.

Still, Eliza knew that no amount of security could absolutely guarantee that something wouldn't happen to her child. She had to live with the fact and try not to dwell on it.

"Mrs. Garcia," called Eliza as she saw her driver pull up, "I'm leaving."

The housekeeper came out of the kitchen and put her arm around Janie's shoulders as Eliza uttered yet another silent prayer of gratitude that Mrs. Garcia had survived the kidnapping as well. That the FBI had found both before it was too late was a miracle.

"We are going to have a good time while your mommy is out, aren't we, *niña*?" Mrs. Garcia asked Janie. "I think we make some brownies."

"I won't be late," said Eliza as she started for the door.

Janie reached out and grabbed her mother's dress.

"What, Janie? What is it, sweetheart?" asked Eliza, fearing she had been wrong to accept the invitation. Yet Valentina Wheelock had been so insistent that Eliza come to the party, and the Wheelocks' house in Tuxedo Park was only twenty minutes away from Ho-Ho-Kus. Now, as she looked down at her daughter holding onto the red fabric of her dress, Eliza doubted she'd made the right decision to go to this party. "What's wrong, Janie?" Eliza asked again as she bent to look directly into her daughter's eyes.

"What does 'repentance' mean?"

"What?" asked Eliza.

"You said St. Francis taught repentance," said Janie. "What is that?"

"Basically it means being sorry for things you've done," Eliza answered with relief that Janie was focused only on a definition.

"What kinds of things?" asked Janie.

"Sins," said Eliza. "The kinds of things nobody should ever do."

CHAPTER 2

Everything had to be perfect tonight.

Innis Wheelock descended the marble steps of the grand spiral staircase that led from the upper levels of the mansion down to the main floor. In the dining room, caterers were ensuring that all was in readiness for the party. Pots of orchids from the greenhouse and sparkling silver chafing dishes were spread out on the enormous trestle table, which tonight would serve as a huge buffet. From there, Innis wandered down the long vaulted gallery that led to the expansive double parlor. He walked over to the elaborate fireplace and rubbed his hands on the highly polished wood surface of the mantel, admiring the expert craftsmanship of the carvings that adorned it. Four hand-cut blocks, protruding from the front, each with a letter inscribed on its face, spelling "ROMA." A tribute to Innis's beloved city.

Innis sank into one of the down-filled armchairs and looked around, thinking about what had led up to this evening's event: the months of meticulous designing, the many shopping trips in Italy, carefully choosing which architectural elements to ship back to the United States in giant wood and metal containers. Innis had plotted and planned and finally assembled all the elements that would make up his final puzzle.

Executing the renovation had taken professional help from the architect, carpenters, masons, plumbers, electricians, and landscape engineers. Innis had coordinated it all. The result had been worth it. Pentimento was a gracious, unique home, with every modern convenience, yet brimming with Old World charm and character.

The house hadn't always been called Pentimento. Everyone in the park had known it as the Abbate place when Valentina had grown up in the mansion. She hadn't understood when he told her what he wanted to call their newly refurbished home.

"But a pentimento is an alteration in a painting, isn't it? It allows you to see traces of the artist's original work, showing that the artist changed his mind about the composition during the process of painting. What does that have to do with our home?" she'd asked.

"I've changed my mind about the composition of my life, dear one," Innis had answered. "I want to alter it. The work I've done on this house is a start."

Valentina had shrugged and gone along, not pressing him for any details. Innis suspected that Valentina felt that it was easier, and safer, not to press the issue. After thirty-five years of marriage and a political career that had been supported and orchestrated largely by Innis, Valentina seemed satisfied enough with their life. She wasn't interested in shaking things up or changing anything—except perhaps the screeching birds he had stocked in the aviary he'd insisted on building.

The inspiration for the aviary, as for almost everything else Innis had planned at Pentimento, came from St. Francis. While studying Giotto's huge frescoes of the saint's life on the walls of the basilica in Assisi, Innis had become fascinated with the one depicting St. Francis preaching to the birds that had filled the trees on both sides of an

Italian road. Drawn by the power of his voice, the birds surrounded him, listening intently, it seemed, as he reminded them that God had given them everything—rivers and fountains for their thirst, tall trees for their nests, mountains and valleys for their shelter—and that they should always seek to praise the God to whom they owed so much.

Innis had wondered if the episode with the birds had really happened or whether it was just part of folklore. Whatever the case, it was while studying the fresco that Innis decided what he had to do.

He was certain that he hadn't always praised God by his actions, until now. In fact, he knew too well that he'd done things that God would condemn. He had to atone for those things and make up, as much as possible, for the evil he had committed. He had to make sure, as well, that justice was done in the future.

"Pentimento" came from *pentire*, the Italian word for repent. Tonight the repentance would begin. But first he had to hide the video camera, the final puzzle piece.

CHAPTER 3

As the sun set over the Ramapo Mountains, the man in the stone guardhouse leaned forward to peer through the car window, craning his neck to get a better view of the passenger in the backseat.

"Eliza Blake is a guest of the Wheelocks," said the driver.

The security guard was careful to keep his facial expression neutral.

Even in the failing light, she was recognizable. The wide-set blue eyes, the straight nose, the dark, shoulder-length hair. He felt a pang as she smiled at him, the smile that had greeted him so many times from the television screen.

"Good evening," she said.

"Evening, ma'am," he answered, wanting to say more but holding back. He would like to tell Eliza that he was a big fan, that he thought she was the best of all the morning-show hosts, that he appreciated having her input each day, having her keep him company while he drank his first cup of coffee. But it wasn't his place to have any sort of personal conversation with residents or their guests. It had been made quite clear to him when he was hired that his job was to keep anyone who didn't belong in Tuxedo Park out of Tuxedo Park. He was to remain professional and polite and never hobnob or socialize with the people whose security he protected.

Checking his clipboard, he gave the driver directions, pushed the mechanism to raise the gate, and watched as the car drove through, past the massive old stone gatehouse and the tower that flanked the road and onward up the hill.

CHAPTER 4

After Innis finished his task, he found his wife standing at the bottom of the grand staircase. She appeared relieved when she saw him.

"Where have you been?" asked Valentina. "I've been looking for you, Innis. Our guests will be here in a few minutes."

"I had one last detail to take care of," said Innis. "Everything is going to be perfect tonight. It's all going to go according to plan."

Valentina reached out to straighten her husband's tie. "You sound like you're talking about a campaign, not a party," she said.

He stared at her, studied her, trying to press every detail of her face forever in his memory.

"What is it, Innis? Why are you looking at me like that? Do I have lipstick on my teeth or something?"

"No, my dear one, nothing is wrong. You look absolutely beautiful, elegant in your black velvet. I was just thinking about the long journey we've taken together and how lucky I was to be married to a woman like you."

"It hasn't all been a bed of roses," said Valentina. "We certainly haven't agreed on everything."

"I know we haven't."

Valentina turned her back toward Innis. "Zip me up the rest of the way, will you?"

As he caught sight of the soft white skin on her neck, he swallowed. He was going to be leaving her exposed and vulnerable. But he had to be resolute.

"I've tried to shield you from things, Valentina," he whispered. "But there are some things that must be faced, sooner or later."

She spun around to face him. "I thought we agreed not to talk about it anymore."

"Not talk of what?" asked Innis. "Which *one* of the things don't you want to talk about? There have been so many. And others you don't even know about."

"Look, this isn't the time," said Valentina, reaching up to smooth her blond hair. "We've got almost a hundred people coming tonight. Let's not start the evening with another fight."

CHAPTER 5

Eliza sat back and looked out the window at the darkening woods that rimmed the winding road. She marveled at the thought of the roadway's having been forged up the mountain and through the thick virgin forest without the aid of electricity or giant earthmoving equipment. No computer animations had been used to plot the route, no giant trucks had transported building materials.

Hundreds of acres of forbidding terrain with huge granite boulders and rocky soil had been transformed by the great vision and willpower of tobacco heir Pierre Lorillard. What began as a fishing and hunting reserve just forty miles northwest of New York City was transformed into an exclusive year-round enclave for America's elite at the end of the nineteenth century.

The most renowned architects of the time designed massive "cottages," carriage houses, boathouses, and gardens situated to take advantage of the splendid mountains and glorious views of three lakes. Tuxedo Park was listed on the National Register of Historic Places, and as the old mansions set back from the road began to come into view, Eliza was glad. The houses were masterpieces and should be preserved. They represented a unique time in American history, a time when vast fortunes were amassed as the country galloped into the industrial revolution. The imposing structures were built with the cheap labor provided by the immigrant population streaming into the United States from Europe and maintained by that same cheap labor as well—with money not yet subject to the drain of income taxes.

For a while, if you were one of the fortunate, life was just about perfect. Then the government began taxing income. Next came the Roaring Twenties, followed by a decade of economic depression. Residents who had suffered business reversals could no longer afford to live in the park, but it was hard to find buyers for the big houses, even at bargain prices during the Depression and World War II. With workingmen and -women serving in the armed forces and employed in factories, there simply weren't enough servants for the upkeep and the mansions became uninhabitable. The decline of the park lasted for several decades. Some houses were deserted, some burned to the ground, some barely survived as heirs took to living in just a few rooms while they struggled to live on dwindling trust funds. Finally, at the end of the twentieth century, with a booming economy and stupendous fortunes made in industry and technology, sports and entertainment, the big houses became desirable again.

Tuxedo Park was still a privileged and protected world where residents didn't lock their doors or take the keys out of their car ignitions. Guarded by the enclave's own police department, Tuxedo Park's children ran free, their parents feeling safe. There were no leash laws for dogs. And, until recently, the houses had no numbers. Residences were referred to by the family's surname or by the name the house had been given by its original owners.

Before the first interview Eliza had done with Valentina, she learned that it was here in Tuxedo Park that Valentina Abbate and Innis Wheelock had grown up and gone to school together. It was here that they had married at the Abbates' Italianate villa perched on the hillside above Tuxedo Lake. It was to here that they had returned after their stints in the governor's mansion in Albany and the United States ambassador's residence in Rome.

In the twilight a deer darted out in front of the car, forcing the driver to slam on the brakes and Eliza to snap out of her reverie. She caught her breath as she watched the big doe leap across the road before disappearing into the woods.

"Thank God you didn't hit that beautiful creature, Charlie," said Eliza. "That would have been such a horrible way to start the night."

CHAPTER 6

*T*he party guests were arriving, and Valentina and Innis Wheelock were gracious and welcoming. So influential and accomplished were they that no one knew it was a sham. They had a secret. An explosive secret.

Yes, they loved each other; yes, they were devoted to each other. But their marriage was far from perfect. They hid things. They hadn't been fully honest with the public or with those they purported to care about.

You had to give credit where credit was due, though. Innis had insisted on that one-on-one conversation in his study, a chance to air any anger and resentment with no one else around to hear. He hadn't seemed shocked when he heard the feelings that gushed out. It was as if Innis had known exactly what would be said and didn't care. In fact, Innis had seemed pleased to listen as the ugly explanations for what had been done came spewing forth.

Innis responded with a diatribe of his own, promises to go public with everything and to ensure that justice would be done in the end.

And were they even promises—or threats? What did he mean when he said that the world was going to know?

Upon leaving the office, another potential threat appeared.

Eunice was standing outside the door. By the expression on her face and her flustered behavior, it was obvious that the maid had been eavesdropping.

Not that it wasn't understandable that Eunice would do such a thing. Anytime there was a chance to listen in on someone's conversation, it was an opportunity not to be wasted.

Eavesdroppers at Pentimento heard very valuable information.

CHAPTER 7

The car inched along the crushed-stone driveway, behind the other vehicles waiting for the chance to drop off their passengers. Spotlights were trained on the big house, illuminating the stucco façade and the colorful etched-glass windows with decorative crowns, while Corinthian columns stood guard across the full expanse of the entranceway. Red-clay tiles covered the extensive roof. A European garden was plotted at the side of the house. A copy of Bernini's famous turtle fountain in Rome stood in the center.

Valentina and Innis Wheelock were greeting their guests in the spacious entrance hall.

"Eliza!" Valentina's still incredibly beautiful face broke into a broad smile. Her blond hair was perfectly coiffed, swept up in an elegant French twist. Her makeup was expertly applied, making her skin appear smooth and creamy, her eyes a clear, brilliant blue. Sapphire earrings dangled from her lobes. She wore a simple but beautiful black cocktail dress and carried a martini glass in her left hand. Valentina extended her right one to Eliza, drawing her close, kissing her on the cheeks, and then putting her arm around Eliza's shoulder.

"I'm so glad to see you, darling," Valentina announced. "You look absolutely wonderful."

Valentina was known for her tact, diplomacy, and keen sense of what was appropriate and what wasn't. Those qualities, her years as chief executive of the Empire State, along with sizable donations and fund-raising parties given for the winning presidential candidate, had earned her the ambassadorship to Italy, the first woman to hold the post since Clare Boothe Luce did so during the Eisenhower administration.

"Look who's here, Innis," said Valentina, steering Eliza by the arm toward her husband. "Our new neighbor."

"Soon," said Eliza. "We get the place starting next weekend."

Eliza was taken aback as she looked into Innis Wheelock's face. His skin was sallow, his eyes bloodshot. He looked so much older and thinner than the last time she'd seen him. He was gaunt, really. When Eliza gripped his hand, she could feel a slight tremor.

"So good to see you, my dear," he said as he leaned forward and kissed Eliza on the cheek. "I'm so glad you've come."

"I'm happy to be invited," responded Eliza, smiling. "I've never been to a party for a saint before."

Innis smiled weakly. "To tell you the truth, neither have I," he said. "But I thought there was no better time to gather the people who have meant something to me over the years to honor someone who has changed my life."

"You'll have to tell me all about it, Innis," said Eliza.

"Yes, I would like that, Eliza," said Innis solemnly. "I want you to understand." He glanced over at the doorway and saw there were guests still arriving. "Excuse me now, dear," he said. "I'll catch up with you a bit later."

"I'll look forward to it," said Eliza.

As she began walking away, Valentina called after her. "And thanks so very much again, Eliza, for agreeing to be part of our

Special Olympics event next Sunday. People are terribly excited about your being there."

"It's my pleasure," said Eliza. "You know how I feel about supporting such a good cause."

Proceeding into the central room where the party was being held, Eliza wondered if Innis was ill. What else would account for the weight loss, the poor coloring, and his trembling?

She went to the bar and asked for a glass of white wine. While she waited, she surveyed the cavernous space, milling with people. Antique furniture was carefully placed throughout the room, creating different seating areas. The oil paintings on the walls were lit to their best advantage. Candles glimmered from crystal and silver candlesticks arranged on glistening wooden tabletops, while fresh flowers burst from porcelain vases and bowls. The rear wall was made up of floor-to-ceiling windows that revealed a spectacular view of Tuxedo Lake below.

"Thank you," she said as the bartender slid the glass of pinot grigio across the bar.

"You're welcome, ma'am," he said.

Eliza took a sip as she observed the guests socializing in the lush surroundings. "Beautiful, isn't it?" she murmured.

"Yes, it is."

"I guess you go to many of these things," said Eliza.

"If you call working at them 'going to them,'" answered the bartender with a melancholy smile, revealing a gap between his front teeth. "I've been working parties here in the park for many years."

"What are you doing, Bill?" asked a man dressed in a dark suit who walked up to the bar. "You know you shouldn't be bending this lovely lady's ear."

Eliza felt immediately uncomfortable, and she could tell from the flush rising in the bartender's fair-skinned cheeks that he was embarrassed.

"I was bending *his* ear, not the other way around."

"Well, I'm Peter Nordstrut," said the man as he held out his hand. His grip was strong. His face was a bit puffy, and he wore horn-rimmed glasses. The deep lines at the corners of his eyes and across his brow suggested he spent a lot of time in the sun, though any tan he had picked up over the summer had already faded. His hair was blond with gray running through it. Eliza judged him to be in his mid-fifties.

"Eliza Blake," she said, returning his handshake.

"Yes, I know. I'd say everyone in this room knows who you are."

Eliza smiled politely. "How do you know the Wheelocks?" she asked.

"From the club," answered Peter. "I've been trying to teach Innis to play court tennis, but I'm afraid it's a lost cause."

"Isn't court tennis the kind hardly anyone plays?" asked Eliza.

"Well, it isn't the number of people who play, it's the quality of the people who play that counts."

He said it with a smile, but Eliza sensed he was an unmitigated snob.

"Real tennis, royal tennis, court tennis—whatever you want to call it—it's not for the masses," he continued. "Lots of complicated rules. In fact, there are only about thirty-five existing courts for real tennis in the entire world."

"And Tuxedo Park has one of them?" asked Eliza, trying to sound interested.

Peter nodded. "I'd be happy to show it to you. Even better, come over to the tennis house sometime, and I'll teach you how to play."

Eliza laughed. "If Innis can't learn, I'm sure I couldn't either." She glanced across the room. "Speak of the devil," she said, hoping her relief didn't show, "here comes Innis now."

After a few minutes of small talk among the three of them, Innis took Eliza's arm. "Will you excuse us, Peter?" he asked. "I want to introduce Eliza to some of our other guests."

Innis led her off.

"Couldn't wait to get you away from that guy," he said as he guided her through the crowd. "Peter Nordstrut is a pompous know-it-all, and God help me, I've had way too much to do with him over the years. He's a crackerjack political operative, but not a very nice human being. Now, if you don't mind, I want to talk with you alone before I share you with anyone else."

Eliza followed Innis out through the French doors that led to the side garden.

"Only you, Innis, would have a reproduction of Bernini's fountain," said Eliza as she admired the small bronze tortoises and reached out to rub one of their shells.

"It was one of my favorite places in Rome," said Innis. "I could gaze at it for hours. Though I was disappointed to discover that Bernini may not have designed the fountain, only the turtles."

The night air had grown cooler, and Innis offered Eliza his jacket.

"I'm fine, thanks," Eliza said. Innis didn't look as if he could afford to be chilled. He seemed so frail that a heavy cold could lead to something fatal.

"Are you really fine, Eliza?" Innis asked with genuine concern. "I remember when we received kidnapping threats about Russell when Valentina was governor. She could barely function."

"I'm just trying to put it behind us now, Innis," said Eliza. "That's why I've rented the carriage house on Clubhouse Road. Janie and I can get up here easily on the weekends. It feels so protected and serene, as though nothing bad could ever happen here." Eliza shook her head. "You know, we still have people driving by our house in Ho-Ho-Kus and gawking at us. You'd think we'd be old news by now."

"It was a horrible thing, Eliza. They say time heals all wounds, don't they?" he asked pensively. "But there are some things one never gets over."

Eliza gave him time to continue.

"It's no secret that I changed while we were in Italy, Eliza," said Innis as they walked slowly around the fountain. "While Valentina was conducting embassy business in Rome, I filled much of my time walking the streets of the Eternal City and, later, traveling throughout Italy. I spent hours and hours at the Vatican, drinking in the magnificence of the Sistine Chapel and those incredible frescoes of Michelangelo." Innis shook his head in wonderment. "The majesty of them was beyond description, Eliza. Have you ever seen them?"

"Yes. But not since they've been cleaned. I hear they are so brilliant and vivid now. I have to get back to Rome and see them again."

"You must, you must," said Innis. "They'll take your breath away. There are so many glorious, unbelievable things to see in Italy. Not to mention some of the most delicious food in the world. Don't get me started on the food."

Eliza smiled. "Few would disagree with you there, Innis," she said.

"There will be some wonderful ravioli alla norcina and gnocchi with black-truffle cream on the buffet tonight, Eliza. Make sure you try some of both."

"I will," she said. She was waiting for Innis to get to the point.

He gestured at a bench, and they sat down. Gazing at the spouting water, Innis continued. "After the Sistine Chapel, I discovered other churches in Rome. The Basilica of St. Mary Major, where the Bethlehem manger is kept, and St. Paul Outside the Walls, where the apostle was buried—even Sant'Andrea della Valle, where the first act of Puccini's *Tosca* takes place. Then I went on to Florence and fell in love with the Baptistry, and Orvieto's striped Duomo. In the process I became fascinated with the ceremony and history of the Roman Catholic Church. But it was when I went to Assisi that I was moved on a deeply personal level. Studying the frescoes of the life of St. Francis in the basilica, I became so ashamed of myself."

Innis grew quiet and looked down at his hands.

"Ashamed of what, Innis?" Eliza asked gently.

"Of the life I've led," he answered, his head still bowed. "St. Francis was a man from a wealthy background, a guy who was set to inherit the family business and live out his days in a lavish lifestyle, a guy a lot like me. But unlike me, he gave everything up and lived his life without creature comforts, helping his fellow human beings. Then he established a religious order that has helped even more people."

"Somehow I don't see you in a homespun robe, walking barefoot down the road, Innis," said Eliza, trying to get him to lighten up. "Or in some sunless, airless monastery sleeping on the floor."

Innis smiled slightly. "No, I don't see that either. And I've never been overly fond of animals, and St. Francis was crazy for them. There's no way I'd have been able to talk that wolf out of eating those villagers."

"I'd forgotten all about that story," said Eliza, smiling. "Think it was true?"

Innis shrugged. "Who knows? But the essential story of his life is valid. This was a man who did things that truly mattered, and now, at the end of my life, I want to unite myself with him in the most vivid way possible, and to do my part in putting the past to bed and saving the future."

Eliza wasn't sure what he meant. "You certainly have done things that mattered, Innis," she said.

He looked at her incredulously. "How can you say that? Be honest, Eliza, what about my life is there to admire?" He didn't wait for her to respond. "No real accomplishments of my own, no good works to speak of—"

Eliza interrupted. "That's not true. You've donated generously to many charities."

"Anyone at my stage of the game can write a check, Eliza. But what have I done to make a difference in somebody's life? The truth is, I've hurt many people, damaged them, ruined them along the way. Politics is a dirty business. And I've finally admitted to myself that some of the things I told myself were necessary to get Valentina elected governor were done out of pure ambition. And now it's too late to take those things back."

"Innis, why are you telling me all this?" asked Eliza.

"Because I know how my world works, Eliza. Ugly things happen, cruel things, and they never see the light of day. And people get away with things that should never be gotten away with. That isn't right. You know it isn't right. You care about right and wrong. I know you do." His voice cracked.

"What are you talking about, Innis?"

"You'll see, Eliza. You'll see," he said, rising from the bench. "And I know you'll do what needs to be done. You're shivering now, dear. Let's go back inside and join the party."

CHAPTER 8

There you go, sir," said Bill O'Shaughnessy as he put a glass of vodka down on the bar. "Good health to you."

The guest lifted the drink and walked away without saying a word to the bartender. With no one else waiting to be served, Bill sliced another lime. Wiping his hands, he looked up and saw Innis Wheelock walking in from the garden with that woman from morning television.

This was some party. The Wheelocks had invited lots of people from inside the park along with many city people who had come out from Manhattan. He didn't really understand the reason for the celebration; nobody he knew ever threw a party for a saint. But the wealthy were a different breed as far as Bill was concerned. Over the years he'd witnessed rich people trying to outdo one another in coming up with new themes for their parties. He had to give the Wheelocks credit for originality with this one.

Bill bent down behind the bar to open another bag of ice. When he straightened, Valentina Wheelock was waiting for him. As he looked at her, Bill knew she must be in her sixties now, but he thought she was still ravishing. He suspected he would always think so. For Bill, some wrinkles and lines didn't diminish her great beauty.

"How are we doing?" she asked. "Everyone enjoying themselves?"

"Yes, ma'am," he answered.

"We have enough of everything?"

Bill nodded. "Yes, ma'am, I think we're in good shape."

"Good," said Valentina. She turned partially and looked out at the room. "Nice party, isn't it, Bill?"

"Very nice, Mrs. Wheelock."

"Do you think St. Francis would approve?"

Bill felt he should be cautious with his answer. You never knew how they were going to react. It wasn't a good idea to joke, because too many of the people he worked for didn't have much in the way of a sense of humor. Bill knew they didn't think of him as being on their social level and that a joke or a criticism or a display of any sort of familiarity would not go over well. He was the hired help, and his job was to be respectful and pour the drinks.

"I couldn't say, Mrs. Wheelock," Bill answered. He could feel his face flush.

"Oh, yes, you could, Bill," Valentina urged. "You won't hurt my feelings. This was Innis's idea, and I just went along to keep him happy. Go ahead, go out on a limb and tell me what you think."

Bill wished she wouldn't do that, push him, tease him, encourage him. She had done that from the very beginning. He remembered the first time he saw her when she walked into the Black Tie Club on another October night almost thirty years before.

The Fall Ball was always held on the third Saturday of October. One legend had it that at the first Fall Ball back in 1886 the grandson of Pierre Lorillard, along with some of his friends, showed up at the party in cutoff tailcoats, and the tuxedo was born. The presentation of debutantes at the Fall Ball was the start of the New York social season for over eight decades.

Bill was new to working at the club back then. His father, who earned his living as a gardener there, had gotten Bill the job. He could recall how nervous he'd been. He hadn't felt comfortable, didn't feel like he belonged. And he didn't. He could only observe the people in Tuxedo Park and marvel at their world.

But it wasn't the young ladies his age, in their frothy white gowns, making their debuts, who had intrigued Bill that evening. It was a woman fifteen years older than he who caught his attention. When Valentina walked in on Innis Wheelock's arm, Bill and every other man in the room had eyed her with admiration and Innis with envy. When she took to the dance floor in her blue gown, her blond hair long and loose, it had seemed to Bill, stealing glances as he served food and cleared dinner plates, that Valentina moved as if she and the music were one. She mingled with the other guests, confident and regal.

Bill, exceedingly *un*confident, had wanted to disappear under one of the damask-covered tables when his shaking hand spilled a few drops of wine on the sleeve of Valentina's dress. She noticed it immediately, though no one else at the table had. Instead of commenting, she just looked up him, winked, and covered the spot with her napkin. At that moment, as his face flushed bright red, he fell in love.

Later she had pulled him aside. "Don't worry about the dress," she said. "Accidents happen."

"Thank you, ma'am. I'm so sorry, really sorry. Maybe I could have it cleaned for you?"

Valentina smiled. "That won't be necessary."

"I really appreciate that you didn't make a big thing about it at the table or mention it to my boss."

She looked over at her table. "They wouldn't have taken it very well, would they?"

Bill shook his head. "No, and I need this job."

"Are you doing this while you go to school?" she asked.

"No," said Bill, blushing again.

Valentina instantly understood. "Maybe you should think about that. College can make a big difference in somebody's life."

Bill had watched her walk off across the room, and in that instant he stood taller. For a week or two, he had actually considered Valentina's suggestion, but before he could broach the idea of college with his parents, his father suffered a severe heart attack. That was the end of Bill's brief flirtation with higher education, but his fascination with Valentina lived on.

Valentina had charm. Though she had never made a mortgage payment, never worried about paying her property taxes or electricity bills, she had the knack for making people feel that she understood their lives, felt their pain, and dreamed their dreams. Bill knew that the president of the United States himself had been enthralled with Valentina Wheelock.

"Bill?" Valentina's blue eyes were staring directly at his.

"Yes, ma'am."

"You haven't answered my question. Do you think St. Francis would approve of this party?"

Pushed, Bill answered, "I didn't know the man, but I remember from religion class that he was a guy who believed in living very simply." He shrugged. "I wonder if champagne, caviar, and filet mignon were a part of his diet."

Valentina laughed. "That's what I've always liked about you, Bill. In that careful way of yours, you get to the point—in this case, that this is a pretty inappropriate excuse for a party. But Innis really wanted to have this shindig, and he's been so serious and dour since we've come back from Italy that I was glad just to see that he wanted to have people in for a celebration, even if it is for a man who's been dead for almost eight hundred years."

CHAPTER 9

As they took their place on the buffet line, a man of medium height with longish salt-and-pepper hair stood in front of Eliza and Innis.

"Eliza, I'd like you to meet Zachary Underwood," said Innis. "Zack is the architect who worked wonders with this old place."

"The house had good bones to begin with," said Zack, smiling at Eliza. "And Innis had some very intriguing ideas about the renovation. He did a lot of the thinking for me."

"You're being too modest, Zack," said Innis. "You were presented with a real challenge, and you rose to meet it with flying colors." He excused himself and turned to speak to the guests behind him on the buffet line.

Eliza took a plate from the end of the table. "If I ever need an architect, I'll know who to call," she said. "Everything is fabulous— the house, the grounds. You feel like you're in another world in this place."

"That's what the people in the park want," he said. "Those who've lived here forever don't want the world to come in and change it, and most of the new people want to have a place to escape the intense life outside the gates. Everyone has a vested interest in keeping the park pretty much the way it's always been. They feel safe here."

Eliza sensed that he was about to say more, and she steeled herself for the possibility that Zack would bring up the kidnapping that had fascinated the country for the interminable five days while Janie was missing and then for the weeks since she was safely home. When he didn't broach the subject, Eliza felt herself relax.

"This ravioli looks and smells wonderful," Zack said as he took a large silver spoon. "Can I serve you some?"

"Thank you, yes." Eliza held out her plate. "What was the most interesting thing you discovered while you worked on this place?" she asked as they moved along the line.

Zack shook his head. "It's hard to pick just one thing. There were so many. I've worked on several renovations here in the park, and each of the houses has its own intriguing structural details, not to mention fascinating stories about previous residents. But Pentimento is special to me because it's not just about the past glories of the building and the people who lived here. It's the future of the house that could actually turn out to be the far more interesting and important phase."

"How so?" asked Eliza as she gathered up a fork and napkin at the end of the buffet table.

"Innis has big plans for this house, though even I don't know all the details. He's kept me in the dark about the reason for some of the things he asked me to design. He also had me sign a confidentiality agreement. I can't talk to anyone about the plans and designs for Pentimento." Zack motioned to the double parlor, and Eliza followed him to a love seat in the corner.

"Isn't that unusual?" asked Eliza as she sat down and spread her napkin on her lap. "Are architects usually asked to do that?"

"Not usually, but it does happen. People build their dream houses, and they can be very proprietary about them. They want their homes to be unique, and at the very least they don't want their architect doing the same design for the family down the block."

"I can understand that," Eliza said. "Yet if you don't know the details of what Innis is planning for the house, you wouldn't be breaking a confidentiality agreement by doing a little speculating, would you?" She smiled.

"You're not going to get anything out of me," Zack answered, smiling back. "Innis told me he has a big surprise planned for later tonight, and I don't want to take the chance of spoiling it."

CHAPTER 10

C lose to one hundred well-dressed and well-connected guests gathered in the vaulted gallery to listen to their host.

"I'd like to thank Valentina for putting up with me all these years and for agreeing to have this party, because she knew it was important to me. And I want to thank each and every one of you for being here tonight to celebrate with us and our son, Russell."

Heads turned to look at the tall, powerfully built young man standing against the wall. He smiled and nodded at his father.

Innis stood under a massive Venetian-glass chandelier and held up his drink while the guests raised theirs.

"All of you have meant something special to us. Valentina and I have known some of you most of our lives. Others we've met over the years through Valentina's time in government, and some are relatively new friends that we've gained since we returned from Italy."

There were beads of perspiration on Innis's brow as he continued speaking. "Valentina, *carissima*, come over here."

He kissed his wife on the forehead and put his arm around her.

"I want to take a moment to talk about the reason we are here to-night. St. Francis of Assisi."

"Ah, Innis," Valentina pleaded. "Do we have to ruin the evening with religion?"

The assemblage laughed. Innis smiled weakly.

"I promise I won't go on too long, dear," he said, as he took his arm away. "I know that most of you are aware I've become devoted to St. Francis, and I guess some of you might find that strange."

The room was quiet as everyone listened.

"All of us have done things which we'd do differently if given a chance. But that's not the way it works. You don't get a do-over. All you can do is repent, try to make up for it, and do what you can to ensure that the future is safeguarded. Yet sometimes there are things that, no matter how sorry you are, can't be rectified."

Innis looked down at his shoes and stood wordless for a moment.

"Anyway," he said as he lifted his face again, "what I'm trying to say is, I'm so grateful that I've been given this opportunity to redirect my life, that this humble Italian saint has shown me what I need to do going forward. As St. Francis said, 'Our actions are our own; their consequences belong to heaven.'"

There was an awkward silence in the room as Innis looked out with glistening eyes at his audience.

"Here's to St. Francis," someone called out, breaking the tension. The guests raised their glasses to their lips and drank with enthusiasm and relief.

"Has Innis totally lost it?" Eliza heard one of the guests ask another.

"He's always been an eccentric, but this is really strange. He must be driving Valentina out of her mind."

"I'm sure. Valentina has never been much of a churchgoer, except when she was running for office."

Both of the guests laughed.

CHAPTER 11

He was fairly certain that he had slipped out of the house unnoticed. On his way to the greenhouse, Innis looked back over his shoulder. Pentimento glowed as golden light drifted out from the many large windows. He could see his guests talking and laughing inside. Oblivious.

Under a full moon, he walked across the property and behind the high shrubs that hid the greenhouse from view. Light came through the glass-paned walls of the building, but Innis knew the way without it.

The hunting knife was in the drawer of the intricately carved Italian worktable, just where he'd put it after he'd had it cleaned and sharpened. A dull blade would have difficulty piercing the skin.

CHAPTER 12

Why was Innis creeping about late at night, on his own property, while a party was going on inside?

The man knew everything. He knew much too much, and if he was true to his word, he was going to make sure that the whole world knew, too.

Innis said he wanted justice.

That would ruin everything. All the meticulous planning, all the preparation, all the carefully crafted lies would be for naught. If everything was made public, the dream would be crushed.

What was he up to now? Why had he stolen away, and where was he going?

The sound of the greenhouse door closing indicated where Innis was, but what on earth was he doing in there?

CHAPTER 13

I have been all things unholy. If God can work through me, he can work through anyone."

Innis heard the saint's words over and over in his head.

"I have been all things unholy."

He picked up the knife and gripped the handle. He held it for a moment and closed his eyes, trying to summon the courage.

"I have been all things unholy."

He had to do this. He couldn't think of another way to repent, to make things right. Innis was sorry about the things that were going to come out, sorry to reveal such grave sins—and who had committed them. And he didn't feel right about what Valentina was going to have to face.

It couldn't be helped.

He could have left a written account of everything that had happened, laying the whole sordid story out at once. Instead, Innis had chosen a puzzle as his method. As each part of the puzzle was revealed, a little at a time, each guilty party would have a chance to come forward, confess, and repent.

"If God can work through me, he can work through anyone."

He wouldn't exit this world without leaving a record of all that had happened. What transpired after his death was in God's hands and he hoped Eliza Blake would be the instrument used to make things right.

As the blood oozed bright red against his pale flesh, Innis knew he wasn't part of the select group of holy men and women who had been chosen by God, the ones who had experienced the mystical appearance of the wounds. There had been over sixty of them, St. Francis being the first, with no logical explanation for the angry tears in their skin at the carefully chosen spots on their bodies.

Innis wasn't like them. There was nothing mystical about what was happening to him. He was doing it to himself.

He had read that the fluid that flowed from their cuts and punctures might not have been blood, but Innis was certain that it was blood leaking first from one foot, then from the other as he plunged the hunting knife into his extremities. He cried out with pain that shot through his mutilated body. Perspiration dripped from his brow and tears seeped down his cheeks.

Innis heard himself groaning loudly again as the knife he held pierced his left palm. He forced himself to repeat the process on his right hand.

"Dear God, dear God, help me," he prayed. "Help me get through this. I need your help, Lord, to make things right."

Switching grips again, and breathing heavily, Innis took the knife and leaned over awkwardly. He had practiced getting into position before, but it was a much different situation when both hands were bleeding and throbbing. Innis reached around and found a spot between his ribs on the left side of his body and pushed the knife through.

As he lay on the ground in the greenhouse, life draining from him, Innis wondered if St. Francis had felt this way when he had experienced the stigmata. Did the unexplained marks corresponding to the wounds of Christ that had appeared on the saint's body six years before he actually died hurt as much as the ones Innis had inflicted on himself in the very same places?

CHAPTER 14

Eliza was standing by the fireplace admiring the beautiful carvings that decorated it when she heard the clock on the mantel begin to chime. She glanced at the Roman numerals edging the face. Ten o'clock.

She was ready to go home.

As she tried to find her hosts to thank them for a lovely evening, Eliza was stopped several times by people who complimented her on her work on *KEY to America*.

"If the percentage of people at this party who say they watch our broadcast was representative of viewers nationwide, we'd have nothing to worry about with the ratings," she told them, laughing.

"But I really *do* watch your program," insisted a diminutive woman with steel gray hair arranged in a classic chignon style. She wore a simple navy dress with a vintage Hermès scarf tied loosely at the neck and sensible black leather pumps on her feet. "Fitzroy and I watch KEY News every morning."

"And I thank you for that," said Eliza. "Now, if we could just get the ones younger than us to watch, we'd be in great shape. As it is, network news viewership is declining, even in the morning. Cable news is part of the problem, but more and more people are also getting their information via the Internet."

"Well, we don't get cable and we don't know how to use a computer," said the woman. "Fitzroy and I are satisfied with things just the way they are. Where is he, anyway?" She craned her neck to search the room. "Oh, there he is."

The man who approached them had thinning white hair and a lined and thin yet still handsome face, and he walked with a slight limp. Standing erect, he firmly shook Eliza's hand.

"I'm Fitzroy Heavener, and it's such a pleasure to meet you," he said in an even, well-modulated voice. "We are great fans."

"I've been telling Miss Blake that, dear," said his wife. "I told her we watch her every day." The woman's facial expression clouded, and she lowered her voice. "Of course we were glued to our chairs in July. I prayed for you every night."

"Unity, I'm sure Ms. Blake doesn't want to be reminded of all that," Fitzroy chided.

"Please, call me Eliza," she said, not commenting on the kidnapping. "And I wish I could stay and talk some more, but I have a driver waiting outside and a little girl at home who might not fall asleep until I get there. I just want to find Valentina and Innis and thank them."

Just then a shout came from across the room.

"In the greenhouse! Innis is lying in a pool of blood in the greenhouse!"

A stream of guests ran out the French doors and across the property.

CHAPTER 15

"E xcuse me. Pardon me."

Eliza made her way through the crowd that had gathered at the door. When she managed to get inside, she walked past the pots of plants and bags of soil and fertilizer. As she drew closer to the cluster of people gathered at the rear of the greenhouse, she noticed a single black shoe on the floor in front of one of the antique worktables.

She could hear Valentina murmuring, "Oh, Innis, Innis. What have you done? What have you done to yourself?"

Valentina was sitting on the ground, rocking back and forth gently and cradling her husband's head in her lap. Her legs and hands were smeared with blood. All color had drained from her face.

Innis, too, was very pale, his mouth open, his head drooping to one side. His limbs were splayed. His hands and bare feet bled from the deep incisions that pierced them. The left side of his crisp white shirt was drenched in blood.

It took a while for Eliza to grasp what she was seeing. Altogether there were five places where the skin had been sliced open. Innis bore the five wounds that Jesus had suffered at Calvary the day he was crucified. Eliza knew there were stories about holy men and women who had mysteriously suffered the same wounds—wounds appearing seemingly without cause but known by them to have come from God as a bizarre sort of blessing.

But seeing the hunting knife with its long, sharp blade lying beside his still body, Eliza immediately sensed that Innis had administered the wounds himself.

Poor, sad, troubled man.

Is that what Innis had meant when he said that he wanted to unite himself with St. Francis in the most vivid way possible?

She cringed at the thought. Had Innis gotten so carried away with his religious fervor that this is what he'd done to himself?

Eliza thought about their walk around the turtle fountain together earlier in the evening. Innis had been distressed, saying he was ashamed of himself. It had never even crossed her mind that he was desperate enough to kill himself. What had happened that was horrible enough to make suicide the only answer?

Watching the emergency medical technicians arrive and begin working on Innis, Eliza realized that she could have been the last person that he'd spoken to in more than amiable cocktail-party conversation. If she had understood the depth of his anxiety, she would have done something to help. Instead, thinking Innis just needed an opportunity to vent, she'd only listened.

"It could have nicked the heart."

Eliza heard the medical technician's words and felt anguish along with guilt and responsibility. If she had reacted differently, this horror might have been averted. She tried to remember every bit of their conversation. What had Innis been talking about when he insisted that she cared about right and wrong and said he knew that Eliza would do what needed to be done? What was it that he wanted her to do?

Instinctively, Eliza felt that someone should be making a record of what was happening. She took out her cell phone and began snapping pictures. Trying to be unobtrusive, she managed to take a few shots before a uniformed Tuxedo Park police officer intervened.

"No pictures, ma'am," he said, in a tone that left no doubt he was deadly serious.

Glancing over at the covered figure that was now lying on the stretcher, seeing the tears streaming down Valentina's face and her son awkwardly trying to comfort his mother, Eliza didn't fight. She slid her cell phone back into her purse.

She wasn't even going to tell Linus about the pictures, because if the *KTA* executive producer knew about them, he would insist on using them.

But for some reason she was glad to have them.

CHAPTER 16

*I*n their final conversation in his study, Innis had said he was going to make everyone sit up and take notice. He'd certainly done that.

It wasn't easy watching the stretcher carrying his body being rolled out of the greenhouse. There was too much history between them not to feel regret and some sorrow. But there was also relief.

There would be no need now to eliminate Innis before he revealed everything. He had done that to himself.

Innis wasn't going to be around to be the righter of wrongs. Life could go on as it had, with nobody the wiser.

But what if this act of suicide, so grotesquely executed, was just the prelude to something more? What if he'd planned to grab everyone's attention before disclosing the devastating thing he'd threatened to tell? What else had Innis planned?

In addition, there was Eunice to worry about. The maid had overheard all the sordid details and could wreck everything if she came forward with what she knew.

And something else was troubling. Eliza Blake had never seemed to be one of those media hounds who would take pictures of someone, especially a friend, bloodied and dead on the ground. And yet that's exactly what she'd just done.

MONDAY
OCTOBER 5

CHAPTER 17

B.J. D'Elia groaned. "These hours kill me."

"Think what misery it would be to be stuck on this shift," said Annabelle Murphy as she and the producer-cameraman sat in a KEY News Broadcast Center editing room. "Thank God we're on dayside. It's bad enough we have to fill in once in a while."

"Ever notice that 'once in a while' seems to be turning into 'all the time' lately?" asked B.J. "Somebody's always on vacation or on assignment, and we're stuck plugging up the holes."

Annabelle took a sip of the thick, bitter brew that came from the aluminum coffeemaker sitting on a cart in the hallway. "Ugh," she said after she swallowed. "Remember the good old days when the cafeteria was open twenty-four hours, when you could get a decent cup of coffee whenever you needed it, and there were actually more than enough people to get the jobs done around here?" Annabelle didn't wait for B.J. to respond. "That's why we get saddled with this overnight stuff, Beej. The budget cuts. Cutbacks in personnel. Cutbacks in overtime hours. The same amount of work to be done—even more—but fewer people to do it."

"Bitch and moan, bitch and moan." B.J. smiled as he leaned forward and played with the knobs on the monitor.

"I'm serious, Beej."

"I know you are, Annabelle. But what's the alternative? You think it's any better at ABC, CBS, or NBC? Every network has tightened things up. All we can do right now is smile, do our jobs, and pray we get to keep them."

"I guess you're right," said Annabelle begrudgingly, "but if I can't complain to you, who can I complain to?"

"You can complain to me all you want, but just don't let Linus hear you."

"What do you think I am, an idiot?"

"Who's an idiot?" Annabelle and B.J. jumped as they heard another voice. Eliza was standing in the doorway.

Annabelle relaxed when she saw who it was. "What are you doing here so early?" she asked. "Did you even have any sleep?"

"Not really," said Eliza, closing the door of the editing room. "But I wanted to get in before Linus does and show you guys something." She handed her cell phone to B.J. "Download the last pictures, will you, Beej?"

Standing with Annabelle and B.J., Eliza felt a reassuring camaraderie. The three of them, along with Margo Gonzalez, had gone through so much together over the last months. Each of them had contributed to solving the murder of Eliza's predecessor at *KTA*, Constance Young. And they had bonded around Eliza, supporting her personally and using their considerable professional skills to help when Janie and Mrs. Garcia were kidnapped. They had jokingly dubbed themselves the Sunrise Suspense Society because of the ridiculous hours they kept and the anxiety-filled and sometimes dangerous situations they'd found themselves in.

While they waited for B.J. to do what needed to be done, Eliza told them what had happened.

"I heard on the radio in the cab coming in that Innis Wheelock had offed himself, but I didn't know you were at the party when he did it," said Annabelle. "Linus must be beside himself at the prospect of your giving our audience an eyewitness account."

"He was thrilled when I called him at home and told him," she said. "But I didn't tell him I took these."

Eliza nodded toward the monitor where the first of the cell-phone pictures appeared. The grainy image showed the body of Innis Wheelock, covered in blood, stretched out on the floor next to a large terra-cotta pot.

"Nasty," said B.J., grimacing as he studied the picture. "This one scores high on the gore meter. But I guess we can crop the picture and fool around with it so it doesn't show all that blood."

"Don't go to the trouble," said Eliza. "We're not going to air these."

Annabelle and B.J. both turned to look at Eliza. "I'm assuming that nobody else was taking pictures," said Annabelle.

"The cops took some, but I think I was the only guest who got any," said Eliza.

"So we're exclusive with these, right?" asked Annabelle.

"Right," Eliza answered.

"Are you kidding? We *have* to air these," Annabelle insisted.

"Innis Wheelock was a friend of mine, Annabelle," Eliza said quietly. "It was the journalist in me that made me pull out my phone, but now I almost regret it."

Annabelle looked back at the violent image on the monitor and tried to imagine how she would feel if a friend of hers had committed suicide. She wouldn't want the disturbing and profoundly private pictures broadcast and published around the world. She said nothing as B.J. displayed the next image.

The second shot zeroed in on one of Wheelock's pierced hands.

"What's that he's holding in his hand?" asked B.J.

"I don't know," said Eliza. "I didn't even notice that last night."

"Why would you?" asked B.J. "There was too much else to capture your attention."

"It looks like he's clutching a handful of dirt," said Annabelle.

The next image appeared on the screen. "What a mess," said B.J., grimacing. Innis Wheelock's white shirt was drenched in blood.

"The blood is coming from the left side," said Annabelle. "He stabbed himself in the hands and the left side?"

"And feet," said Eliza.

All three were quiet for a moment as they thought about it.

Annabelle broke the silence. "The radio didn't say anything about stigmata."

CHAPTER 18

Eliza Blake's voice announced the top stories of the morning.

"The president attends a three-day Middle East peace summit in London.

"Consumer confidence and spending climb as new and positive economic figures are released.

"And a tragic death amid a bizarre set of circumstances as the spouse of one of the nation's most accomplished public figures appears to have committed suicide.

"Good morning, it's Monday, October fifth, and this is *KEY to America*."

The director cut from the *KTA* logo to a two-shot of the show's hosts sitting behind the news desk.

"Hello, I'm Eliza Blake, here with Harry Granger, and we have lots to tell you about this morning, don't we, Harry?"

"We certainly do, Eliza, starting with the president's historic trip to London, where he arrived overnight. U.S. officials have high hopes that the multilateral talks between the United States and the governments of Israel and several Arab nations will bear fruit. We have a report from KEY News Foreign Correspondent Mack McBride."

Eliza listened intently for Mack's opening words, relieved to his hear his voice, even if only delivering a dispassionate account of what was happening among world leaders. The video on the screen showed the president of the United States climbing down the stairs of Air Force One. Midway through the piece, Eliza leaned closer to the monitor as Mack appeared on the screen. He was standing on the banks of the Thames, Westminster Abbey behind him.

She inhaled and smiled when she saw him, looking tanned, fit, and confident. She missed him so much. They hadn't been together in over a month, and Eliza was counting the days until they would be united again and the weeks until his contract would be up for re-negotiation. Mack was adamant that he was not going to sign up for another overseas assignment. He wanted to return to New York. Eliza ached for him to come back as well.

After Mack's piece wrapped up, Harry introduced the next story, which was an explanation of what the newest fiscal figures meant. While viewers were shown a series of graphs and charts illustrating the upturn in the economy, Eliza was off-screen, silently rereading the narration she would soon deliver over the pictures and video that would accompany the story of Innis's death.

"Five seconds," the voice of the stage manager boomed.

Eliza sat up straighter and cleared her throat as the economic story ended and the stage manager cued her to begin.

"Innis Wheelock, best known as the husband of former governor of New York and ambassador to Italy Valentina Wheelock and the political genius behind her success, died last night in what appears to be a suicide. The manner in which he may have taken his own life has caused shock waves."

Video from the KEY News archives appeared on the screen showing Innis standing next to his wife as she took the oath of office in Albany more than twenty years earlier. The picture was remarkable for the time, not only because it showed the first female governor of New York but because that governor was clearly pregnant.

Eliza continued narrating. "Wheelock was found lying on the ground in the greenhouse on his property in Tuxedo Park, New York, his body stabbed five times. The wounds to both hands and feet and to his left side copied the wounds Jesus Christ suffered at his crucifixion. The wounds in this pattern are known as stigmata."

Eliza knew that Annabelle had been stumped on what to show to cover those words and was finally satisfied to find some video taken in Vatican City when Valentina and Innis had had an audience with Pope John Paul II.

"In the interest of full disclosure," Eliza went on, "I was attending a party at the Wheelocks' home last night when Innis Wheelock seemingly took his own life. While medical professionals examine his body to determine if the wounds were self-inflicted, people who knew Innis Wheelock are asking themselves why a man of his stature and experience would end his life, why he would have done it in such a bizarre fashion, and they are wondering what they could have done to stop him."

The last shot on the screen showed spare video that had been shot but never aired before. Eliza was walking alongside Innis and Valentina in the garden of the U.S. ambassador's residence in Rome. It was taped when Eliza had conducted her first interview with Valentina shortly after she began the diplomatic posting. That professional assignment had resulted in a personal friendship with both of the Wheelocks, ultimately leading to the talk at the fountain with Innis when he'd told her he was ashamed of himself and let her know that he believed she cared about right and wrong and would do what needed to be done.

As Harry began to read the next story, Eliza felt she had some sort of responsibility. For what, she was not sure.

CHAPTER 19

Snapping off the television set, Susannah Lansing got out of bed, picked up her coffee cup, and walked over to the doors that led out to her terrace. She pulled her robe closed as the cool morning greeted her. When she reached the wrought-iron railing, she looked down the mountain. She could see the red-tile roof of Pentimento below her.

Susannah marveled that just last evening she had stood in this very same spot and watched the stream of cars arrive at the mansion. She'd felt rejected and discouraged and hurt. Now she tried to contain her satisfaction.

Innis Wheelock had been on the board that had denied her and John admission as members of the exclusive Black Tie Club. No official reason had ever been given, but Susannah suspected she knew why.

CHAPTER 20

T hey got off to school all right?" asked Annabelle.

She held the phone to her ear and listened to her husband's answer. "Yeah, except for the fighting about Halloween. Tara is determined to be Hannah Montana, and Thomas keeps telling her that's dumb."

"What else is new?" said Annabelle. "But at least now that they're gone, you can try to get some sleep. Hopefully, I'll be home soon and can crawl in beside you."

Annabelle hated it when they both drew overnight shifts at the same time. It fouled up everything. Her body clock didn't adjust easily—or, for that matter, at all. The focus of life became sleep and how to get it. While that was bad enough for a single individual, add to the mix two active grade-school kids with their accompanying activities and homework that had to be paid attention to, babysitters who had to be carefully rescheduled to cover any gaps in parental presence, along with the grocery shopping and other errands, and you had a household struggling to keep it together.

But she felt worse for her husband than she did for herself. Mike did overnight shifts at the firehouse much more than she did at KEY

News. Unlike Annabelle, Mike never complained. He just accepted the fact that the tough hours came with the job. He'd known that going in.

Annabelle glanced at her watch. The broadcast would be over soon, and then, with any luck, she just had to hang around for another hour or so and wait for the dayside staff. Annabelle would turn over her video and logs to the producer assigned to the next Innis Wheelock story, and then she could get going.

While she was putting the videotapes and discs she'd used in a box, B.J. came into the newsroom. When he saw her, he beckoned to her.

"I want you to see something," he said.

Annabelle followed him out of the newsroom, down the hall, and into the elevator. "What's up?" she asked.

"I want you to take a look at this and tell me what you think."

"Take a look at what?" asked Annabelle.

"One of the pictures Eliza took at the Wheelocks'."

B.J. shut the door after they walked into the editing room. As Annabelle sat down, he brought up the image on the monitor screen. It was the first picture Eliza had taken, the one where Innis Wheelock's body was stretched out on the floor next to the terra-cotta pot.

"Notice anything?" asked B.J.

Annabelle looked carefully at the grainy image. "I don't see anything that I didn't see this morning," she said.

"Look at the pot," he said.

"Yeah? What about it?"

"See the numbers on the side?" asked B.J.

Annabelle squinted. "I guess they're numbers, but I sure can't read them."

"Neither could I," said B.J. "So just for kicks, I enlarged them." He pushed a button on the console, and a magnified image appeared.

Annabelle read the numbers out loud: "41-11 8-3508 and 74-13

9-0552." She looked at B.J. "I don't get it," she said. "Nine digits. The only nine-digit numbers I know are Social Security numbers."

"But the spacing's all wrong. And the dashes aren't in the right places either," said B.J.

"Well, it beats me," said Annabelle, "and to tell you the truth, I'm too sleep-deprived to try to figure it out." She got up from the chair. "But remember, you'd better make sure nobody else sees these pictures," she said as she started to leave. "We don't want to have them turn up on the air unless Eliza okays it."

CHAPTER 21

Throughout the broadcast, whenever she wasn't on camera, Eliza checked the screen beneath the news desk to see what the wire services were saying about the Wheelock story. Just before 9:00 A.M., the Associated Press reported having a source who revealed that the medical examiner could tell that Innis Wheelock's wounds were self-inflicted. After teasing the viewers about what would be on the next day's broadcast, signing off for the morning, and waiting for the stage manager's signal that they were off the air, Eliza removed her microphone and let out a long, deep sigh.

"Man, that poor bastard," said Harry, shaking his head as he gathered up the pages of his script. "What was the matter with him? He had everything—success, money, family. What could be so bad that he'd go and stab himself—and like Jesus Christ no less? Was he sick?"

"I don't know," said Eliza, "though he looked unwell when I first saw him last night." Eliza was on the verge of telling Harry about the conversation she'd had with Innis in the garden, but then she thought better of it. She enjoyed working with Harry, but he couldn't always be counted on to keep a confidence. He'd go to jail—and had—to protect a news source, but when it came to KEY News and insider gossip, Harry enjoyed trading tidbits with the best of them.

"Well, it will all come out," said Harry with a shrug as he started to walk away. "It always does."

As Eliza cut across the studio on the way to her office, she bumped into Linus Nazareth emerging from the control room.

"Well, the video could have been better, but it was cool that you could say you were there when Wheelock died," the executive producer said with satisfaction.

"I don't know if 'cool' is the word I'd use, Linus."

"You know what I mean, Eliza."

"Yes, I'm afraid I do," she said. "Reporter involvement and all that."

"Don't say it with such disdain," said Linus. "That's our business."

"Maybe so," said Eliza. "But there have to be limits. Let's let them grieve in peace, Linus."

Linus shook his head, a look of bewilderment on his face. "Come on, Eliza," he said. "You know that's not going to happen."

Paige Tintle was waiting with a handful of messages when Eliza arrived at her office.

"We've already gotten a call from Valentina Wheelock's secretary," said Paige. "Mr. Wheelock's funeral will be held on Wednesday morning at eleven o'clock at Our Lady of Mount Carmel Church in Tuxedo."

CHAPTER 22

Lacing up his athletic shoes, Zack Underwood was determined to go for a nice long jog. He had tossed and turned all night and was physically tired. Yet he knew that pushing his body for a couple of miles would make him feel better. Once he got into the run, he might be able to get his mind off the horrible thing that had happened the previous night.

How perverse of Innis to say he had something special planned for the evening, knowing full well what he was going to do.

During the months of work as architect on Pentimento's renovation and restoration, Zack had spent hours and hours with Innis Wheelock. He was a strange duck, but it was his eccentricity and creativity that drew Zack to him. Innis was extremely bright, quite knowledgeable, and some of the things Innis had asked Zack to incorporate into the architectural plans had been challenging to execute but satisfying upon completion.

It had also been a pleasure for Zack to spend time talking with Innis. The man had had such a fascinating life, growing up in privilege, living with power. Innis Wheelock was a man whom others would say had everything—and then some.

Zipping up his hooded sweatshirt, Zack was at the front door when the thought occurred to him. *Could some of the things that Innis wanted incorporated in the Pentimento designs have anything to do with his death?*

CHAPTER 23

Eliza paced her office, stopping to look out the huge window. The cloudless October sky was clear and bright blue. The Hudson River sparkled below, reflecting the mellow autumn sunshine.

She still couldn't decide which space she liked better. When she'd been anchor of *KEY Evening Headlines,* her office had been right above the central newsroom, and she could look down and watch the staff on the phones, at their computers, scurrying from desk to desk and interacting with one another. It was a constantly moving scenario that never ceased to fascinate and energize her.

When she'd come back to hosting *KEY to America,* she'd handed off her prized piece of Broadcast Center real estate to Anthony Reynes, her successor at *Evening Headlines.* Her new office, on a higher floor, was spacious and flooded with natural light. The view, looking out over the river to the shores of New Jersey, was more peaceful and serene, and she felt somewhat insulated and removed from the thick of things. That had its advantages.

But today the view did little to soothe her.

Eliza walked to the office door and leaned out toward the vestibule where her assistant sat. "Paige, will you see if Margo Gonzalez is here today?" she asked.

"Thanks for coming, Margo," said Eliza as she gestured toward one of the upholstered chairs positioned on the other side of her desk. "Don't tell Linus, because he's under the impression that your job here is to act as a *KTA* mental-health contributor. He doesn't understand that I need you to perform a far more important function. It's nice to be able to call on my own in-house psychiatrist."

Margo smiled. "Glad to be of assistance," she said as she sat down. "What's up?"

"Innis Wheelock was a friend of mine," said Eliza.

Margo's smile faded. "I gathered that might be the case after I heard you say on the air this morning that you'd been at a party at his home last night. Oh, I'm so sorry, Eliza."

"And I had a private conversation with him shortly before he killed himself."

Margo nodded. "So you're feeling guilty, as though you could have done something to stop him."

"How'd you guess?"

"Tell me what happened," said Margo.

Eliza recounted the walk in the garden at Pentimento. "He came out and told me he was ashamed of himself, Margo. That he'd done things that were wrong, that he'd hurt and ruined people. I could tell he was troubled, but I never thought he was a candidate for suicide."

"Why do you think he confided in you?" asked Margo.

Eliza considered the question. "I guess he trusted me," she said. "He said I cared about right and wrong and that I would do what needed to be done."

"What do you think he meant by that?" asked Margo. "What do you think he thought needed to be done?"

"I have absolutely no idea," said Eliza.

Margo sat back in her chair and ran her fingers through her short red hair. "You know, Eliza, suicide is not a random act," she began. "And the fact that Innis Wheelock actually chose the stigmata as a way of killing himself means he had planned this out very carefully."

"I suppose that's true enough," said Eliza. "He told me he wanted to be like St. Francis, wanted to 'unite himself' with him in the most vivid way possible. By choosing the stigmata, he did that. But *why*? Why would Innis do it?"

"Suicide represents an answer to a seemingly insoluble problem; it's a choice that the person makes thinking death is preferable to facing whatever it is in life that seems so dreadful."

"Maybe Innis was sick, had some terminal illness," said Eliza. "Maybe he didn't want to face a pain-filled future and a miserable death."

"Perhaps," said Margo. "But the most common reason for suicide is intolerable *psychological* pain. Shame, guilt, anger, fear, sadness, in excruciating degrees, very often serve as the foundation for self-destructive behaviors. Suicide is the most self-destructive you can get."

Eliza considered Margo's words. "You know, when I look back on it, I think Innis *did* have a plan, a plan beyond taking his own life. I feel like he was trying to tell me something, something he wanted me to follow through on, something he was counting on me to do after he was gone."

CHAPTER 24

Listening to Mike snoring beside her, Annabelle could not get to sleep. She was no closer to reaching a stage of suspended consciousness than she'd been when she snuggled in several hours before. She looked at the clock on the bedside table and realized that the kids were going to be getting out of school in just over an hour. Even if she finally fell asleep now, she would only be roused from slumber when they came bounding in. Sometimes getting a little sleep was worse than getting no sleep at all.

Thinking that a long, hot bath would make her feel better, Annabelle went in and started the water and poured into the tub some of the lavender-scented bath salts the twins had given her for Mother's Day. She noted that the bottle was still more than half full five months later.

While the old white tub filled, Annabelle went to the living room. Her canvas tote bag was on the sofa where she'd thrown it. She extracted the complimentary copy of *Us Weekly* magazine she had taken from the newsroom.

Annabelle sank into the calming water, luxuriating in the warmth and the soothing scent. She put her head back against the rim of the tub and closed her eyes to rest. Hard as she tried, she couldn't keep the images of Innis Wheelock lying on the ground from replaying in her mind. Suicide was bad enough, but the bizarre manner in which he'd killed himself made her shiver even in the heated water.

There was no point in going over and over it. Annabelle reached out and grabbed the magazine from the floor next to the bathtub. With wet fingers she began to page though it. She noted those who had dressed the best that week and those who hadn't lived up to the judges' standards and were mocked accordingly for it. She read about which stars were having babies and which ones were getting divorced. She learned who was using Botox and who was going all out for the face-lift. Annabelle stopped and looked at the pictures before starting to read the article about Angelina Jolie.

Annabelle marveled at the full-length pictures of Angelina. The woman's figure seemed even better after she'd given birth to her children than before. How was that possible?

Sighing deeply, she turned the page. The next glossy picture showed Angelina wearing a black strapless cocktail dress that was hemmed just below her knees. She stood tall, elegant, and erect with her body angled toward the camera. Her long dark hair was swept to one side, leaving the top of her left arm and the tattoos there exposed. The caption explained that the rows of tattooed numbers displayed the map coordinates of the places where her children were born.

Sleep-deprived and staring at Angelina Jolie's thin arm, Annabelle figured out the meaning of the numbers painted on the terra-cotta pot next to Innis Wheelock's bloody corpse.

CHAPTER 25

With the midterm elections fast approaching, political guru Peter Nordstrut had plenty of work to do, but he couldn't concentrate. He hadn't been able to focus on the latest polling numbers all day. His mind was tortured with the image of Innis Wheelock lying on the greenhouse floor.

Peter got up from his desk and walked over to the mirror hanging on the wall next to the office door. He peered at himself through his horn-rimmed glasses. His blond hair was going gray; his face looked puffy, his eyes a bit bloodshot. No wonder: He'd barely slept the night before.

He paced across the blue carpet, his eyes avoiding the pictures that lined the office wall. There were too many photographs of Innis and Valentina and him there. In Tuxedo Park, in Albany, in Washington, in Rome.

Peter had been with the Wheelocks since he was a very young man, just a few years out of law school. He'd signed on as a volunteer when Valentina made it clear that she intended to run for governor. He knew that he'd proved himself invaluable in that campaign, ensuring that he would be along for all the others. It had been a wonderful ride for as long as it lasted.

Since the Wheelocks had returned from Italy, things hadn't been the same. Peter had first thought that it was his imagination, but it became clear that Innis was simply not returning his calls and was avoiding every opportunity to meet with him. It had become so obvious that Peter had been stunned to receive an invitation to the St. Francis party at Pentimento. He had eagerly accepted.

Now, however, Peter suspected that he'd been invited to the party because Innis wanted him to see what he did to himself. Perverse, yet perhaps fitting, considering everything else they'd been through together. Every ugly thing.

Walking over to the American flag that stood in the corner of the room, Peter began counting the stars on the field of blue. He kept losing his place, forcing himself to start all over again.

What are you doing, Peter? You need to get some help.

He couldn't go to a psychiatrist and unburden himself. Confidentiality laws or no, a doctor's records could always be subpoenaed. The last thing Peter could survive was having what he'd done revealed in a court of law.

Where can you get relief? Who can help you?

Impulsively, Peter told his assistant to hold his calls. Then he called 411 for the number of Mount Carmel's rectory in Tuxedo. When the parish secretary answered, he asked to speak with Father Michael Gehry.

Peter didn't identify himself. "Father, I'm not a churchgoer, but I need to go to confession. I knew Innis Wheelock, and his death has me feeling I should make things right with God. Innis always said he found confession to be such a relief. I want relief, too, Father. I need forgiveness."

"I can hear your confession," said Father Gehry. "Would you like to make an appointment to come to Mount Carmel?"

"Before I say anything, Father, I have to ask you something." Peter paused before putting his question to the priest. "You can't reveal anything you hear in confession, can you?"

"Absolutely not," Father Gehry said firmly. "The sacramental seal is inviolable."

"That's what I've been told, Father, but if you knew something that would save someone's life, wouldn't you speak up?"

"No," said Father Gehry. "But I could pray that those responsible would do the right thing."

Peter considered the priest's words. The thought occurred to him that Innis might already have told Father Gehry about what Peter had done. With that possibility in mind, Peter had to reflect on how he wanted to proceed. "You know what, Father? Thanks for your time, but I think I'm going to hold off confessing anything after all."

Father Gehry checked the ID window on the telephone and recognized the name of the caller.

Innis Wheelock had spoken quite a lot about Peter Nordstrut. Father Gehry could well understand why Peter Nordstrut would feel he needed to go to confession.

CHAPTER 26

The hybrid sedan stopped in the driveway.

"See you in the morning, Charlie," Eliza said as she got out.

"Too bad, it will be here before we know it," the driver said good-naturedly.

"Isn't that the truth!" said Eliza, smiling wanly.

She was exhausted as she walked wearily up the slate path that led to the large Federal-style brick Colonial. The security car wasn't stationed in front of the house. It was parked outside Janie's school now and would remain there until Janie came home.

Eliza let herself in through the front door. She greeted Mrs. Garcia, discussed the dinner menu, and then went upstairs to wash the heavy TV makeup off her face. She changed into a pair of blue sweatpants and a long-sleeved University of Rhode Island T-shirt. She didn't really feel like it, but she knew she should get some exercise. It would make her feel better now and help her sleep later.

She went across the hallway to the bedroom she had converted into a small gym, outfitted with a treadmill, some light weights, and a miniature trampoline. Going to the wall unit, Eliza selected a disc and placed it in the DVR. As the lithe yoga instructor appeared on the screen, Eliza spread out her mat and got down on the floor. She followed along as the instructor guided her through the series of stretching and breathing exercises.

The last few minutes of the yoga session were devoted to relaxation and meditation. Try as she might to find peace and calmness, Eliza's mind strayed. Instead of concentrating on the voice of the instructor, she kept thinking about what Innis Wheelock had done.

"I'm home, Mom."

The sound of her daughter's voice called from downstairs. Eliza was glad to be diverted.

"Up here, sweetheart," she called back as she got up from the mat.

Janie came running up the stairs and bounded into the room. Eliza held out her arms, and mother and child gave each other a long hug.

"How was school?" Eliza asked.

"All right," said Janie. "Mrs. Wojciezak gave us the October calendars today." She zipped open her backpack and took out an orange piece of paper. "We're going to have a Halloween party in a few weeks."

"I guess we better start thinking about your costume, huh? Do you have anything in mind?" asked Eliza.

"Well, I can't decide. I was thinking about being Dorothy in *The Wizard of Oz*, but then I thought maybe it would be better if I was Glinda the Good Witch, but, you know, the Scarecrow is really my favorite."

Eliza laughed. "Any of those would be great, sweetheart. But let's decide by next week so we don't have to run around and come up with a costume at the last minute." She put the yoga mat in the corner. "Any homework tonight?" she asked.

"Just my reading."

"Want to do that now?" asked Eliza, worried that she might not be able to stay awake after dinner.

"Do I have to? I just got home from being in school all day long. I need a break." Janie's facial expression was earnest.

Eliza smiled and patted the top of her daughter's head. "Okay, kiddo. Everybody deserves a break. Let's go downstairs and see what Mrs. Garcia has for a snack."

As the two of them sat in the kitchen and ate warm oatmeal cookies, Janie broached the subject.

"Rachel's family is going to Hershey Park this weekend. They're sleeping over there."

"Oh, that's nice," said Eliza. "We'll have to go there, too, someday."

"Rachel wants me to come with them." The child paused for a moment, watching her mother's face. "Can I, Mommy? Can I?"

Eliza was taken aback. There hadn't been a day since the kidnapping when Janie hadn't slept in her own bed, when Eliza hadn't tried to see her daughter as much as possible during their waking hours. The fact that Janie seemed eager to go away for the weekend with her little friend, was ready to leave the security of their home, that was a good sign. But Eliza wasn't sure that she herself was prepared.

"You know, this is the first weekend we were going to try our little house," said Eliza. "Don't you want to do that?"

"I do, Mom, but you told me we are going to be able to go there *every* weekend," said Janie. "And this is the *only* weekend I can go to Hershey with Rachel."

CHAPTER 27

Valentina Wheelock stood inside the walk-in closet and stared unseeingly at the precisely arranged men's suits that hung there.

How could Innis have done this to himself, to both of us?

She couldn't remember a time when Innis hadn't been part of her world. She'd known him since she was a young girl, and he, five years her senior, had been self-assured and smart and popular among all the young people in the park. Someone the girls had a crush on. When they grew older and five years was no longer an enormous chasm in age, Valentina was thrilled when Innis began paying attention to her.

They'd been through it all together—marriage and the birth of a child after years of infertility, professional and political triumphs and disappointments, life in the public arena, the private struggles that were part of every life and some that were unique. When they returned to Tuxedo Park after their years in Italy, Valentina had assumed that they would grow very old together in this house.

How wrong I was.

She reached out and took hold of the arm of one of Innis's jackets and held it to her nose. Smelling him in the soft fabric, Valentina began to cry.

"Let me help you, Valentina."

Valentina stiffened. "You know I don't like it when you call me that, Rusty. I think it's disrespectful." She looked into her son's eyes. "Please, dear, call me 'Mother.'"

Russell Wheelock put a strong arm around Valentina's shoulder, steered her out of the closet, and guided her to the chaise in the corner of the master bedroom. He went over to his father's dresser and removed a snowy white handkerchief from the top drawer.

"Here," he said.

Valentina took it and wiped at her eyes.

"Why don't I choose what Father will wear?" he suggested.

"All right," said Valentina. "Thank you, Rusty."

He flipped through the suits, narrowing the choices down to a navy silk and a charcoal wool pinstripe. He took both of them off the rack and brought them out to his mother.

"Which do you think is better?"

Valentina considered the options. "The blue one." She sniffed. "Your father had that made in Rome before we left. He loved that suit."

Russell hung the gray suit back in the closet and laid the navy one out on the bed. He went back into the closet, chose a starched white shirt, a blue-and-beige Marinella tie, and shoes of soft black Italian leather. Then he went to the dresser again and selected underwear and dark blue socks.

"What about a watch?" he asked.

Valentina thought for a moment. "I don't see any point in that. You should have all your father's watches, Rusty."

She watched her son zip the garment bag closed. "Thank you, dear," she said. "I'm so grateful to have you with me."

Russell didn't look at her.

"What is it?" she asked.

"I can't stay. I've got to go back to the city, Mother."

She regarded him quizzically.

"You know I've scheduled all my classes on Mondays, Wednesdays, and Fridays," he said. "I missed today's, and I'll be missing Wednesday's because of the funeral. I have to go in and borrow someone's notes and get caught up."

"Surely your professors will understand."

"Mother, please, I've got to go back. Columbus Day is next week. I can come home for a nice long weekend then."

Valentina pressed. "Well, can't you have someone e-mail you the notes?"

Russell closed his eyes and took a deep breath. "I'm doing the best I can, Mother," he said through clenched teeth. "Try to understand. If you want me to get into law school and have the political future you say I deserve, I have to make school my priority."

Valentina sighed heavily. "Of course, dear. You're right."

But as she started to gather up her husband's clothes to take to the undertaker, Valentina was mindful of the possibility that, despite Rusty's keen desire for it, a life in politics might not suit him at all.

Valentina shrank back in the chaise. She knew the signs. It was better not to press him anymore.

TUESDAY
OCTOBER 6

CHAPTER 28

Nobody locks their doors in this park. Anybody could just walk into a place like Pentimento. Later, when it was done, anyone could be suspect.

This morning is as good a day as any to deal with the nosy maid. She can't be allowed to reveal what she heard.

CHAPTER 29

The cab dropped Annabelle off in front of the Broadcast Center. She pushed through the heavy revolving door to the lobby and looked up at the big clock on the wall. It was 2:15 A.M. Annabelle scanned her identification card over the security turnstile.

"Hi, Herman," she said to the guard as she pushed through. "How's it going tonight?"

"Fine, ma'am, fine."

"We've got to stop meeting like this, you know."

The guard smiled broadly.

"The sooner the better," added Annabelle. "I'm crazy about you, Herman, but this is my last overnight, I hope, for a very long time."

"Good for you, ma'am. Have a nice night, then."

"I'll try, Herman. I'll try."

How does Herman manage to be so unfailingly pleasant at these god-forsaken hours? Annabelle had all she could do to keep from tearing somebody's throat out.

She dropped off her jacket and tote bag in the newsroom and checked her computer to see what she was scheduled to do. There was nothing that couldn't wait for the next fifteen minutes. Annabelle walked to the elevator and took it down to the editing floor.

B.J. was in the same place he had been the last time she saw him. Now his feet were up on the desk and he was leaning back doing a sudoku puzzle.

"Do you ever work?" she asked.

"Not if I can help it." He held up the newspaper, preening. "I finished this in under three minutes."

"I've figured out something much bigger," said Annabelle with a smirk.

"Yeah? What?"

"The numbers on the pot near Innis Wheelock's body. Look." She handed him the magazine opened to the picture of Angelina Jolie.

"She's hot, all right," said B.J.

"Look at her arm, Beej. Look at her arm."

"Thin, toned, tattooed."

"That's what I'm talking about," Annabelle said with urgency. "Look at the tattoos."

She watched as B.J. studied the picture and then read the caption.

"Get it? The tattoos are the map coordinates of where each of her kids was born," said Annabelle with enthusiasm. "The numbers on the greenhouse pot could be longitude and latitude numbers."

"Let's see," said B.J., sitting forward. He brought up on the monitor the picture Eliza had taken, zooming in on the grainy photo, and the numbers painted on the terra-cotta pot appeared on the screen. "They look like 41-11 8-3508 and 74-13 9-0552," he said. "I don't know much, but that isn't how longitude and latitude coordinates look."

"Well, let's see if we can get some help on the Web."

Together they turned to a computer terminal and quickly discovered that the terra-cotta pot that lay next to Innis Wheelock's body pointed the way to a spot on West Lake Road in Tuxedo Park.

CHAPTER 30

The clock screeched, rousing Eliza from a deep sleep. She groaned as she reached out and turned off the alarm. Then she rolled over and pulled the down blanket close around her, trying to get herself psyched to get out of bed.

Four-thirty. Who was up at four-thirty? Nurses, police, firefighters, bakers, waitresses who made their living in all-night diners, and others staffing the places that were open twenty-four hours a day. The news business was operating all the time as well, and this was the career she'd chosen.

She had no right to resent these miserable hours. After all, she'd asked to host the morning program again. And she was being paid *far* more than anyone else she could think of who worked while it was still dark outside.

When the phone rang, she dived for it before it could sound a second time. She knew who was going to be on the other end.

"Good morning," she said sleepily.

"Hello, honey," said Mack. "How are you this morning?"

"Better, now that I hear your voice," said Eliza.

"I wish I were there with you."

"I wish you were, too," she said, rolling onto her side and fluffing her pillow. "I so wish you were here. How's everything going over there in jolly old England?"

"The rumor is that the president is making some real progress with these guys," said Mack. "In fact, I'm in the middle of writing a piece about it for your show."

"That's mighty kind of you," said Eliza.

"Anything for you. And while we're on the subject of what I can do for you, how about if I fly home this weekend and we can come up with a list of other things you need doing."

Eliza smiled in the dark as she thought about the prospect. If Janie was going away with the Cohens for the weekend, she and Mack could drive up to Tuxedo Park and have the carriage house all to themselves.

"I could definitely go for that," she said. "And I'll start making that list."

Her hair was still damp from the shower when the car left Eliza off in front of the Broadcast Center. She walked briskly through the lobby, the guard pushing a button so she didn't have to show her identification card to get past the security post. She strode directly to the makeup room.

Ruthie Pointer was waiting to blow out Eliza's shoulder-length hair before it dried completely. Eliza put a nylon robe on over her clothes and climbed into the elevated chair. While Ruthie worked on her brunette locks, Eliza read through the notes for the broadcast.

When Eliza's hair was styled, Doris Brice took over with her makeup kit. Wearing a zebra-striped jumpsuit and Chanel sneakers, Doris applied foundation, blush, and powder. She gave special attention to the eyes, choosing the shade of shadow that she knew from long experience would make Eliza's blue eyes pop on the screen. To make Eliza's eyes seem larger and more open, Doris used white powder to highlight the skin beneath her eyebrows.

"What do you think?" asked Doris as she stood back and surveyed her artistry.

Eliza looked up from her reading material and regarded herself in the mirror.

"I look tired," she said. "But I'll make up for it over the weekend."

Doris was unconvinced. "That doesn't work," she said. "Once you've lost sleep, you've lost it. And that's not good for your skin. It's not good for you, period."

"Yes, Mother," said Eliza. "I promise. I'll try to do better."

"See that you do," answered Doris with mock severity, wagging her finger up and down.

Eliza noticed the *Daily News* on the counter. She leaned forward and picked it up. The paper was still headlining the Wheelock story.

"'Suicide by Stigmata.'"

"Creeps me out," said Doris. "I always think that if I ever want to commit suicide, I'm going with the car-exhaust-in-a-closed-garage plan. The carbon monoxide leaves your skin all pink and glowing."

Annabelle and B.J. were waiting for Eliza when she arrived at the *KTA* studio.

"We've got something to show you," said B.J. "Can you come downstairs for a minute?"

Eliza looked at the clock. Fifteen minutes till airtime.

"All right, but let's make it fast."

As they rode down in the elevator, Annabelle explained about the numbers on the side of the terra-cotta pot in the greenhouse.

"I didn't even notice those," said Eliza.

"Why would you?" asked Annabelle. "With a dead body and five stab wounds oozing blood staring you in the face, who would notice some numbers on a flowerpot?"

"Obviously you two did," said Eliza.

"Actually, believe it or not, it was B.J. who noticed them," said Annabelle, feigning disbelief. "He enlarged the picture to see them better."

"And it was Annabelle who figured out what the numbers meant," said B.J. "Her obsession with those gossip magazines finally paid off."

In the editing room, Eliza looked at the photo enlargement.

"All right, I give up," she said. "What do the numbers mean?"

B.J. handed her the computer printout. "Those are the latitude and longitude coordinates for a spot on West Lake Road in Tuxedo Park."

Eliza shrugged. "I guess that makes sense," said Eliza. "The Wheelocks' house is on West Lake Road."

B.J. shook his head. "Look at this map, Eliza. You can see an aerial shot of all the houses on West Lake Road." He pointed to one of the larger roofs. "That one is the Wheelock house. But see that X way down at the end of the road, the deserted section at the bottom of the lake, where there are no houses around?"

Eliza nodded.

"That's the spot the numbers indicate," said B.J.

"That's weird, isn't it?" asked Annabelle. "Maybe we should add something about it in our piece."

"Let's hold off," said Eliza, "until we know if it's even pertinent to the story."

CHAPTER 31

Eunice showered and dressed in her basement apartment before going upstairs to the kitchen. She walked to the front of the house, opened the always unlocked front door, went out to the driveway, and picked up the *New York Times*. Going back inside, she took the newspaper from its blue plastic wrapping, spread it out on the kitchen table, and began perusing the front page. The Wheelock story was there again, but below the fold today.

She wondered if anything was going to happen to her job. Would Mrs. Wheelock continue living at Pentimento? Would she find it too hard? Eunice hoped not. Mrs. Wheelock was nice to work for, and Eunice really needed the job, sending money back to Trinidad every month to help support her family there.

Turning to the task at hand, Eunice took the bag of coffee from the cupboard and scooped the appropriate amount into the grinder. While the machine pulverized the beans, she took butter from the refrigerator and left it on the counter to soften.

Mrs. Wheelock had barely swallowed a morsel since everything had happened Sunday night. Eunice planned to prepare a nice breakfast for her and was determined to make sure she actually ate it. She set the coffee brewing and sliced an orange in half. She was twisting it on the juicer when she suddenly sensed that she was not alone.

Her body swung around. When she saw who it was, she held her hand to her chest.

"You scared me," she said.

"I'm sorry. I didn't mean to."

"It's just that it's so early, and I wasn't expecting anyone," said Eunice. "Is there something I can do for you?"

"A cup of coffee would be nice."

Eunice set the sugar bowl and creamer on the table. Her hand trembled as she poured a cupful of the black, steaming liquid.

"There you go," she said.

"Thank you."

"You're welcome," Eunice answered. She waited tensely to see if there was something else required of her.

"Go ahead and do what you were doing, Eunice. Don't mind me. We can talk while you work."

The woman nodded and turned to the refrigerator, taking out eggs, ham, onions, and peppers.

"What are you making?"

"A frittata," she said.

"Sounds good."

Eunice smiled weakly.

"You know, Eunice, we have to talk about it."

Eunice shrugged. "I don't know what you mean."

"Yes you do. I know that you were standing outside the door, listening to my conversation with Innis. Please don't bother denying it."

Eunice answered with silence.

"So you heard everything. You know what I've done. The question is, are you going to tell anyone about it?"

The woman hesitated. She averted her eyes as she answered softly, "No, I'm not going to tell anyone."

"How do I know that you're telling the truth? How do I know that you'll keep your word?"

"Because it's a sin to tell a lie?" Eunice asked uncertainly.

"Not as big a sin as what I've done, Eunice. Right?"

Eunice didn't respond.

"Answer me, Eunice. What I've done is terrible, isn't it?"

Eunice nodded.

"And you are a very religious person, aren't you, Eunice? You go church and pray all the time."

"Yes," said Eunice. "I do the best I can."

"So how does a religious person, a person who believes in God, keep quiet about something like you know about me? How, in good conscience, can you not go to the police?"

She cast her eyes downward.

"That's what I thought, Eunice. You aren't going to be able to keep my secret."

Eunice began backing away, terrified by the piercing eyes that bored into hers. Then she turned to run. As she got to the doorway that led down to her rooms, she felt the hands push against her back.

She tumbled down the stairs, eyes shut tight, feeling her body banging against the wooden steps, over and over, coming to rest at the bottom on the hard, cold cement floor. As she lay there, stunned and already in sharp pain, she could hear the heavy footsteps descending toward her.

There was no place to hide, not enough time to get up and scramble away. Eunice kept her eyes shut, certain that her only chance was to act as if she were already dead. She willed herself to keep still, tried to calm her breathing.

"Nice try, Eunice. But not good enough."

Eunice opened her eyes and began to pray as a pillow from her own bed pressed over her face.

CHAPTER 32

"What took you so long?" asked Unity as her husband entered their apartment. "How much time does it take to go into town and pick up some orange juice?"

"Please, Unity," said Fitzroy. "Don't nag me. People in the deli wouldn't leave me alone. They all wanted to talk about Innis. Let's just have our breakfast."

The apartment upstairs at the Black Tie Club was close quarters. There wasn't much distance between the small table in the dining area and the television in the adjoining living room. The couple ate as they watched *KEY to America*.

"To think that we were talking to Eliza Blake as Innis was taking his own life," observed Unity. "I still can't believe it."

"Shh, dear," said Fitzroy. "Let's hear what she has to say."

Eliza was looking straight into the camera lens. Though she was reading from the teleprompter, it appeared as though she was talking spontaneously to the viewing audience.

"As the shock at the suicide of Innis Wheelock begins to lessen, family, friends, and the authorities are trying to make sense of the event and the method of his death. To begin sorting things out, we have to start by understanding what stigmata are."

Various artists' renditions of the crucified Jesus Christ appeared as Eliza continued speaking.

"The word 'stigmata' comes from the Greek *stigma*, meaning mark. In Christianity it's thought that some people develop wounds like those Christ received at the crucifixion . . . signs from God that the person afflicted with them is holy."

Another artist's rendition, this one of a bearded dark-haired man in a belted long brown robe, popped up on the screen.

"The wounds on both hands, both feet, and one side were suffered by St. Francis of Assisi, the first person recorded to have shown stigmata. St. Francis did not die until several years after receiving the mysterious wounds.

"Innis Wheelock killed himself Sunday night, at a party he hosted at his home, a party in honor of St. Francis, the founder of the Franciscan Order. St. Francis, possibly the most venerated figure in Catholic history, taught repentance and called his followers to embrace a life of poverty and to help others. He was known for his love of nature, and he is the patron saint of animals and the environment."

The same file video that had been shown yesterday morning of Innis, Valentina, and Eliza walking in the Rome garden began to run.

"Innis Wheelock had made it known that he'd become deeply devoted to St. Francis while living in Italy when his wife served as U.S. ambassador there. Coming back to the United States after her assignment was completed, Innis immersed himself in the renovation of an old family home in Tuxedo Park, New York. He named the house Pentimento—a name that comes from the Italian word meaning 'to repent' and is a word that describes an alteration in a painting showing traces of the artist's previous work, illustrating that the artist changed his mind. For many of the guests at the party on the night he died, it was their first glimpse of the place since the restoration was completed."

Eliza peered from the television set again.

"The manner and circumstances of Innis Wheelock's death raise speculation and questions. Was Innis Wheelock trying to leave a message? Was he trying to repent for something? What would he have done over if he could?"

As the broadcast went to commercial, Fitzroy sat back in his chair, the color drained from his face. He was finding it a strain to breathe when the telephone rang. His wife picked it up.

"Unity? It's Valentina."

"Yes, dear. How are you this morning?"

"All right, I suppose," Valentina said softly. "I haven't been able to drag myself out of bed yet, but I hope I didn't wake you."

"No, Fitzroy and I have both been up for a while."

"Oh, good," said Valentina. "It occurred to me in the middle of the night that it would be wonderful if Fitzroy would say a few words at Innis's funeral tomorrow. After all, Fitzroy was his oldest and dearest friend."

Unity looked at Fitzroy, who motioned he didn't want to take the phone call.

"I'm sure Fitzroy would be very touched that you've thought of him like this, Valentina," said Unity. "He's indisposed right now, though, dear. I'll tell him, and he'll call you back as soon as he can. Is that all right?"

When she'd hung up the phone, Unity looked quizzically at Fitzroy. "Why didn't you want to talk to her?" she asked.

"I just didn't," he said flatly.

"Well, she wants you to speak at the funeral."

Fitzroy rubbed the back of his neck. "I guess there's no way out of it," he said. "Did Valentina mention if Innis was being buried or cremated?"

"Buried," said Unity.

"Thank God," said Fitzroy. "I've always felt that 'dust to dust' is better than 'ashes to ashes.'"

CHAPTER 33

Cleo had slept later than usual, allowing her father to get some things accomplished. But now they were rushing to get ready.

Cleo knocked over the box of cereal, spraying Cheerios all over the kitchen floor.

"I'm sorry, Daddy," she said. "I'm sorry."

Clay sighed tiredly, barely able to bring a smile to his craggy, care-worn face. "That's all right, honey," he managed. He finished buttoning the jacket of his police uniform before going for the broom in the closet down the hall. *Might as well keep it propped up in the corner,* he thought. Cleo was always dropping things and spilling things and making a general mess. But usually he didn't get angry with her. She couldn't help it. And Cleo was always so contrite after she made a mistake that Clay didn't have the heart to make her feel any worse than she already did.

As he swept up the cereal, Clay wondered why he never completely came to terms with the fact that his daughter was mentally disabled. He'd long since gotten over the fact that his wife, Cleo's mother, had left them when Cleo was only six years old. He accepted that the last sixteen years had been spent raising Cleo by himself. He was all right with that and loved his child more than he would ever have thought possible. But every time he saw Cleo's contemporaries doing things she would never be able to do, Clay was filled with sadness.

Life wasn't fair. It wasn't fair that Cleo had been singled out to have the life she did. It wasn't fair that she wouldn't drive a car, or go to college, or have a big wedding with babies to follow.

Clay had talked to Father Gehry about his feelings, and the priest had told him that Cleo was a gift from God. Clay didn't disagree; Cleo was the most precious gift of his life. But what was *her* gift? In Clay's opinion his child had been stiffed. Cleo hadn't been given a fair shake. Not at all.

"Get your jacket on, sweetie. The van will be coming soon."

He helped his daughter zip up her Windbreaker and handed her the bag lunch he'd prepared.

"What is it?" she asked.

"Bologna and cheese," answered Clay. It was always bologna and cheese, day after day. That was the only thing she wanted.

Cleo's face broke into a big smile, delighted that she would be eating her favorite at her desk at the workshop today. Did she remember she'd had the same thing yesterday? For certain, he'd be making it for her again tomorrow.

Tomorrow.

Tomorrow was the funeral.

Clay thought of Russell Wheelock, just two years younger than Cleo. When they were young, Valentina and Innis had insisted that the children get together to play. If you could call it play. Rusty would do all the playing. Cleo would just watch him.

Now Rusty was without a father.

But, in a way, it was a relief that Innis was dead. One less person alive who knew what had happened all those years ago.

CHAPTER 34

There was hot coffee waiting, and an empty cup on the table, but the kitchen was vacant. Valentina called out for Eunice but got no response as she searched through the rooms on the first floor.

Maybe Eunice was upstairs cleaning or downstairs doing the laundry. Valentina didn't have the energy to look further. She would turn up soon enough.

Taking a deep, resolute breath, Valentina slid open the wooden pocket doors that led to the old smoking room, which had become Innis's study. The room was dark and still, the only sound the clicking pendulum of the antique grandfather clock that stood solidly in the corner. She entered slowly, keenly feeling her husband's presence.

How many times had she watched him working at that desk or reading the leather-covered books that lined the walls? How many times had Innis paced the Oriental carpet that covered the floor? She could picture him now, his brow knitted in concentration.

Innis was a worrier, and therefore Valentina had been spared. All during their lives together, Valentina had known that Innis would take care of things. What was she going to do now? Without Innis, who was going to worry for her?

Valentina shook herself. No good could come from riding that train of thought. She walked to the window and drew back the drapes, letting the bright morning sun flood the room. Seating herself in Innis's well-worn leather chair, Valentina sank into the indentation made by his repeated use. She reached down and pulled back the lower drawer of the desk and began flipping through the carefully organized files. The one marked "Cemetery" was near the front.

She extracted the folder and opened it. The deed to the burial plot was right on top. Valentina was about to close the folder and put it back in the drawer when she saw the long white envelope with the word *"Wishes"* written across it in Innis's scrawling script.

Her hands trembled as she ripped open the envelope, unfolded the piece of paper inside, and began to read.

AT THE TIME OF MY DEATH, I REQUEST THE FOLLOWING AT MY FUNERAL:

ON MY COFFIN I WOULD LIKE AN ARRANGEMENT OF WILD NARCISSI AND THE RED POPPIES THAT ARE FOUND GROWING IN THE MEADOWS NEAR MY BELOVED ASSISI. IN LIEU OF OTHER FLOWERS, I WOULD LIKE DONATIONS TO BE MADE TO UNESCO FOR THE PRESERVATION OF ASSISI AND THE BASILICA OF ST. FRANCIS AS A WORLD HERITAGE SITE.

I WOULD LIKE TWO SONGS WITH TEXTS BY ST. FRANCIS TO BE SUNG AT MY FUNERAL: "ALL CREATURES OF OUR GOD AND KING" AND "THE PRAYER OF ST. FRANCIS."

I WOULD ALSO LIKE SMALL PRAYER CARDS TO BE DISTRIBUTED TO EVERYONE WHO ATTENDS THE SERVICE. ON THE FRONT OF THE CARD SHOULD BE A PICTURE OF THE GIOTTO FRESCO OF ST. FRANCIS PREACHING TO THE BIRDS. ON THE BACK OF THE CARD, I WOULD LIKE THE FOLLOWING VERSES FROM ST. FRANCIS'S CANTICLE OF THE SUN:

ALL PRAISE BE YOURS, MY LORD, THROUGH OUR SISTER
MOTHER EARTH, OUR MOTHER, WHO FEEDS US IN
HER SOVEREIGNTY AND RULES US, AND PRODUCES
VARIOUS FRUITS AND COLORED FLOWERS AND
HERBS.

ALL PRAISE BE YOURS, MY LORD, THROUGH BROTHER
FIRE, THROUGH WHOM YOU BRIGHTEN UP THE
NIGHT. HOW BEAUTIFUL HE IS, HOW GAY! FULL OF
POWER AND STRENGTH.

ALL PRAISE BE YOURS, MY LORD, THROUGH SISTER
WATER; SO USEFUL, LOWLY, PRECIOUS, AND PURE.

ALL PRAISE BE YOURS, MY LORD, THROUGH BROTHERS
WIND AND AIR, AND FAIR AND STORMY, AND ALL
THE WEATHER'S MOODS, BY WHICH YOU CHERISH
ALL THAT YOU HAVE MADE.

Valentina reread the verses. Puzzled, she got up from the desk, went to the shelves, and quickly found the section Innis had reserved for the treasured volumes about his beloved saint. Pulling a random book from the collection, she consulted the index and found the page where the lyrics of St. Francis's most famous song were written.

Sure enough, Innis had edited the canticle, changing the order of the verses, leaving some of them out altogether. Why had he done that?

Valentina put the book back in its place on the shelf. She folded Innis's instructions and slipped them into the pocket of her skirt.

All right, Innis, she thought, *if that's what you want, that's what you shall have. After what I put you through, you deserve anything you ask for.*

CHAPTER 35

Linus Nazareth strode right past Paige's desk without acknowledging her and giving her no time to warn Eliza that the executive producer was coming. He rapped on the door frame with his knuckle but didn't wait to be asked to enter. Linus looked annoyed when he saw that Eliza was on the phone.

"That sounds like a good idea," Eliza was saying. "Why don't you call Shaw's Books in Westwood and see what he has? If Janie is interested, I think we should encourage it."

Eliza looked up and held up her index finger, signaling that Linus should wait. He took a seat, his bulging stomach spilling over his belt. He crossed his legs, and his foot began tapping up and down. Unable to ignore his impatience, Eliza wrapped up the call.

"I'll be leaving in a little while, Mrs. Garcia," she said. "I'll see you later."

Before Eliza could put the receiver in the cradle, Linus began to speak.

"I want you to cover the Wheelock funeral."

Eliza frowned. "I *am* going to the funeral, Linus," she said. "But I'm going as a friend, *not* as a reporter."

"You can attend the funeral and still cover it," said Linus. "Slip out toward the end and shoot a stand-up when the mourners come streaming out of the church."

"Uh-uh," said Eliza, shaking her head.

"I really don't see the problem," said Linus. Color rose in his pock-marked cheeks.

"I'm sorry, but I do," Eliza said firmly. "If you want a story done, this time somebody else is going to have to do it. I intend to concentrate on the funeral, and I don't want to be distracted by the knowledge that I have a deadline to meet."

Eliza looked evenly at him while Linus glared back until he stood up and stalked out of the office without saying another word.

CHAPTER 36

Standing on her terrace in her cashmere robe, her short dark hair still disheveled, Susannah Lansing looked down at the cars coming in and going out the Pentimento driveway. She used her binoculars to get a clearer view of the faces of the people who got out of those cars, walked to the front door, and were admitted inside. She recognized most of them, and they would recognize her, too—though Susannah also knew from experience that they would act as if they didn't. They were experts in looking straight ahead and pretending she didn't exist.

Susannah hated to admit it to herself, but she envied them and had wanted so much to be one of them. She wished that she were down there right now, with all the others paying their respects to Valentina Wheelock. Not that Susannah was sad that Innis was dead, but because she yearned to be with the people whose acceptance she craved.

"Mrs. Lansing?"

Jumping at the sound of her housekeeper's voice, Susannah was embarrassed to be caught monitoring what was going on at the

Wheelock home. She turned from the railing and walked back into the master bedroom.

"Yes, Bonnie, what is it?" Her voice was husky.

"We need some things at the store, Mrs. Lansing. Paper towels, detergent, furniture polish. I'm going to go out and get them now, if that's okay with you."

"All right, thank you, Bonnie."

"Is there anything else you would like me to get while I'm out?"

"Yes, if you think you can find someplace that sells peace of mind," said Susannah.

The housekeeper looked at Susannah with concern.

"Don't worry, Bonnie. I'm all right. Go ahead and go to the store."

"Maybe we could go together?" Bonnie suggested. "Maybe go for a ride? It's such a pretty day out."

Susannah put her arm around the younger woman's shoulder. "Why are you so good to me?" she asked. "It must be misery working here, week after week, while I drag around and feel sorry for myself."

"No it isn't, Mrs. Lansing," Bonnie lied. "I just wish there was something I could do to make you feel better."

Susannah took her arm away and sat on the king-size bed. She looked up and said, "You know, Bonnie, you're the only friend I have anymore."

"That's not true, Mrs. Lansing. You have many friends."

Susannah shook her head and studied her fingers. "No, I don't. The people in the park have nothing to do with me, and my old friends don't bother calling to make plans anymore. I can't say I blame them. I wouldn't want to spend time with me either. I've become such a downer."

"Don't say that, Mrs. Lansing," Bonnie soothed. "You're just having a bad day. Why don't I run a hot bath for you? It will make you feel better. And I'll bring up a nice cup of tea for you to drink while you soak."

But Susannah wasn't listening. She lay back on the bed and stared up at the ceiling. "Bonnie, did they have cliques when you were in high school?" she asked. "You know, 'in' crowds that excluded people because they weren't cool enough or didn't fit in with the others in the group for any reason at all?"

Bonnie considered the question before answering. "Well, there were the popular kids and the not-very-popular ones. The popular people hung out together. Everybody else kind of watched them and wished they were in that group, I guess."

"You know, Bonnie, believe it or not, I used to be one of the popular ones," said Susannah as she continued studying the ceiling. "When I think back at how I used to ignore some of the poor kids who my friends and I considered losers, I'm ashamed of myself, because now I know exactly how they must have felt. Do you think God is punishing me for what I did back then?" asked Susannah.

"No, Mrs. Lansing. When I look around at this house and all the gorgeous furnishings and see your beautiful child and your handsome husband, I wouldn't ever think that God is punishing you. I think God has been very, very good to you. You have everything anyone could ever want."

Susannah sat up and hugged her knees. "Then why can't I feel satisfied, Bonnie? Why am I so obsessed with the fact that we weren't admitted to the Black Tie Club? Why am I letting it get to me?"

Bonnie's tone was apologetic. "I don't know, Mrs. Lansing. I don't understand it, because if somebody didn't want me to be part of their club—please excuse me for saying this, Mrs. Lansing—I'd say to hell with them."

CHAPTER 37

As the hybrid sedan crossed over the George Washington Bridge, Eliza sat back and looked out the left-side passenger's window. The conversation with Linus had left her rattled. She didn't like to say no when he had an assignment for her. Eliza felt that she and her coworkers were all on the same team, and if Linus was the *KTA* coach, then she wanted to execute the plays he called. On the other hand, she expected him to be respectful and understanding when she expressed her reticence about a particular story. But Eliza knew there was no middle ground with Linus. You were either with him or against him. He got his way, or sooner or later there would be a price to be paid.

If Linus knew about those cell-phone pictures he would be livid. To Linus those pictures would be invaluable, exclusive images that KEY News could use again and again to illustrate the story, elements that the competing news organizations didn't have. No matter how private or painful the pictures were. Eliza was relieved that she had shared them only with Annabelle and B.J. and was confident they would go no further.

But as she thought of the pictures of Innis Wheelock's blood-stained body, Eliza remembered what Annabelle and B.J. had discovered. The numbers had very deliberately been painted on the pot that was positioned next to the spot where he lay—and it was Innis himself who had made certain of that.

Innis Wheelock was trying to tell them all something. But why not come right out and say whatever it was? Why take the chance of nobody's noticing the pot or the numbers? Innis was known to be eccentric, but his dying actions had gone beyond merely strange to bizarre.

During their final conversation, Innis had told her that he knew she would do what needed to be done. Eliza wasn't sure what that would be, but she did know that the first chance she got, she was going to check out that spot on West Lake Road.

CHAPTER 38

Peter was watching MSNBC on his office television set and thinking that they hadn't called him in a while to be a guest on *Hardball* when his assistant's voice came over the intercom.

"Valentina Wheelock is on the line."

He quickly clicked off the TV and grabbed the phone.

"How are you, Valentina?" he asked. "Are you holding up all right? What can I do to help?"

"It's good to hear your voice, Peter. No matter how many things went wrong over the years, you were always able to make me feel better."

"You pay me a very great compliment, Valentina," he said. "I would have called you, but I wasn't sure you'd want to hear from me."

"Nonsense," said Valentina.

"You don't know how much it means to me to hear that," said Peter.

"I'm puzzled, though, Peter. I knew that things had been strained between Innis and you since we came back from Italy, but Innis wouldn't tell me why. Do you know why, Peter?"

"I have some idea, Valentina," said Peter, "but it really isn't anything I want to talk about or anything that Innis would want you to be involved with. You'll just have to trust me on that."

"All right," said Valentina. "But it would make me very happy if you would serve as an honorary pallbearer at the funeral tomorrow. However things ended up, you and Innis still shared so many triumphs in the past. And when this is all over, I want you to talk to Rusty about his future. Impress on him that he has to fly right if he ever plans to be elected to anything. With Innis gone, I hope I can count on you to be a male influence for my son."

"I'm flattered," responded Peter. "And believe me, I'll do all I can to make sure Rusty gets to where he should go."

Valentina hung up the phone.

Something was wrong. Something was definitely very wrong.

Eunice would never have left Valentina alone to deal with the neighbors who were stopping by to pay their respects.

During a lull in the stream of visitors, Valentina had been able to make important phone calls, and the time had slipped by. She'd been preoccupied, but now a feeling of dread washed over her.

Valentina opened the door, switched on the light, and looked down the steps.

"Oh, my God, no!" she cried as she rushed down the staircase.

CHAPTER 39

T
he walls of Zack Underwood's office were decorated with old architectural renderings along with a diploma from Pratt, a Historic Preservation Prize, and a certificate citing Zack as a finalist for the Cooper-Hewitt Architecture Design Award. Zack knew he could find a position with just about any of the most prestigious architectural firms in Manhattan, but he preferred to work for himself. For the most part, he liked working *by* himself, too.

Standing at his large drafting table, Zack spread the plans for Pentimento before him. After the completion of every job, Zack made sure that pictures were taken of the finished product. The photos were carefully arranged in books that could be shown to future clients who would be interested in seeing samples of his work. Going to the case, Zack took down the bright turquoise album. The shade of blue reminded him of the waters of the Mediterranean, and that's why he chose it for the photos of Pentimento. Zack began turning the pages.

The images of the expansive double parlor were particularly impressive. Zack managed a slight smile when he thought of how enthusiastic Innis had been when the special quarter-sawn Tuscan walnut had arrived from Italy to replace the old flooring that was too warped to be refinished. And when that same container had brought the carved blocks that Innis planned to have as part of the decoration on the fireplace, he'd been almost gleeful. Zack hadn't had the heart to tell Innis that having "ROMA" inscribed on the mantelpiece did nothing at all for him.

Zack winced when he got to the pictures that had been shot at the greenhouse. Innis had taken such an interest in the place where he would grow his beloved orchids and other beautiful plants. Sighing deeply, Zack thought it a shame that such a delightful living space would be forever linked with death.

He was about to close the book when he noticed it. The terra-cotta pot with the numbers on the side was positioned on the floor near the potting table. Zack had never cared for that pot, feeling that the bold black numbers on the side were jarring, standing out too much and not in keeping with the soft hues throughout the rest of the space. He had moved the pot to a less conspicuous place, shoving it beneath one of the long benches covered with plants. Innis had been almost apoplectic when he came into the greenhouse and noticed that pot was gone and had insisted that it be repositioned right where it had been before. Zack had shrugged and accepted it as just another one of Innis's peculiar preferences.

But now, as he took a magnifying glass out of his desk drawer to get a better look, Zack wondered if the pot and its black numbers could have some sort of significance.

WEDNESDAY
OCTOBER 7

CHAPTER 40

Reporters, producers, and camera crews were staked out in front of Our Lady of Mount Carmel Church, anticipating the arrival of the hearse carrying the mortal remains of Innis Wheelock. While waiting, they made sure that video was taken as the funeral attendees entered the church. Most of the faces were not immediately recognizable, but the current governors of New York, New Jersey, and Connecticut arrived with their spouses. The mayor of New York City came, and a large Secret Service contingent escorted a former president of the United States and his First Lady.

The church was located in the village of Tuxedo, outside the gates of Tuxedo Park and open to the public. The local population, cordoned off by police, watched the activity from the other side of the road. Bill O'Shaughnessy stood behind a wooden barricade, aware his time was limited. He had to get back to the Black Tie Club, where he was scheduled to tend bar at the repast following the funeral.

Moira's funeral had been in the same church just six months before. It was a much simpler funeral, but Bill had been touched by the people who'd attended. Most were friends that Moira and he had known for many years, people from the area but not from the park.

Like Bill, many of them made their living working for the park's residents, but at the end of the day they left the private enclave to eat and sleep in their more modest dwellings outside the gates. There was a decided divide and sometimes tension between the parkies and the townies.

Few members of the Black Tie Club, people he had served for years, had bothered attending Moira's funeral. Bill hadn't really been all that surprised, but he *had* been hurt. The hurt turned to anger and resentment when he let himself think about the request he'd made a few years before her death.

When Bill celebrated his twenty-fifth anniversary as a club employee, he was asked what he would like as a gift. He responded without hesitation. His wife had always wanted to come and take a tour of the club, have a cocktail on the stone terrace overlooking Tuxedo Lake, maybe have dinner in the dining room. That's what he most wanted to mark his quarter-century of service.

The request was denied.

CHAPTER 41

Even without an invitation, Susannah was determined to attend Innis Wheelock's funeral. She stood to the side and waited. When she saw a group approaching the church, she joined them, slipping by unnoticed as the overwhelmed usher busily checked his list. She took a seat in a pew toward the back.

Pulling the skirt of her dark knit suit over her knees, Susannah surveyed the scene. The church was filling with familiar faces from both the Tuxedo Park community and from the larger world outside the gates as well. Susannah noticed a few women look her way, but when she nodded and smiled at them, they averted their eyes. They knew she had been denied membership to the Black Tie Club, but if Innis was true to his word, he had never made public why he'd black-balled the Lansings. With Innis no longer around, Susannah felt secure. He could never reveal what he'd seen.

Those women had made up their minds about her, but Susannah believed she could win them over—if she won over Valentina Wheelock first. The event she had organized for the mentally handicapped was the first step. Surely when they saw that she was trying to do good work, they would come to change their opinions of her.

Already the planning had benefited her. When she'd written to Valentina Wheelock and explained her desire to host a local Special Olympics–like event and needed help with the venue, Valentina had agreed to sponsor and hold the games at the tennis house. Just the response Susannah had been hoping for. Eliza Blake's promise to attend had been a bonus. Susannah was certain that having the celebrity there was ensuring a bigger turnout.

Appealing to Valentina's generosity had been a gamble. Either Valentina hadn't mentioned Susannah's event to Innis or Innis hadn't wanted to quash such a worthy cause just because it was being organized by a woman he'd caught shoplifting.

Watching people take their seats in the church, Susannah felt her face grow warm as she recalled the instant she knew that Innis had seen her. She'd just stopped at a nearby convenience store to pick up some milk and bread. While she stood in line to pay for them, she'd taken a pack of gum and a candy bar from the display beneath the counter and slipped them into her purse. When she looked up again, she saw Innis staring at her.

The lift she usually got from stealing something undetected was replaced with mortification. Getting something for nothing was like giving herself a reward. It didn't matter how valuable the thing was— or wasn't; the act itself just made her feel better, a momentary relief from the anxiety she often suffered.

Innis's facial expression told her all she needed to know. She'd ruined her family's club-membership chances over a pack of gum and a Milky Way.

But now it seemed that Innis hadn't mentioned the incident to Valentina. Susannah said a prayer of thanks for that.

She also prayed that Valentina would still attend on Sunday afternoon. Valentina's attendance, despite her husband's death, could be interpreted as a signal that she didn't necessarily agree with Innis's decision to bar the Lansings from membership.

With Innis Wheelock no longer blocking the way, there was hope. And Susannah was going to do anything else she could to get into Valentina's good graces.

CHAPTER 42

I t's going to be okay, Mother," said Russell, patting her hand as they sat in back of the limousine. "It will all be over soon."

Valentina nervously pulled at the skirt of her tailored black suit and looked out the window. "*This* will be over," she said, gesturing at the people entering the church and assembled outside. "But what will life be like without your father? And now to have lost Eunice, too . . ." Her voice trailed off as she reached out and touched her son's cheek.

As the rear door was opened by the driver, Valentina wiped a tear from the corner of her eye and climbed out of the car.

Mother and son waited together in the church vestibule while the casket was unloaded from the hearse and carried inside by the funeral home's pallbearers. After the coffin was placed on the trolley, the honorary pallbearers lined up alongside the casket to escort Innis Wheelock's body to the altar.

As she stood with the rest of the assembly, Eliza recognized all four of the men coming up the church aisle. She had been introduced to three of them at the party. The fourth was the police officer who'd insisted she stop taking pictures inside the greenhouse.

Fitzroy Heavener, his face pale and eyes downcast, looked grief-stricken as he walked slowly alongside the coffin carrying his dear and longtime friend. Zack Underwood, the Wheelocks' architect for Pentimento, was solemn, his gaze focused straight ahead. Peter Nordstrut's face was devoid of expression, but he cast furtive glances around the church, trying to see who else was there. *Why was he chosen as a pallbearer?* Eliza wondered. She'd gotten the impression that Innis didn't like his political cohort very much at all.

Following the casket, Valentina faltered slightly but was steadied by her son. He was a tall, handsome young man, with broad shoulders and auburn hair. Eliza recalled Valentina's telling her that her baby had been born with soft red down on the top of his head and that she and Innis had immediately started calling him Rusty. They had decided the more formal Russell would be the name on the birth certificate—a name more fitting for the man of substance the Wheelocks expected their son to be.

Watching the young man standing by his mother's side and bracing her as they walked toward the altar, Eliza was so glad that Valentina had her son to comfort her now.

Father Michael Gehry stood at the baptismal font in the center of the church, with the tall paschal candle to his left, waiting to greet the body of Innis Wheelock. After sprinkling the coffin with holy water and placing the white funeral pall over it, the priest led the procession up to the altar, his eyes welling with tears at the sound of St. Francis's "Make Me a Channel of Your Peace." Every funeral service he performed moved him, but this one was already affecting him profoundly.

Father Gehry was absolutely sure that Innis had received God's mercy. Innis was truly sorry for his sins, and he'd done penance for them. But for Innis that wasn't enough. He wouldn't believe that God had forgiven him, and he couldn't forgive himself.

The gruesome suicide had gotten a lot of coverage in the newspapers and on television. Father Gehry knew that there were still many people, even Catholics, who mistakenly believed that suicides forfeited their chance to have a church funeral. The church's change in practice had been such a solace for the families and friends of those who took their own lives.

As he reached the altar, Father Gehry was thinking about his homily, hoping he was in no way responsible for Innis's death. "Come to me all you who labor and are burdened, and I will give you rest." Innis had ignored Christ's invitation, but the priest prayed that the Gospel would bring Valentina—and himself—some comfort.

CHAPTER 43

His palms were clammy as he waited for his turn to speak. Fitzroy reached over and patted his chest to reassure himself that the remarks he'd written down were in the pocket of his suit jacket.

After Communion, Father Gehry glanced his way. Fitzroy rose slowly, left the pew, and walked up to the lectern at the side of the altar. He made himself look out at the assembly, but, seeing all the faces, he quickly lowered his gaze and studied his speech. His hands gripped the sides of the pulpit as he began.

"When I think of Innis Wheelock, I think of so many things. He was a faithful husband to Valentina and a wonderful father to Russell." Fitzroy lifted his head, looked at Innis's widow and son sitting in the front pew, and said, "And I'm sure I speak for all of us sitting here today when I extend our very deepest condolences for your immeasurable loss."

Valentina gave him a sad little smile. Russell studied the program in his lap.

"Innis was a true friend to so many of us. I had the pleasure and privilege of enjoying his friendship longer than anyone else. We grew up together in the park, we went to school together, learned to play golf together, fished and sailed on Tuxedo Lake together. When Innis first noticed Valentina, he confided in me that he thought he'd met the girl of his dreams. I was best man at their wedding and was so flattered and touched when they asked me to be Russell's godfather. With no children of our own, my wife, Unity, and I were thrilled when Innis and Valentina included us in family celebrations and holidays so we could experience the joy of watching their son grow up.

"Much has been written about Innis and his political acumen and how he contributed his genius to Valentina's stellar rise, so I won't go into all that today. But his was a mind that assessed a situation quickly, set high goals, and reveled in the achievement of them. He enjoyed the challenge of a political race, was fascinated by current events, and worked tirelessly to understand the issues in our ever-changing world."

Fitzroy paused and gazed out at his audience, waiting until every person was looking his way. "Many of you know, of course, what gave Innis the most pleasure. On weekends he didn't even look at the front page until he finished the Sunday *New York Times* crossword puzzle. He waited all week for that thing to arrive and tossed the rest of the paper aside, going straight to the back of the magazine. He didn't even get dressed until he'd finished the puzzle."

Everyone smiled; some even chuckled.

"Innis loved puzzles. Any kind would do. Acrostics and jumbles, Scrabble and sudoku, Sherlock Holmes and Hercule Poirot, labyrinths and scavenger hunts—you name it and Innis would be all over it. When he and Valentina were in Italy, Innis even got special permission to visit the Vatican's Secret Archives. Mysteries delighted him. In fact, he once told me that figuring out the puzzles in people's personalities helped him with politics."

Fitzroy looked up again and noticed that some of the faces looking back at him wore expressions of concern and dismay. Did they think he would be insensitive enough to bring up the mystery of the stigmata? Of course he wasn't that callous.

"I was Innis's closest friend, but clearly there were things he could not share with me. That puzzles me now as I try to make sense of what happened. But there was never any puzzle about my devotion to Innis. There was nothing I wouldn't do for him, and when Valentina asked me if I would say a few words today, I couldn't refuse. It seemed somehow fitting, I think, that the person who knew him from the very beginning would be able to eulogize him at the very end. How fortunate I feel, how fortunate we all are, to have known a man like Innis Wheelock."

CHAPTER 44

Leaving the dimness of the church, Eliza squinted as she came out into the bright sunshine. She could see B.J. and Annabelle across the parking lot, stationed with the other members of the media. She went over to talk with them.

"How was it?" asked Annabelle.

"It was a funeral," said B.J. "How do you *think* it was?"

Annabelle ignored him.

"It was moving and sad," said Eliza, "yet uplifting at the same time. The priest did a very nice job."

"What's that in your hand?" asked B.J.

Eliza held up a small holy card. On the front was an image of the Giotto fresco of St. Francis talking to the birds, and on the back were stanzas from the saint's Canticle of the Sun. "I'm going to keep this," Eliza said as she slipped the card into her purse.

She looked around. "Where's Bruce?"

"He's over there, talking to the guys from CBS," said Annabelle. "I gotta go get him and see if we can snag some interviews."

Eliza watched her go. "I feel like Bruce got stuck with this assignment because I said no," she said to B.J.

"Are you kidding?" asked B.J. as he hoisted the camera to his shoulder. "Bruce Harley loves to get on television. He'll cover a dog show, a car show, or a fashion show, just as long as he gets his mug on the screen and scores another piece for his 'story count.' He doesn't resent you for refusing to cover this funeral—he loves you for it."

CHAPTER 45

As Eliza was driven inside the gates of Tuxedo Park, she noticed that in just the few days since she'd been here last the trees had gotten more colorful.

The car pulled into the cobblestone-lined courtyard in front of the Tudor-style clubhouse. The mansion's stucco walls were painted a creamy yellow and were punctuated by leaded-glass windows. A slate roof crowned the stately structure.

"I'll be out in less than an hour, Charlie," said Eliza as she exited the car.

Valentina and Russell Wheelock stood in the gracious entry hall, shaking hands and accepting condolences. While she waited for her chance to speak with them, Eliza noted the antique English furnishings, tufted leather chairs and settees, and heavy draperies made of tapestry. A large silver loving cup was displayed on the mantel of a huge fireplace in the center of the room, and old, well-polished brass chandeliers hung from the ceiling.

"Thank you for coming, Eliza," said Valentina when Eliza's turn came.

"I'm just so, so sorry, Valentina," said Eliza.

"I know you are, dear. I know you are." Valentina squeezed Eliza's hand. "But Innis wouldn't want us to wallow too long, would he?"

"No, I doubt that he would," said Eliza. She turned to the young man at Valentina's side. "I'm so sorry about your father," she said as she held out her hand.

Russell Wheelock shook it firmly. "Thank you," he said. "It's very kind of you to come. I know my father thought very highly of you."

"Well, I was a big fan of his, too," said Eliza.

Eliza turned to Valentina again. "How are you holding up?" she asked, looking into Valentina's eyes.

"Our maid died yesterday," Russell interjected.

"Oh, that's horrible. I'm so sorry to hear that," said Eliza. "Eunice, right?"

Valentina nodded. "Yes, poor, dear thing. She fell down the basement steps. A dreadful accident—and the timing is just unbelievable."

"Maybe it *is* unbelievable, Mother," said Russell. "Maybe it had something to do with Father's death."

"I can't talk about that now, Rusty," said Valentina. "Are you still taking the carriage house, dear?" she whispered.

"Yes," said Eliza.

"Good. I want you to make sure you and Janie come over and visit this weekend. I could use the company, and it would be wonderful to have someone young in the house."

"Oh, no, Valentina," Eliza protested. "I wouldn't think of intruding at a time like this."

"You'd be doing me a favor," said Valentina. "I really don't want to be alone right now."

"You'd be doing both of us a big favor," said Russell. "I have to get back to school, and I'd be very grateful if you'd be able to spend time with Mother."

"Well, all right," said Eliza uncertainly. "Janie won't be with me, though. She's going away with her friend's family this weekend. But Mack McBride is coming home."

"Please bring him along," said Valentina. "It will be good to have a man around."

Silver chafing dishes of chicken Florentine, rice, and asparagus were arranged on a long table set up in the ballroom. The funeral service had left most people who'd attended with a hearty appetite and thirst. Seeing the line at the buffet, Eliza decided to get a drink first.

"A Bloody Mary, please."

"Yes, ma'am."

As the bartender dropped ice cubes into a glass, Eliza found his face familiar.

"You were at the Wheelock party the other night, weren't you?" she asked.

"Yes," he said, keeping his focus on mixing the drink.

"I thought so," she said. "Who'd have predicted that we'd be *here* just a few days later, huh?"

"You never know," said the bartender as he slid Eliza's drink toward her.

At that point Eliza could have turned and walked away, but it occurred to her that people talked freely and openly to bartenders, and this guy could be a potential source of information.

"I'm Eliza Blake," she said. She held out her hand.

"Bill O'Shaughnessy," he said as he wiped his hand dry and shook Eliza's quickly. She noticed that he looked around furtively. He didn't want anyone to see that, she thought.

"Nice to meet you, Bill," she said. "Have you worked here a long time?" she asked.

"Thirty years, give or take."

"Wow, I bet you've seen a lot," said Eliza.

"I guess you could say that," said Bill. "But Mr. Wheelock killing himself by stigmata pretty much takes the cake."

She nodded. "Yes, I suppose it does. I can't begin to imagine why in the world Innis would do such a thing."

"Something had to be bothering him pretty deeply," said Bill quietly. "I guess you never know what's really going on in another guy's head."

Eliza took a sip of her drink. "It's just hot enough," she observed. "Thank you."

"You're welcome." Bill put the cap back on the bottle of Tabasco.

"Since you've worked here in the park for such a long time, would you mind if I tapped your memory?" she asked.

He looked at her warily. "I guess not," he said.

Eliza opened her purse and took out the map that B.J. had given her, illustrating the point on West Lake Road indicated by the latitude and longitude numbers. She handed the paper to the bartender.

"Do you know where that spot is?" she asked.

He squinted at the map. "Sure." He nodded. "That's the spot of one of the biggest mysteries Tuxedo Park has ever seen."

"Really? Why? What happened?" asked Eliza.

"It was just over twenty years ago now," said Bill as he handed the map back to her. "That was where the police found the totaled vehicle. It was smashed like an accordion, but there was no blood and there were no bodies inside."

"And there were no witnesses to the accident?" asked Eliza.

"Nope, that's a pretty isolated stretch of road there," said Bill. He shook his head. "You know, it's funny. You're the second person to ask about that today."

"I am?" asked Eliza with real interest. "Who was the other one?"

Bill nodded in the direction of the buffet table. "Zack Underwood, the big-shot architect, was just asking me about what happened on West Lake Road, too."

CHAPTER 46

The gold walls, the rose-based Oriental rug, the drapes printed with a botanical pattern of orange, crimson, and green butterflies and hibiscus, and the gilded chairs in the ballroom of the Black Tie Club were a welcome relief from the darkness of the church and the sadness of the occasion. The men and women who had come to pay their respects to Innis Wheelock and his family were relieved that the funeral was over and they could rejoin the land of the living. They ate, drank, chatted, and joked, happy for their reprieve and proving to themselves that life goes on.

Valentina traveled from table to table, accepting condolences and good wishes, expressing her gratitude to people for making the effort to come and pay tribute to her late husband. Between tables, Zack Underwood took her arm.

"Could we talk for a few minutes?" he asked.

"Of course, Zack," said Valentina. "Why don't we go into the bar?"

They seated themselves on the tufted leather sofa against the wall just inside the entrance. At the side of the room, the bartender continued to serve the guests who came in with their requests for wine, beer, and soft drinks.

"That's an attention grabber," said Zack as he observed the mounted bigmouth bass that hung on the persimmon grass-cloth-covered wall.

"Something tells me you don't want to talk about taxidermy, Zack," said Valentina.

"You're right," said Zack. He angled his body toward hers and leaned a bit closer. "First of all, I wanted to tell you, though I'm sure you've never had any doubt, that Innis loved you very much, Valentina. We worked quite closely together over the last year, and sometimes his eyes would fill with tears when he mentioned your name. It was touching." Zack reached over and took her hand. "I know that this must be so hard for you, Valentina, and I'm hoping there's something I can do to help."

Valentina smiled weakly. "Thank you, Zack. I just have to take it day by day."

"What if Innis was trying to tell us all something, Valentina?"

She looked up at him, unaware of anyone standing at the bar or coming in or out of the room. "I don't understand," she said.

"Innis had me sign a confidentiality agreement about the work I did on Pentimento, but I guess when someone dies, the pledge of secrecy dies with him."

"Meaning what?" Valentina asked apprehensively.

"Meaning I think that Innis was constructing some sort of puzzle, and I think I know what the first clue might be."

She waited. He explained about the numbers on the greenhouse pot and how he'd discovered that they were the map coordinates for the spot where the crashed car had been found twenty years earlier.

"But why would Innis point to that?" Valentina asked tensely.

"I don't know," said Zack. "But I have a feeling that there are other things—other clues—that are going to tell us what he wants us to know."

CHAPTER 47

Was that what the great Innis Wheelock meant when he said he was going to make sure that people found out? When he said that time was running out to confess and repent? Had he left behind one of his crazy puzzles that would lead to exposure?

How dare he! A puzzle was a cowardly way to do it. Instead of standing up like a man and dealing with everything, Innis had chosen to remove himself but leave a posthumous trail behind for others to follow.

That bastard wasn't going to win.

Innis sensationalized his death so that all eyes would be on Tuxedo Park. But if the stigmata was the way Innis chose to grab attention, he could certainly be one-upped.

Suicide by stigmata was grotesque enough. What would Innis think about carrying the theme further? Murder by stigmata—not just using the five bodily wounds but incorporating some of the other physical and psychological injuries Jesus suffered? Even Innis wouldn't have thought of something as perverse as that!

Clearly Zack Underwood didn't understand how stupid it was to talk where he could be so easily overheard. But that didn't mean Zack was stupid.

If he was onto West Lake Road and thought there were more clues built into Pentimento, he would surely follow through and try to figure things out.

This had to be taken care of right away, before it went any further.

The Internet made so much fascinating information available so easily.

Wikipedia, the free encyclopedia, had entries on stigmata and the Passion, the Christian theological term used for the physical, spiritual, and mental suffering Jesus Christ endured at the time of the crucifixion. The wounds he suffered while on the cross weren't the half of it.

How convenient it was to have a list of the Instruments of the Passion. Among them: the chains used to bind Jesus overnight in prison; the whip used for the thirty-nine lashes at his scourging; the reed that was mockingly placed in his hand as his royal scepter; the hammer used to drive the nails into his hands and feet; the robe of Jesus and the dice that the soldiers cast for it; thirty pieces of silver, the price of Judas's betrayal; and the shroud used to wrap Jesus's body before burial.

There was more, much more. Each of the cruel and vicious acts that Jesus endured had the potential to be acted out in a different way, in a different time, on a different victim—if it came to that.

CHAPTER 48

At one of the round tables, there was an empty seat next to Zack Underwood. Eliza went over.

"May I?" she asked.

Zack looked up, his expression welcoming when he saw her. "Please join me," he said, standing up and pulling out the chair.

Eliza sat down, and they made small talk while they ate. When they had finished, she brought up their first meeting at the party.

"I remember you saying that Innis told you he had something special planned for that night," she said.

Zack sat back in his chair and shook his head. "God, if I'd known what he meant, maybe I could have done something that would've stopped him. I feel terrible about this."

"Me, too," said Eliza. She told Zack about her conversation with Innis at the fountain. "I could tell that something was bothering him, but I had no idea of the depth of his despair."

"I don't think anyone did," said Zack. "I keep asking myself why. Why would Innis do something like this? He'd been so happy when we finished the renovations. In fact, I recall him telling me that he had never been more satisfied."

"Zack," began Eliza, "I want to talk to you about something. We have a picture taken in the greenhouse that shows a pot with numbers on it. Numbers that correspond to a spot where a mysterious accident occurred two decades ago."

Zack sighed deeply, a sigh Eliza interpreted as relief. "I'm so glad you know about it, too," he said. "I just figured out what those numbers meant myself. And only this afternoon I spoke with Bill the bartender, who's been around this place forever, and asked if that West Lake Road location meant anything special to him. When he told me about the accident that had taken place there, I got this horrible feeling. As if Innis were trying to tell me something. Tell us all something."

"Did you put those numbers on the pot?" asked Eliza.

"No, Innis did," said Zack. "Even though I told him that they were distracting, he insisted on keeping the numbers and the pot on display. But, you know, there were other things he asked me to do that didn't make a whole lot of sense to me."

"Like what?" asked Eliza.

Zack looked around the room. "I don't really feel comfortable talking about them here."

"Would you be willing to talk to me about it in private?" asked Eliza.

"Yes, I think I would," said Zack. "If Innis is leaving us some sort of message from the grave, that isn't something I'd want to deal with alone."

CHAPTER 49

Eliza finished her coffee and looked around the ballroom. She spotted Russell and went over to speak with him again.

"I want to say good-bye to your mother, too," she said. "But I can't find her. Would you thank her for me and tell her I'll call when I get back this weekend?"

"I will," said Russell. "I know she's so happy that you'll be spending time up here. I am, too. She needs her friends now. Bad enough she lost her husband, but now this Eunice thing. I don't know what she's going to do."

"Your mother is a strong woman," said Eliza. "I hope you have people you can lean on, too, Russell. I know how hard it is to lose someone you love very much."

Russell nodded, and Eliza saw him swallow hard as he tried to keep his emotions in check.

"Don't go out the way we came in, Charlie," said Eliza, taking the map B.J. had printed out for her from her purse. "Turn left when you leave the courtyard and follow the road around the lake."

They passed the swimming pool and the outdoor tennis courts and an enormous white Greek Revival–style building in which court tennis and squash were played. Then the road curved and rose and fell gently, as if inviting the travelers to slow down and enjoy the loveliness of the surroundings. One after another, each different in architecture and coloring, some of the prime residences of Tuxedo Park appeared: Tudor, Dutch style, Federal Colonial, English Arts and Crafts, Spanish Mission style, Jacobean Revival, and French Château. Some had single gables; some were built of stone and shingles or brick and granite. All of them were carefully placed on a unique parcel of land and were designed to satisfy their demanding original owners. The homes continued to please the residents who came to live in them for the century afterward.

As the car climbed upward, it came to Pentimento. Eliza looked out the window at the Italianate mansion as they passed. Such a beautiful house, perched in the hills in such a glorious spot, and yet the owner of the home had been so hopelessly troubled.

If only I had known, if only I had known.

After Pentimento there were a few more mansions tucked away behind the trees. Then a long stretch where there was nothing but hills and vegetation on one side of the road and the shore of Tuxedo Lake on the other.

"Can you slow down, Charlie?" Eliza asked as she consulted the marked map.

As the car crept along, Eliza craned her neck to get a better view. Trees, bushes, some large boulders, and, through the growth, the sparkle of the sun on the lake.

There was nothing else to see.

CHAPTER 50

O nce the last of the luncheon guests had departed, Russell escorted his mother home from the club.

"Are you sure you're all right with my going back now, Mother?" he asked when they entered Pentimento.

Valentina squeezed her son's hand. "Yes, dear, I understand. You've so much to do, and those professors at Columbia don't want to hear any excuses about not having your work done. And if you want to go on to Harvard Law, every single grade counts. But do you have a few minutes to sit and talk before you leave?"

"Sure I do," said Russell.

Valentina led the way down the long hall and into the main living area. She stopped at the bar, took the cover off the ice bucket, and looked inside. "No ice," she said. "Eunice would have made sure there was ice ready and waiting for the drink she knew I'd need. She took such good care of me, thinking of everything."

"We'll find a replacement, Mother," said Russell. "Try not to worry."

They sat in the two armchairs that flanked the fireplace. Valentina began the conversation.

"Everyone had such good things to say about your father, Rusty. You've got a lot to live up to."

"I know that, Mother. I've always known that."

"The world is your oyster, Rusty. Your father and I have so many friends from our years in politics, and if your turn comes to run, they'll be there to help you."

"If?" Russell asked sharply.

"You are in a very privileged position, Rusty. 'Of those to whom much is given, much is expected.'"

Russell nodded solemnly.

"Always remember: Any sort of scandal could ruin everything."

CHAPTER 51

C hief Clay Vitalli reviewed the security logs, checking to make sure that the nonresidents who had entered the park for the funeral luncheon were safely out now. Satisfied that everybody had left, Clay turned to the guard at the security gate.

"I'm taking a ride into town," he said, running his finger under the starched collar of his shirt. "Then I'm going home and getting out of this uniform."

"Yes, sir."

As he was exiting the guardhouse, a car was coming down the hill. The late-model, dark green Audi convertible slowed to a stop next to Clay. Russell Wheelock was behind the wheel.

"I want to thank you again for all you did to make things go smoothly today, Clay," said Russell. "My mother and I really appreciate it."

"Your father meant the world to me, Rusty," said Clay. "I'd do anything for him and your mother."

"And you have," said Russell. "Thanks a lot for helping me out with that other thing."

"Which one?" asked Clay.

"The speeding ticket, of course." Russell grinned.

"Oh, yeah. It's not funny, Rusty. Watch that heavy foot of yours, will you? It could get you in trouble."

Russell raised his hand. "I hear you. I hear you," he said.

"Good."

"Another thing, Clay. With Eunice gone, my mother is all alone in that house—"

Clay cut him off before he could continue. "Don't worry. I'm putting more security on the house. My guys will be checking on her."

As the young man drove away, Clay was filled with resentment. A kid in college tooling around in an expensive ride like that. That kid didn't know how lucky he was. His parents had given him everything, made sure that all his problems were solved, paved the way for him in every possible respect.

Rusty Wheelock was the chosen one, the heir apparent. And he took too much for granted.

Meanwhile Clay's own child, his twenty-two-year-old daughter, Cleo, would never drive a car and never go to college. Hell, he'd be thrilled if Cleo could learn to read.

It wasn't fair at all.

CHAPTER 52

Once Bonnie had let her know that there was a lot of talk in town about the death of the Wheelocks' maid, Susannah knew she had an opportunity to further ingratiate herself. After talking it over with Bonnie, Susannah called and offered her maid's services to Valentina until she could find a replacement.

"Would you really do that for me?" asked Valentina. "How generous and thoughtful of you, Susannah. I can't thank you enough."

"It would be my pleasure and privilege, Valentina. I want to help you in any way I can."

After they decided when Bonnie would arrive at Pentimento, Susannah hung up, hoping she was one step closer to being part of the "in" crowd. She hurried to find Bonnie and let her know.

Though she was careful not to show it, Bonnie was relieved to be getting away from the Lansings. She welcomed the chance to escape Susannah's constant neediness and insecurity, her moping around and her complaining that she wasn't a part of the Black Tie Club.

She was also worried that eventually Susannah was going to be caught shoplifting. Bonnie had seen her do it repeatedly, though she never let on to Susannah. Bonnie didn't want to be associated in any way with that.

CHAPTER 53

When he arrived at his office in town, Zack returned a few phone calls and read through some mail, but he was unable to concentrate on the plans he was working on for another restoration. By five o'clock he realized it was useless and gave himself permission to wrap things up. At least he could get in a jog before it got too dark. He changed into the sweats and running shoes he kept in the office and told his secretary to go home.

After a day like this, there was no better thing to do than get some exercise. It was life-affirming to run, surrounded by the brilliant red of silver maples and the gold and yellow of the tall oaks. The crisp, cleansing autumn air pulsed through his lungs, and his legs felt strong as they pounded on the pavement.

The light was beginning to fade when he reached what he knew to be the two-mile mark, and he turned around. By the time he got back to his building, it was almost dark. Zack walked for a while to cool down before he went inside.

The door was unlocked, but he didn't think much of it. His secretary must have left it that way, knowing that he would be coming back but aware from experience that he might have forgotten his keys.

It was quiet as he entered the vestibule. Zack turned on a light and proceeded to his office.

The moment he walked into the room, he felt tense. The papers on his desk, always stacked so precisely, were scattered and messy. Books from the shelves were lying on the floor. Some of the file drawers were pulled open. Architectural renderings were strewn around the room.

Instinctively, Zack reached for the telephone to call 911, but before he could dial, something encircled his neck. Stunned, he reached for the ligature as it was pulled, shocking him, keeping him from breathing. He gasped for air as he clawed at the leather cord wrapped around his throat, tearing into his skin, getting tighter and tighter.

Before Zack lost consciousness, a distinctive flash of color caught his eye, and it registered in his mind that the turquoise-leather-covered album containing the pictures of Pentimento was lying on the office floor.

Zack was a lot heavier than he looked. Pulling his body over to the chair required too much strength. It was easier to bring the chair to Zack.

It was a perfect throne, high-backed with armrests.

Maneuvering the dead weight onto the seat took some effort. And the body kept slumping over to the side each time it was positioned upright.

A king had to sit erect, or the effect would be lost.

Finally the remains of Zack Underwood were balanced, his eyes open, his mouth agape as if caught in the middle of issuing a royal command.

Before leaving, there was one last thing to do. A reed, pulled from a field in Tuxedo Park, was placed in Zack's hand and his fingers forced around it.

CHAPTER 54

A s she walked through the front door, Eliza was greeted by the aroma of Mrs. Garcia's scrumptious lamb stew. Seconds later Janie ran up to her and gave her a kiss and a long hug.

"Mrs. Garcia took me to Shaw's after school, and look what we got," said Janie, holding up two children's books.

Eliza took them and read the titles aloud. "*St. Francis of Assisi: A Life of Joy* and *Francis: The Poor Man of Assisi.*" She flipped through the pages. "Wonderful illustrations," she said.

"Want to read them with me?" Janie asked hopefully.

"All right, but let me change first." She was eager to get out of the clothes she'd worn to the funeral.

Eliza stopped in the kitchen to check in with Mrs. Garcia. "How'd it go today?" she asked as she took the cover off a pot on the stove and looked inside.

"Everything is fine, *señora*," said the housekeeper as she measured out some cornmeal and poured it into a mixing bowl. "The plumber came and fixed that dripping faucet in the bathroom."

"Good," said Eliza, taking a spoon and sampling the gravy.

"And I went to the market and bought some things to stock the kitchen of your new place. I thought it would be good if I make a few dishes for you to keep in the freezer there to have when you need them."

"Great idea," Eliza said with enthusiasm. "Do you think you could make that chicken that Mack likes so much? That would be nice to have on Friday night."

Mrs. Garcia smiled. "I was already planning to do that. I went to the liquor store, too, and bought a case of wine and a bottle of Dewar's."

Eliza knew that Mrs. Garcia liked Mack and approved of the relationship.

"Thanks for taking Janie to get those books," said Eliza, changing the subject. "We have enough time to read one before dinner, don't we?"

Mrs. Garcia looked at the clock. "About half an hour," she answered.

Janie was sitting on the bed waiting for her mother, scanning the pages of her new books. The way St. Francis looked was different in each. In the first book, Francis seemed very real. In the other he was more like a cartoon character. In both he had a dark beard and a round haircut, and was wearing a long brown robe tied at the waist with a piece of rope. There were sandals on his feet.

In some pictures St. Francis was talking to animals; in others he was talking to his brother friars. Some showed him praying; some showed him working and helping men and women who looked like they were poor and hungry. The one that showed St. Francis being visited by an appearance of the Christ Child in a cave on Christmas morning particularly appealed to Janie's imagination.

By the time she heard her mother coming up the stairs, she had decided. When Eliza entered the master bedroom, Janie made her announcement. "Mom, I want to be St. Francis for Halloween."

CHAPTER 55

Unity was grateful that they'd had such a big lunch. Now she would just have to heat up some soup and put some cheese and crackers on a plate, and dinner would be served.

Standing in the efficiency kitchen and twisting the handle of the opener as it rounded the rim of the soup can, Unity remembered with longing the life she used to have. The kitchen at Nine Chimneys had been larger than their entire apartment was now. The pantry alone was bigger than her present kitchen. For the early years that Unity lived at Nine Chimneys, she never gave the kitchen a thought, because she had never had to cook. The Heavener women had always had help.

When she'd taken her marriage vows, for better or worse, for richer or poorer, Unity really hadn't dwelled on the meaning of the words. Fitzroy came from a wealthy family that had maintained a house in Tuxedo Park almost since its inception. Of course their new life would be good.

At first it was all that Unity had hoped it would be. She loved being the lady of the manor. She supervised the staff, entertained well and often, decorated and gardened and spent time at the club playing bridge and tennis or taking the boat out on the lake.

Fitzroy was a pleasant partner, available to play with her since he didn't go to an office or other place of business each day. Having family money meant he spent his time managing his investments and generally doing as he pleased. He hadn't been raised to do anything other than that.

Where was he anyway? Unity wondered as she sliced some cheddar cheese and arranged it on crackers. When the luncheon was over, he'd told her that he had something he needed to do. That was several hours ago now.

She began to worry. Fitzroy was taking Innis's death hard. Unity hadn't seen him this upset since Nine Chimneys had burned to the ground. Back then, Fitzroy had had Innis to lean on. Now he had only her to help him in getting over the loss of Innis.

Unity knew that it was her duty to comfort her husband, yet she was overcome with hidden but seething anger. Fitzroy was responsible for the situation they found themselves in now. He was the reason they were forced to live in this little upstairs apartment over the club. Fitzroy could cloak it any way he wanted, but nobody was fooled.

For years he'd known that their investments were dwindling, that they were struggling to heat and maintain and pay the taxes. Even when, one by one, he let members of the staff go, he tried to paint it as his choice. He just didn't feel right, he said, keeping all those people working at the house when only he and Unity lived there. It was unseemly to have more servants than residents.

Getting rid of the servants didn't solve their problems. The cavernous rooms had to be heated, the old plumbing leaked, the roof needed repair. As the bills mounted, first one wing and then another was closed up until, finally, Unity and Fitzroy were living in just three rooms.

As far as Unity knew, in all that time Innis Wheelock had never offered to come to Fitzroy's aid, never extended financial assistance. Even though Fitzroy had done everything he could over the years to help Innis and Valentina's political aspirations, even though he was godfather to their son, when the chips were down, Innis hadn't written a check to help the Heaveners. What kind of best friend was that?

The second section of the *KEY Evening Headlines* featured a report on the Wheelock funeral. Unity recognized many of the people shown entering Our Lady of Mount Carmel, she and Fitzroy among them.

Just as the report came to a close, Unity heard the key in the lock. "Where were you, Fitzroy? I was worried about you."

He didn't answer right away. His face was flushed, and a shock of white hair fell across his forehead. The suit he'd worn since the funeral was rumpled.

"Were you drinking?" Unity asked suspiciously.

"No, I wasn't drinking," said Fitzroy as he limped across the room and collapsed in a worn armchair. "I needed to reflect on what I've lost."

"For almost four hours?"

"I walked around the lake several times, and I stopped here and there to rest and think about all the things that Innis and I did together. I have to admit, they weren't all happy memories."

CHAPTER 56

For the third time in a row, Peter served the handmade tennis ball, but it failed to touch the sloping roof to his left.

"What's the matter with you tonight?" called his opponent from the other side of the indoor real tennis court. "You get here late, you look like a wreck, and now your playing sucks."

Peter walked toward the net. "I don't know," he said. "I guess it was just a horrible day, and I'm topping it off with a horrible match."

"Well, we've only played two sets. Buck up, Peter."

"I'm sorry. I just don't have it in me tonight."

THURSDAY
OCTOBER 8

CHAPTER 57

It was midmorning when the first wire-service story ran about Zack Underwood. It consisted of only three short, clipped sentences.

THE BODY OF AN ARCHITECT EMPLOYED BY INNIS AND VALEN-
TINA WHEELOCK WAS FOUND THIS MORNING IN HIS TUXEDO,
NEW YORK, OFFICE. SOURCES SAY THAT THIRTY-EIGHT-YEAR-
OLD ZACHARY UNDERWOOD WAS MURDERED. THE DISCOVERY
COMES FOUR DAYS AFTER INNIS WHEELOCK COMMITTED SUICIDE
BY STIGMATA.

After reading the story on the computer at her desk, Annabelle Murphy picked up the telephone and called Eliza's office.

"Hi, Paige. It's Annabelle. Is Eliza available?"

As Annabelle waited, another story popped up on her computer screen. She read through it quickly. Zack Underwood had been found by his secretary when she came in to work. The office had been ransacked, and police were trying to ascertain what, if anything, was missing. The story also stated that Underwood had recently completed the architectural renovations on Pentimento, the Wheelocks' estate.

"Did you see it?" Annabelle asked as soon as Eliza answered.

"Yeah, I just read it," said Eliza. "I was talking to the guy only yesterday. He had agreed to let me see the architectural plans for Pentimento." Eliza shook her head. "I can't believe this."

"Something's more than a little funky here," said Annabelle. "This murder has got to be connected to Wheelock's death."

"I'm thinking the same thing," said Eliza. "Zack told me yesterday that he'd figured out that those numbers on the greenhouse flowerpot had been the coordinates for the spot on West Lake Road. I hadn't had the chance to tell you yet, Annabelle, but that was the location of an accident that happened over twenty years ago. They found a complete wreck—but there were no passengers in the car. And despite the fact that the car was totaled and the windshield smashed, there was no blood."

Annabelle digested the information. "But does that have anything to do with his murder? Would he be killed because he knows that?"

"I don't know," said Eliza. "But he told me that Innis had him incorporate other features into the plans for Pentimento."

"What kind of features?" asked Annabelle.

"Zack agreed that he would tell me, but obviously that's not going to happen now," said Eliza. "I think Zack Underwood may have been killed because somebody thought he knew too much."

"So what do we do now?" asked Annabelle, thinking out loud. "Maybe B.J. and I should take a ride up to Tuxedo and see what we can find out."

"Good idea," said Eliza. "And see what you can learn about that accident. I have a feeling that what happened back then is directly related to what's happening now."

CHAPTER 58

On the ride out from Manhattan, Annabelle and B.J. came up with their plan of action. First they would go to Zack Underwood's architectural office, get some exterior shots, and see if they could talk their way inside.

"Don't hold your breath," said B.J. "I doubt the cops are gonna let us anywhere close to their crime scene."

"You're probably right," said Annabelle, "but we can try. At least we can be thankful that Underwood's office is outside the park. If it were inside, we'd have no chance of getting any video at all."

Any hopes Annabelle and B.J. had that KEY News would be alone in thinking that the Zack Underwood murder could be related to Innis Wheelock's suicide evaporated when their vehicle pulled off at the Route 17 exit. They spotted two local-news satellite vans and a couple of cars they recognized to be carrying crews from other networks.

While B.J. shot video of the office building, police cars, and yellow tape cordoning off the crime scene, Annabelle made the obligatory plea to the officers guarding the building to allow KEY News to get some interior shots.

"No dice," said one of the cops.

"How about giving us an interview?" suggested Annabelle.

"Nope."

"Just a short one?"

"What part of the word 'no' don't you understand?"

Annabelle shrugged. "Thanks so much for your cooperation," she muttered as she walked away.

The only reassuring thing was that none of the other newspeople seemed to be getting anywhere either. Annabelle and B.J. sat in their car watching as, one by one, representatives of the competition made their case to law enforcement and were duly rejected.

"I'm not going back until we have something the other guys don't have," said B.J.

"Yeah, but what?" asked Annabelle. She stared out the window, trying to think of what else they could pursue. "Maybe we could take a stab at getting into the park and see if we can get some reaction from the rich residents."

B.J. shook his head. "Ain't gonna happen, and you know it."

"All right," said Annabelle, coming up with an alternate suggestion. "Let's get some reaction from the locals in town."

"What do we have to lose?" asked B.J. as he turned the key in the ignition. "It's better than sitting around here and doing nothing."

As B.J. steered the car from the parking lot onto the busy road, Annabelle spotted a woman on the other side of the street. She was leaning against a tree and staring at the office building. Something about the distressed expression on the woman's face caused Annabelle to reach out and grab B.J.'s arm.

"Hold it," she said.

"What?" asked B.J., keeping his foot on the brake.

"See that woman over there?" Annabelle nodded across the road. "Let me go over and talk to her."

She got out of the car and crossed over to where the woman was standing and smoking a cigarette. A bunch of discarded butts were scattered at her feet. Annabelle sensed the woman's vulnerability.

"Hello. I'm Annabelle Murphy, and I'm with KEY News," she said.

"Nice to meet you," the woman answered automatically as she shook Annabelle's hand weakly.

"It's such a terrible thing," said Annabelle, pointing toward the building across the road.

"It is terrible." The woman's voice cracked. "Awful, awful."

"Did you know Zack Underwood?"

The woman closed her eyes and whispered, "He was my boss, and I think I might have been the last person to ever see him alive."

Eureka!

This woman was definitely not the last person to see Zack Underwood alive. His killer held that distinction. But all the same, Annabelle tried not to show her enthusiasm as she got the woman to reveal her name and agree to an interview.

"Would you be willing to go to a more private place to talk?" asked Annabelle. "We'd rather not do this standing on the side of the road with cars passing by and making noise." She failed to mention that she also didn't want to do it within sight of their media competition or the police.

Aurelia Patterson appeared uncertain. "Where would we go?"

"I'm afraid I have to look to you for a suggestion," said Annabelle. "I'm not really familiar with the area. Is there a park we could go to? Or someplace else that would be quiet?"

When Annabelle brought Aurelia over to the car and introduced her to B.J., he was impressed. It wasn't just luck that had led her to approach the troubled-looking woman across the street—it was an ability to read people and an innate sense of what leads to follow in pursuit of a story.

But when the two women got into the car and Annabelle announced that they were going to Aurelia's house in Tuxedo Park for an interview, B.J. knew that luck, fate, the news gods, or whatever you wanted to call it was on their side. Sometimes it just worked out like that.

As the car drove north on Route 17, Annabelle wanted to make sure they weren't taking advantage of the upset woman.

"I know that the park frowns on cameras coming inside," she said. "Are you sure you're all right with this?"

"They don't have to know," said Aurelia. "I just want to get to my own place, where I feel safe. And if something I know or say can help find out who did this horrible thing to Zack, then I want to make it public. We can do the interview inside the house, and nobody will be any the wiser."

The guard at the security gate recognized Aurelia and waved the car through.

The Patterson home was not grand. It was a standard-size ranch built in the 1960s.

"When people think of Tuxedo Park, they automatically imagine 'mansion,'" said Aurelia as the car turned into the driveway. "They don't realize that there are some smaller houses, too. Not everyone is rich, and not everyone is a member of the Black Tie Club." She leaned forward in her seat. "Pull around to the back so no one will see you bringing in the camera."

A black-and-white border collie greeted them when they entered the house. Aurelia bent down and hugged the dog, not letting go for several moments. While she guided her pet out into the yard, B.J. determined the best place for the interview and set up the lights.

"She seems like a decent sort," B.J. whispered conspiratorially to Annabelle as he plugged an electrical cable into the wall. "Trusting, too, leaving us alone in her house like this."

"Yeah," said Annabelle. "Why do I feel like I should be protecting her?"

"Get over it," said B.J.

Annabelle began with the standard questions, asking Aurelia to state and spell her name and identify herself in regard to her relationship with Zack Underwood.

"I've been his secretary for six years," said Aurelia. "I've been with him since he opened his office in Tuxedo."

"Did you enjoy working for him?" asked Annabelle.

Aurelia's eyes filled with tears, and her lip quivered. "I can't believe we're talking about him in the past tense," she said. "Zack was a wonderful boss, very easygoing, at least as far as working with people is concerned. I started with him just after my husband left me. I hadn't been in the workforce for a very long time, and I was unsure of myself. I knew nothing about architecture, but he was very patient with me, explaining terms that I needed to know and procedures that needed to be followed. But Zack was no pushover. When it came to his work, he was exacting, a perfectionist."

"That's why Innis Wheelock hired him," observed Annabelle.

"Yes," said Aurelia. "And because Zack had spent time training in

Italy. Mr. Wheelock liked that. I used to hear them talking about the things they loved in Roman architecture."

Annabelle was about to begin what she knew would be the toughest part of the interview for Aurelia.

"Would you like some water before we go any further?" she asked.

Aurelia shook her head. "No. I'm all right. Go ahead."

"Can you tell us about the last time you saw Zack?"

Aurelia gripped the arms of the chair. "It was late yesterday afternoon. Zack had gone to Mr. Wheelock's funeral and then the lunch at the Black Tie Club afterward. He came back to the office, but I don't think he got any work done. I don't think he could concentrate. Around five o'clock he told me to pack it in for the day and that he was going to go for a run. That was the last time I ever saw him alive."

Tears flowed down her cheeks. "I think I could use that water now," she said. Aurelia got up, walked into the kitchen, and took a bottle from the refrigerator. When she returned, she had composed herself.

"I left after he did," she said, "and I wasn't sure if he'd taken his keys with him or not. He'd forgotten them other times, so I left the door unlocked. I figured he'd be back in a half hour or so and that it would be all right." She stopped talking and considered what she'd done. "If I had only locked up," she said finally, "Zack might still be alive."

"If somebody wanted to kill him, they were going to find a way," said Annabelle gently. "A locked door wasn't going to stop that."

"Thanks," Aurelia said, sniffling. "I appreciate that."

"Let's go to what happened this morning," urged Annabelle.

"All right," said Aurelia. She took a deep breath. "I came to work at the regular time, but as soon as I got there, I should have known that something was wrong."

"Because the door was still unlocked?" asked Annabelle.

"Not just unlocked—it had been left ajar. Zack's car was in his parking space, so at first I thought he'd come in early. I called out to him, but nobody answered. I should have called the police right then. I wish I had, but I went into Zack's office."

Aurelia stared straight ahead, re-creating the scene in her mind.

"I know this is very difficult," said Annabelle, "but can you describe what you saw?"

Aurelia nodded, closing her eyes for a moment before continuing. "The office had been ransacked," she said. "There were papers and books strewn around everywhere, drawers had been pulled out and their contents thrown all over the floor. The first thought I had was that I was going to have a terrible job cleaning it all up." Aurelia began to cry in earnest. "Can you believe that? I was worried about the mess."

Annabelle and B.J. waited for Aurelia to compose herself so that she could go on to describe the discovery and condition of Zack Underwood's body. But when she did speak again, she deliberately changed the subject.

"Once the police are finished searching the room, they want me to come in and figure out if anything is missing."

B.J. pulled his head back from the camera and looked at Annabelle. They each knew what the other was thinking. They had to press Aurelia for the details of the murder scene. The trick was not to alienate her; they wanted to be able to call on her in the future. She might confide in them what, if anything, was taken from Zack Underwood's office and perhaps be a source for information about the police investigation into his death.

"I know this is very difficult, Aurelia," said Annabelle. "But can you describe what else you saw?"

"You mean how Zack looked?" asked Aurelia.

Annabelle nodded. "Yes, and whatever impressions you had."

Aurelia shifted her gaze from Annabelle and concentrated instead on her hands, which she twisted in her lap. "At first I just got the sense that somebody else was in the room. I could see something in my peripheral vision." She paused for a moment. "It turned out to be Zack."

"On the floor?" asked Annabelle.

Aurelia shook her head, still staring at her hands. "No. He was sitting in an armchair."

"So you think he was killed as he sat there?"

"Oh, I don't think so," said Aurelia. "Zack hated that chair. He never sat in it." She continued, with some hesitation, "I think he was . . . *positioned* there."

"What do you mean?" asked Annabelle.

Aurelia nervously cleared her throat before speaking. "I think somebody wanted Zack to look like he was posing as a king."

"A king," Annabelle repeated. "I'm sorry. I don't get it."

"Zack looked like he was sitting on a throne, holding a scepter in his hand."

"A scepter?"

Aurelia nodded.

"What was it made of?" asked Annabelle.

"It wasn't a real scepter," said Aurelia. "More like a reed or a stalk."

"A plant of some kind?" suggested Annabelle.

"Yes."

"Could you tell how Zack had been killed, Aurelia?"

The woman closed her eyes. "There were marks around his neck," she whispered. Her hands trembled, and her face was ashen.

"Aurelia, are you all right?" asked Annabelle with concern. "Are you up to going back to the office?" She motioned to B.J. to stop recording. "The police are probably ready for you to take stock of what's in there. We can talk more sometime after that."

CHAPTER 59

After dropping Aurelia back at Underwood's office, Annabelle called the newsroom and listened to instructions.

"Linus definitely wants a piece for the show tomorrow morning," she told B.J. when she got off her BlackBerry.

Both of them calculated what elements they already had.

"Obviously, the best thing we've got is the interview with Aurelia," said Annabelle. "But the only other element is the office exterior video. We can pad the piece with the file of Innis Wheelock's funeral when we explain the supposed connection between Wheelock's and Underwood's deaths."

B.J. frowned. "That's all right, I guess. But I wish we had more."

"Well, the cops aren't saying anything yet."

"We could go ahead and try to get some MOS," suggested B.J.

Annabelle sighed. "All right, but all the others will go for man-on-the-street reactions. I'd like to have something else."

As they drove toward the center of town, it occurred to her. "I know," she said. "Turn around."

"Where are we going?" asked B.J. as he slowed down.

"The library," said Annabelle. "We passed it as we drove here this morning."

The stone exterior of the Tuxedo Park Library was in keeping with the historic tone of the area.

Except for the woman behind the circulation desk, Annabelle and B.J. had the library to themselves. They approached the librarian, who looked up from what she was doing and smiled.

"We're looking for some information on an accident that happened about twenty years ago in Tuxedo Park," said Annabelle. "I did a Google search but found only a short mention of it in a *Times Herald-Record* article out of Middletown, New York."

"I didn't live here then," said the librarian. "But maybe there's some account of it in the *Tuxedo News.* It's not available online, so I'll have to do a manual search. Do you have an approximate date when the accident happened?"

Annabelle told the librarian when the article had run. She and B.J. followed the woman to the other side of the library.

"This is the Tuxedo Park History Collection," said the librarian, gesturing to the shelves. "Let me check through our archives for the *Tuxedo News* editions that ran around the time you're interested in."

Fifteen minutes later the librarian returned, carrying a stack of old newspapers.

"Start with these," she said. "But please be careful with them. They're the only copies we have."

Annabelle and B.J. began flipping through the pages.

"Here's something," B.J. said with excitement. "It's buried in the back of the paper."

"Read it out loud," said Annabelle.

B.J. cleared his throat. " 'A blue Ford Mustang convertible was found, abandoned and badly damaged, on an isolated stretch of West

Lake Road. A search of the area found no possible driver or passengers. Authorities are investigating to find out the owner of the car. Officer Clay Vitalli responded to the scene after a passing motorist alerted Tuxedo Park Police.' "

"Good," said Annabelle. "Now we know to look in the editions after this one."

The following edition featured a bigger story, right on the front page. Annabelle read it aloud.

" 'The crushed blue Mustang convertible, found abandoned on a secluded section of West Lake Road in the park last week has been identified as belonging to 31-year-old Martin O'Shaughnessy, a town resident employed as a landscaper for many Tuxedo Park estates, among them the house of Innis and Valentina Wheelock. Mrs. Wheelock is widely considered a favorite in the next gubernatorial election.

" 'Police are looking for Martin O'Shaughnessy, but so far have been unable to find him.' "

Annabelle could find only one more article. It ran the following week.

" 'Police may be near to closing the case of the mysterious abandonment of a car on West Lake Road two weeks ago. Tracing the car to Martin O'Shaughnessy, a landscaper and village resident, police now suspect that O'Shaughnessy has fled to Ireland. Martin O'Shaughnessy's brother, William, told police his sibling had been dissatisfied with his work situation. He also said Martin had been talking for quite some time about going to live in Ireland, the country from which their parents had emigrated.

" 'Officer Clay Vitalli stated that since no real crime was committed, other than abandoning the car in a ditch, authorities are satisfied and do not plan to pursue matters further.' "

Annabelle removed a reporter's notebook from her bag and opened to a clean page. Taking her pen, she began writing notes as she spoke:

"Wrecked car found. Car belongs to Martin O'Shaughnessy. O'Shaughnessy isn't found. Police call off inconclusive search."

"Sounds fishy," said B.J.

"Ya think?" said Annabelle. "Let's make copies of these articles and bring them back to Eliza."

CHAPTER 60

Aurelia Patterson was in tears when she finished taking inventory of Zack Underwood's ransacked office. She handed the short list of missing items to Chief Vitalli. Then she wanted to go home and lie down. Vitalli assigned one officer to drive her and another one to follow along in her car.

"You're in no condition to drive, Mrs. Patterson," said Clay. "Thank you for your help today, and needless to say it would be best if you didn't tell anyone any details."

Aurelia was afraid to mention that she'd already told the KEY News people what she'd seen.

As soon as he could get to a location where no one would hear his conversations, Clay took out his cell phone to make two phone calls.

He said the same thing to both people. "We have to get together and talk. The three of us have a lot to figure out. Things are busting wide open."

CHAPTER 61

Eliza was in her office talking with Margo Gonzalez when Annabelle and B.J. arrived. They recounted what Aurelia Patterson had told them.

"Zack was positioned like a king on a throne?" Eliza asked uncertainly.

"Sounds more like a mock king," said Margo.

"If the killer was staging things," said Eliza, "what was that supposed to mean?"

"I don't know," said Annabelle. "But let me show you what we found at the library." She handed the *Tuxedo News* articles to Eliza.

When she finished reading the third article, Eliza made two connections.

"First of all, Officer Clay Vitalli mentioned here in the article is Chief of Police Clay Vitalli now. He was one of the honorary pallbearers at the funeral."

"And the one who was unhappy with you taking those pictures in the greenhouse?" asked B.J.

"The very same," said Eliza. "The other thing that strikes me is that Martin O'Shaughnessy's brother was named William. The bartender at Tuxedo Park who told me about the accident is Bill O'Shaughnessy. I'd say he's in his fifties, so that would line up with having a brother who would now be fifty-one or fifty-two. But if Bill's brother was the owner of that abandoned car off West Lake Road, why didn't Bill tell me about it when he told me about the accident?"

"He's hiding something," said B.J.

"Or maybe it's a painful memory," suggested Margo.

"Whatever his reason," said Annabelle, "it would be interesting to confirm that Martin is his brother and, if so, whether he ever had any contact with his brother again. Want me to try to get ahold of him?"

Eliza thought about it for a moment. "If Bill O'Shaughnessy omitted mentioning his brother's involvement, he has his reasons. We phone him and we might upset him or give him a chance to come up with some sort of story if he doesn't want us to know the truth. I just have a hunch it might be better to talk to Bill O'Shaughnessy in person. How he reacts when confronted with our suspicions will tell a lot—perhaps even more than what his words express. Let's see what he has to say when he has no warning."

"All right," said Annabelle, "but how are we going to catch Bill O'Shaughnessy by surprise? Find out where he lives and stake out his house?"

"We're in luck this time, dear members of the Sunrise Suspense Society, since it seems we have another case to solve." Eliza smiled. "I'll have the perfect chance to speak to Bill O'Shaughnessy when I go up to Tuxedo Park this weekend. But I'm going to give Chief Vitalli a call right now."

CHAPTER 62

He had tried to put her off—evading her questions or giving her vague and incomplete answers—but she was determined to find out what had happened on West Lake Road. She wanted to begin by seeing the police report. If he wouldn't fax it to her, she said, she'd stop by the station when she came up this weekend to take occupancy of her leased carriage house.

Cursing under his breath, Chief Vitalli put down the telephone. He didn't like Eliza Blake trawling for information on the old accident. He didn't need this aggravation.

Well, she can't see what doesn't exist.

Clay found the old case file and fed it into the shredder.

CHAPTER 63

Spreading the collar of his white shirt on the ironing board, Bill thought about the countless times his wife had done this for him while she was alive. The little tasks, day in and day out, that she'd performed to keep their lives going. Clipping supermarket coupons and searching for sales, figuring ways to get three different meals from a single roasted chicken, keeping the thermostat as low as they could stand it all through the cold winters, Moira had never complained that they had to live carefully, that a big treat for them was spending a weekend at the Jersey shore.

Like him, Moira had not been brought up to expect more. If the rent could be paid, if there was food on the table and the other bills could be managed, she was satisfied, even grateful. When she was so sick and the medical bills kept mounting, Moira was beside herself. Bill knew that the worry and stress she experienced when the insurance company kept denying coverage exacerbated her illness and finally hastened her death.

He took the can of spray starch and shook it, hard. Every time he let his mind travel to the months of fighting with the insurance company, he felt both enraged and helpless. But he hadn't let Moira down, at least he could comfort himself with that. He had worked out payment plans with all the doctors and the hospital. Though he would be paying off the bills for the rest of his life—and maybe they wouldn't even be paid off then—he had the satisfaction of knowing that Moira had gotten the treatments that had given her the best chance of recovery.

As he slid the hot iron back and forth over the white cotton, Bill's mind turned to the subject he'd been trying to push from his thoughts since this morning, when everybody was talking at the deli he went to for his morning coffee and hard roll. Zack Underwood was dead.

Bill had just the day before told Zack about the accident on West Lake Road. He hadn't told him everything—he wouldn't dare to do that. But after all these years, he didn't think it would do any real harm to tell Zack *something*. The accident was no secret. What had happened to the owner of the car was.

But when Eliza Blake had asked the same questions Zack had, Bill knew that it was more than a coincidence. Now, with Zack's murder, Bill was terrified he'd said too much.

As he buttoned up his shirt and finished dressing for work, Bill realized the only times he'd been this frightened were when the doctor had told him that there was nothing left to be done for Moira and, twenty years ago, when Officer Clay had told him what would happen if he continued pressing for answers about his missing brother, Marty.

CHAPTER 64

The tennis house, with its white columns and piazza, was a gracious enormous old building fronting on Tuxedo Lake. With its myriad courts and rooms, it provided the privacy needed for the meeting.

Peter Nordstrut led the way down the long corridor to the back of the building and into the enclosed racket court. There were no windows to let in any of the fading October light. Peter knew where the light switch was and flipped it on as the heavy, solid steel door closed behind them with a haunting thud, the sound echoing through the chamber.

"This place gives me the creeps," said Clay. "It's like a big old crypt."

"How appropriate, considering what we've come here to discuss," said Fitzroy.

"Legend has it that there are spirits in this place," said Peter. "Chairs move, balls fall, doors slam—all without explanation."

"I don't buy any of that crap," said Clay, opening the collar of his uniform. "When you're dead, you're dead. And if there *is* an afterlife, *that's* where you go. You don't stay floating around here."

"I don't know about that," said Peter, picking up a racket from the floor and executing a few practice swings. "Marty O'Shaughnessy seems to be haunting us now."

Fitzroy nodded solemnly. "I always knew this would catch up with us."

"It *hasn't* caught up with us yet," said Clay, "and we have to make certain that it never does. Eliza Blake called today asking questions about the accident. When I asked her why KEY News was interested in a local story that happened two decades ago, she told me about some numbers that were found in the Pentimento greenhouse, numbers that mapped out the spot on West Lake Road. She already knew about the accident, but she wanted more details."

"What did you tell her?" asked Fitzroy.

"What do you think? Nothing," Clay declared. "Do you think I was going to tell her that I staged the whole thing? That I smashed the Mustang into that tree? Of course I told her that I couldn't tell her any more than she already knew."

"How'd she take that?" asked Peter.

"She didn't buy it," said Clay. "She wanted to see the police report—which I promptly destroyed. But I'm sure she's not going to give up on trying to find out what happened."

"And with all the resources of KEY News behind her, she very well could," said Fitzroy defeatedly.

"Not if we take steps to make sure that she—or anyone else, for that matter—doesn't find out," said Clay. "But what worries me most is that Innis, after his big religious epiphany, may have decided to come clean and make it right with God before he stabbed himself. If he left those numbers at Pentimento leading to the crash site, what's to say he didn't leave clues leading to what you guys did, too?"

Peter and Fitzroy were silent as they digested the thought.

"And let me tell you this," said Clay. "According to his secretary, the only things missing from Zack Underwood's office were the architectural renderings and an album cataloging the work done at Pentimento. What if Innis had decided to leave the world one last giant puzzle and used Zack Underwood to help him design it?"

"Well, Zack is dead now," said Peter. "So he's not going to be revealing any of our secrets."

"What do we do?" asked Fitzroy, his face ashen.

"We wait and watch," said Clay. "But each of us has skin in this game. If one of us goes down, we all go down. Nobody can find out what happened back then."

CHAPTER 65

After dinner Russell went back to his Columbia University residence hall and called his mother. With no more funeral preparations to make and the deluge of condolence calls down to a trickle, his mother would have time to think about the enormity of what had happened.

"How's it going, Mother?" Russell asked, stretching out on the single bed.

"All right, Rusty," Valentina said listlessly. "The new maid started today."

"How is she?"

"She's not Eunice, but she's good enough for the time being. She's helping me get some things in order. I'm actually thinking of going away next week," she announced.

"Where are you going?"

"Italy."

"Do you think that's a good idea?" asked Russell.

"Why wouldn't it be?"

"Because it's so soon and it will remind you of Father so much."

"Everywhere reminds me of him, Rusty. And besides, with all that's happening around here, I want to get away. Before I leave, I can make arrangements to have Eunice's body shipped to Trinidad when the medical examiner's office releases it. I don't want to wait around for the autopsy results. I just want to escape for a while and get my bearings."

"The funeral's over now, Mother. Things will be quieter," said Russell.

"Didn't you hear?"

"Hear what?" asked Russell. "I've been in classes and at the library all day."

"Zack Underwood was killed."

"My God. What happened?"

"Somebody came into his office last night and murdered him," she said. Russell could hear the sound of Valentina swallowing something. He would bet it was vodka.

"What do the police think?" asked Russell. "Have you talked to Clay?"

"No, I haven't talked to Clay," said Valentina. "I don't know what the police think, but I think it has to have something to do with your father's death."

"Do you want me to come home tonight, Mother?" asked Russell. "I can be there in an hour."

"No, dear," said Valentina. "It's sweet of you to offer, but the most important thing you can do is stay there and pay attention to your studies. But I would appreciate it if you came home this weekend. I miss you and I love you, and I worry about how all of this is affecting you, too."

Russell's eyes moved over the words in the political-science textbook, but he wasn't comprehending anything he read. Innis's death, the way he'd done it to himself, the funeral, Eunice's death, and now Zack Underwood's murder. It was all too much.

Realizing that he wasn't going to get any work done, Russell closed the book. He went to the bathroom and splashed cold water over his face. He felt the need to go out and have some fun. There was nothing wrong with that, he told himself. Innis was dead, but *he* had to go on living.

Taking the subway just two stops south, Russell got out of the train and climbed up the stairway to the sidewalk. He walked for two blocks, looking into windows and doorways as he went. When he came to a place that felt right, he entered.

The Broadway Dive on 101st Street was dim and noisy. Russell maneuvered his way through the crowd and leaned against the bar.

"I'll have a Rolling Rock," he told the bartender.

As he drank his beer, Russell surveyed the room. Satisfied that no one he knew was there, he concentrated on picking out a likely woman to approach. At a booth near the back, three attractive young women were laughing. The brunette was really pretty, but Russell decided against going over. He didn't want an audience judging him as he tried to pick her up.

He ordered another beer, drank it, and was about to leave for some other place when the petite blonde came through the front door.

CHAPTER 66

It was Janie's last evening before going off to Hershey with the Cohens. Though her daughter would be away for just two nights, Eliza couldn't help but be anxious. Janie, on the other hand, seemed only excited.

Mrs. Garcia had packed a small suitcase for Janie, which Eliza checked.

"What about Zippy?" asked Eliza, holding up the bedraggled-looking stuffed monkey. "Do you want to take him with you?"

Janie cocked her head as she considered it. "No, I think it's all right if I leave Zippy here. I might be getting too big to take Zippy with me."

"All right," said Eliza, touched by her daughter's attempt to be grown-up, but not really certain that leaving behind her nightly bed companion was a good idea. Maybe Eliza would ask Mrs. Garcia to wrap him up when Janie was at school tomorrow and give him to Susan Cohen to keep in the trunk of her car in case Janie ended up wanting him.

After Janie had taken a bath and brushed her teeth, Eliza settled in bed next to her daughter. Janie handed her *The Poor Man of Assisi.*

"We just read this last night," said Eliza. "You want to read it again?"

Janie nodded.

As Eliza opened the book, it occurred to her that in the not-too-distant future Janie wouldn't want to be read to at night. Her baby couldn't be a baby forever.

Together they took turns reading the text and talking about the pictures that illustrated the life of St. Francis. At the end of the book, the Canticle of the Sun was printed.

"What's a canticle?" Janie asked.

"It's a song," said Eliza. "Should I read the words to you?"

Janie nodded as she pulled the covers closer.

Eliza began.

> Most high, all-powerful, all-good Lord! All praise
> is yours, all glory, all honor, and all blessing.
> To you alone, Most High, do they belong. No
> mortal lips are worthy to pronounce your name.
> All praise be yours, my Lord, through all that you
> have made, and first my Lord Brother Sun, who
> brings the day; and light you give to us through
> him. How beautiful he is, how radiant in all his
> splendor! Of you, Most High, he bears the likeness.
> All praise be yours, my Lord, though Sister Moon
> and Stars; in the heavens you have made them,
> bright and precious and fair.
> All praise be yours, my Lord, through Brothers
> Wind and Air, and fair and stormy, and all the
> weather's moods, by which you cherish all that
> you have made.
> All praise be yours, my Lord, through Sister Water;
> so useful, lowly, precious, and pure.
> All praise be yours, my Lord, through Brother Fire,
> through whom you brighten up the night. How

BEAUTIFUL HE IS, HOW GAY! FULL OF POWER AND
STRENGTH.

ALL PRAISE BE YOURS, MY LORD, THROUGH OUR SISTER
MOTHER EARTH, OUR MOTHER, WHO FEEDS US IN HER
SOVEREIGNTY AND RULES US, AND PRODUCES VARIOUS
FRUITS AND COLORED FLOWERS AND HERBS.

ALL PRAISE BE YOURS, MY LORD, THROUGH THOSE WHO
GRANT PARDON FOR LOVE OF YOU; THROUGH THOSE
WHO ENDURE SICKNESS AND TRIAL. HAPPY THOSE WHO
ENDURE IN PEACE, BY YOU, MOST HIGH, THEY WILL BE
CROWNED.

ALL PRAISE BE YOURS, MY LORD, THROUGH OUR SISTER
DEATH, FROM WHOSE EMBRACE NO MORTAL CAN
ESCAPE. WOE TO THOSE WHO DIE IN MORTAL SIN!
HAPPY THOSE SHE FINDS DOING YOUR WILL! THE
SECOND DEATH CAN DO NO HARM TO THEM.

PRAISE AND BLESS MY LORD, AND GIVE HIM THANKS,
AND SERVE HIM WITH GREAT HUMILITY.

When she finished reading, Eliza looked over at Janie. The child was asleep. Eliza got up carefully and turned off the light. She went to her own bedroom and began to undress. As she did, she thought about the length of the canticle she had just read. It was so much longer than the one on the program at Innis's funeral.

She thought no more about it as her mind turned to Innis and Zack Underwood and the spot on West Lake Road where the car had been abandoned. All of it was connected in some way, she was sure. And maybe the death of the Wheelocks' maid was no coincidence. But as she lay in bed and waited for sleep to come, Eliza tried to direct her mind to something much more pleasant.

Mack was coming tomorrow.

CHAPTER 67

I didn't have lunch today, or dinner either," said the blond woman after finishing her second cocktail. She swayed toward Russell. "This is really affecting me."

"How about we get out of here and I take you somewhere to get something to eat," suggested Russell.

"All right," said the woman. She slid off the barstool and grabbed onto Russell's arm until she balanced herself.

"I want you to know that I usually don't go off with a man I've just met at a bar, Samuel, but you're so clean-cut and polite. I just get the feeling that you're safe."

When they came out of the bar, they stood on the sidewalk together. She looked up at him. "I like tall men," she said.

Russell took her arm and began guiding her west.

"Where are we going anyway?" she asked after they walked a few blocks.

"There's a little place I know in Riverside Park. It's got the greatest view of the Hudson River. They also make a good burger."

"I didn't know there was a place like that this far north," said the woman, her speech slightly slurred.

"Good," said Russell. "I'll be showing you something new." He took off his jacket and draped it around her shoulders. The coat looked enormous on her. "It's gotten cold, but we're almost there," he said.

They entered the park and followed the path that sloped downward toward the river. A man walking a dog passed them, then a jogger. The woman strained to get a view of what was up ahead.

"I don't see anything," she said.

"Just a little bit farther," he said.

"I don't like this," said the young woman, pulling away from him. "I want to go back."

"Come on," urged Russell, holding on to her tightly. "We're almost there. You'll see."

"Let go of me!" cried the woman, reaching out and clawing at his face.

Just then another dog walker came into view, and Russell decided to let the woman go.

CHAPTER 68

One of the things that never ceased to amaze Clay was that Tuxedo Park residents didn't bother locking their doors or taking the keys out of the ignitions of their cars. He didn't understand that sort of trust and confidence. In his world it was always necessary to be on guard.

The conversation with Eliza Blake had made him nervous.

It was essential to keep track of what she and her friends were doing, what they knew.

He let himself into the carriage house. Searching the rooms with a flashlight, Clay determined the place he would put the listening device.

CHAPTER 69

E *ach laminated page of the turquoise-leather photo album taken from Underwood's office had to be carefully studied. Interiors and exteriors, close-ups and long-distance shots, photo after photo cataloged the myriad details that made Pentimento unique—a showcase, a masterwork.*

Not everything that was photographed, however, would be a key to the mystery. If that were the case, the puzzle would have too many pieces and could never be solved. But surely some of the pictures in the album illustrated clues to Innis Wheelock's puzzle—and his plan to reveal what shouldn't be revealed.

The proud new owner of the photo album turned to the pictures taken at the greenhouse, and there it was! Clue Number One: a crystal-clear shot of the flowerpot, the numbers appearing dark and distinct against the terracotta.

What was Clue Number Two?

There were so many pages, so many architectural details, so many possibilities at Pentimento, but none of them leaped off the page as a clue. How could you find the next clue if you had no idea what you were looking for?

So many needles hidden in a turquoise haystack!

One thing was comforting, though: The album wasn't in Zack Underwood's office any longer. It was safe and sound in its new home, and no one was going to find it. Nobody else would be studying its contents and trying to figure things out.

Along with the final page came a chest-pounding realization: This album wasn't the only record of the clues to the Pentimento puzzle!

Below the last photo in the album, the photographer identified herself.

Aurelia Patterson had proudly taken the pictures at Pentimento, and she advertised the fact on a yellow Post-it note addressed to her boss, explaining that she would be willing to print out other copies if needed.

Did she know what she had?

There was a good chance she didn't realize—at least not yet.

But given time, she could begin to, just as Zack Underwood had.

FRIDAY
OCTOBER 9

CHAPTER 70

In the moments after the alarm clock sounded, Eliza moved from grogginess to full awareness and excited anticipation as she remembered what was going to happen today. As much as she had some anxiety about Janie's weekend away, Eliza was relieved that Mack and she would finally have some time alone together. She felt strongly that it wasn't right for Mack to stay overnight when Janie was home. It would give the child the wrong signals. Eliza and Mack had already split up once, over an indiscretion of Mack's. Janie had been confused when she was told that Mack wasn't going to be coming around anymore. As glad as she seemed to be that Mack was part of their lives again, she was still a little girl, unsophisticated and emotionally vulnerable. Until Eliza was certain that she and Mack were making a permanent commitment to each other, he wouldn't be staying over at the house in Ho-Ho-Kus.

Eliza's assignment last month to interview Carla Bruni, the glamorous wife of French president Nicolas Sarkozy, had provided an opportunity for Mack and Eliza. Mack came to Paris to meet her. It had all been very romantic. Holding hands as they walked along the

Seine, dining amid the flickering, sparkling lights at the Eiffel Tower, two incredible nights at a luxurious hotel off the Place Vendôme.

This weekend would be different but, she hoped, wonderful in its own way. She and Mack would have some of the time and privacy they desperately craved. They'd be all alone in the carriage house in Tuxedo Park.

Eliza went into the bathroom and turned on the water in the shower, testing the temperature before she got into the stall. She shampooed her hair and let a deep conditioning lotion remain on her head as she shaved her legs. While she was rinsing out the conditioner, she thought about what was coming up at work. She had to get in there and get the narration done on the latest developments in the Innis Wheelock story.

She was sure that B.J. had done a rough cut, recording the narration himself and then editing the video over his own voice. There was a better-than-even chance that everything wouldn't sync up when Eliza recorded her version. Variations in pacing from one narrator to another could affect the length of the narration, even by just a few seconds. And those few seconds could throw everything off. B.J. was one of the most skilled and fastest editors in the building, but it wasn't fair for her to come in late and make him rush to re-edit if it could be avoided.

She selected the blue cashmere sweater that Mack had given her and took a straight black skirt from the closet. Pulling the towel off her head, she dressed and ran a comb through her hair. Styling and makeup would be done when she got to the Broadcast Center.

She turned off the lamp in the bedroom and walked out into the hallway. It was dimly lit by the light that filtered up from downstairs. Eliza knew that Mrs. Garcia was already in the kitchen and that she would have coffee brewing.

Tiptoeing into Janie's room, Eliza leaned over and kissed her child on the forehead. Gently she took the stuffed monkey from beneath Janie's arm. After tucking the comforter around her daughter, Eliza forced herself to leave the room.

CHAPTER 71

The successful Middle East peace talks and the president's arrival back in Washington led the news on *KEY to America*. Wildfires in California ran second. The story Annabelle and B.J. had produced was third to air.

Eliza had recorded the narration, a script written by Annabelle, the moment she arrived at the Broadcast Center. B.J. had edited the video to it in just over a half hour.

In the control room, Linus kept one eye on the monitors tuned to ABC, CBS, NBC, Fox, and CNN.

"Good!" he shouted, pumping his fist in the air. "We're the only ones who got an interview with the dead guy's secretary!"

Though neither Annabelle nor B.J. was in the control room at the time, word of the executive producer's pleasure got back to them.

"For once I can go home for the weekend and not be agonizing over the fact that Linus hates me," said Annabelle as she and B.J. had bagels and coffee in his edit room.

"He doesn't hate you, not really. But even if he did, it doesn't matter to him if he hates you. He hates pretty much everybody. As long as you produce pieces that beat the competition, Linus will never get rid of you," said B.J. He took a bite out of his bagel and sat back in his chair.

Annabelle slowly shook her head and sighed deeply. "He's a freakin' nutcase," she said.

"The devil you know," said B.J. "If the ratings tank, they could bring in somebody else who's even worse. Linus may be a maniac, but he's our maniac."

After the show was over, Annabelle stopped by Eliza's office.

"Nice piece," Eliza complimented her. "Thank you."

"You're welcome," said Annabelle. "I bet you're counting the minutes till you can get out of here today. What time does Mack's plane get in?"

Eliza looked at her watch. "He should be landing at eleven. Then he's coming in here for a meeting with Range Bullock. After Mack is finished in the president's office, we're leaving for Tuxedo Park."

"Well, have a great time," said Annabelle, smiling. "I know you will. And hopefully, if you two can tear yourselves apart at some point, you can track down that Bill O'Shaughnessy and find out what the story is with his brother."

"Will do, boss," said Eliza, exaggerating a salute.

CHAPTER 72

Finished with morning prayer, Father Gehry closed his breviary. He was fully aware that Zack Underwood had been murdered. He had several suspects in mind for the horrendous crime, yet, though he ached to, he would never go to the police with his suspicions.

He leaned back in his chair, feeling the warm leather against his head, and he began to pray silently. *Dear Lord, give me peace of mind. I know I can't break the seal of confession, but so many people might get hurt if I remain silent. Find some other way, Lord, to keep everyone safe.*

Innis Wheelock had confessed everything before he killed himself. Father Gehry knew what had happened twenty years before—things that had haunted Innis all that time, especially after his years in Italy. His devotion to St. Francis had gotten Innis to obey his conscience. It had also taken him too far. Religion had pushed Innis over the edge.

Innis wasn't the only one who had something terrible to confess. But Father Gehry could never—would never—tell another living soul who else had been involved in the murder of Marty O'Shaughnessy and the cover-up that followed.

CHAPTER 73

Knowing that he'd already blown off his nine o'clock class, Russell turned over in bed and decided he wasn't going to his eleven o'clock either. It would be a waste of time. He wouldn't be able to concentrate. He was emotionally and physically spent.

He lay there for a while but couldn't drift back to sleep. He wasn't happy with the way things had gone last night. But it was probably all for the best.

Eventually Russell got up to go to the bathroom, where he caught a glimpse of himself in the mirror over the sink. There were two long, angry scratches cutting across his cheek. The girl had been capable of putting up a fight. She was much stronger than she looked.

He wondered if she had reported anything to the police, but Russell wasn't particularly concerned. It was a big city, and the cops had too much to do. No rape had occurred, not even a mugging, and it wouldn't get a lot of attention. Russell doubted very much that anything he'd said or done last night would lead the police to his door. He was smart enough to know how not to get caught.

CHAPTER 74

Doubting that Aurelia Patterson was going to call and volunteer the information about what was missing from Zack Underwood's office, Annabelle decided to take the initiative. The woman answered on the second ring.

"Oh," said Aurelia when Annabelle identified herself. "I was hoping it would be the police with some news."

"I'm sorry to disappoint you," said Annabelle. "I know how anxious you must be."

"I didn't sleep at all last night," said Aurelia. "I just kept thinking about poor Zack and the way he looked when I found him." Her voice trembled. "I know I'll never be able to forget how he looked."

"It's a terrible, terrible thing," Annabelle said. "Is there anyone you can talk to about it?"

"You mean a shrink?" asked Aurelia.

"Yes," said Annabelle. "Some professional help might be a very good thing for you. You've been through a profound trauma."

"Maybe you're right," Aurelia said uncertainly. "I got through my divorce without a therapist, but I don't know if I can get through this."

"Well, if you decide you want to talk, I have a friend who could probably refer you to someone good up near you."

"Thank you," said Aurelia. "You're very kind."

"Not at all," said Annabelle.

She wished she could claim that she'd been calling to see how Aurelia Patterson was doing, but the fact was, her action was more professionally motivated. She had to get to the reason for the call.

"Aurelia, were you able to figure out what was missing from the office?"

Annabelle sensed that the woman was hesitant to answer.

"Did the police tell you not to say anything about the case?" Annabelle asked.

"Yes," said Aurelia.

"I can respect that," said Annabelle. "But maybe you can confirm something we already have reason to suspect."

Aurelia waited.

"You see, we think that Zack's murder is connected in some way with Innis Wheelock's suicide," said Annabelle. "We also think that Innis orchestrated some sort of puzzle that he built right into his house. Innis would have needed some help to do that. And it makes sense that he would have enlisted his architect, even if the architect didn't understand what he was helping with. What do you think of that scenario?"

"Go on," said Aurelia.

"We know that Zack signed a confidentiality agreement," Annabelle continued. "But, as I understand it, with Innis's death, the agreement could be considered null and void. Suppose Zack was killed because his murderer thought he knew too much about the puzzle and that Zack would talk about the clues that he'd built into the house."

"And the murderer was worried the clues would ultimately lead back to him?" asked Aurelia.

"Exactly," said Annabelle. "So he would want to get rid of Zack and get rid of any evidence of the clues incorporated in Pentimento."

"Like design plans and pictures that were taken of the finished project?" asked Aurelia.

"Yes," said Annabelle. "Is that what was taken from Zack's office? Just tell me if I'm wrong."

Aurelia's silence was her answer.

"Here, Midnight. Come here, boy."

The border collie came right over to Aurelia. She petted the dog's soft coat and then bent down to hug him for her own comfort. She could feel her pulse racing.

If Zack was murdered because he knew too much about Pentimento, then she was in danger, too.

Aurelia hadn't thought to tell the police that she had copies of all the pictures taken at Pentimento and arranged in the turquoise album. In fact, she'd been the one who had taken the photos. They were all stored on her computer.

CHAPTER 75

Mack appeared at the doorway, holding his index finger up to his lips.

"Is she in there?" he whispered.

Paige smiled broadly and mouthed, "Yes."

Quietly Mack walked to the open office door. Eliza had her back to him. She was looking out the window at the Hudson River.

"Hey, you," he said.

She turned quickly, her face lighting up with pleasure.

"Mack."

He dropped his bag on the floor, and they moved toward each other. While they embraced, Paige discreetly shut the office door.

"Oh, I've missed you," he said, closing his eyes and holding her tight.

"Me, too," said Eliza. She pulled her head back and regarded his face. "You look great, but a little tired," she said.

"You look great period," he responded. He leaned down, and his mouth found hers.

"What time is your meeting with the prez?" asked Eliza as she stood before the mirror on the back of the door and reapplied her lipstick.

"Range canceled on me," said Mack. "His secretary said he had some sort of family situation he had to take care of, but I think he might be avoiding me."

"Range Bullock is a pretty straight shooter," said Eliza, pulling a comb through her hair. "If he didn't want to see you, he wouldn't have made the appointment to begin with."

"I'm getting the feeling that he has something to tell me and he knows I won't like it," said Mack.

"Like what?"

"Like despite the fact he's been leading me to believe that when I finish this contract cycle I can come back to New York, he's not going to make good."

"I don't think he would do that," said Eliza.

"Well, you know him better than I do, and I hope you're right, but I'm getting a bad vibe." Mack shook it off. "Forget it. Let's not think about that for the next few days. Let's not let it ruin our time together."

"Deal," said Eliza as she leaned in to kiss him again.

As they left the office and walked down the hallway, they met Anna-belle getting off the elevator.

"I know you guys are anxious to get out of here," she said. "But I just want to tell you, Eliza, that Zack Underwood's secretary found that the plans and photographs of Pentimento were missing from the office."

"She told you that?" asked Eliza.

"Not in so many words, but trust me—that's what she was saying."

Eliza considered the information and its implications. "All right, let me see what else I can come up with this weekend," she said.

"What's this all about?" asked Mack.

"I'll tell you on the ride up to Tuxedo Park," Eliza promised.

They said good-bye to Annabelle, and Mack pushed the button to summon the elevator. Annabelle got only a few steps away when she turned.

"I know the last thing in the world you need is to see anyone else this weekend, Eliza, but if it turns out you need some help up there, don't hesitate to call."

CHAPTER 76

Fitzroy had been very quiet all morning, and Unity was concerned. After lunch, when he said he wanted to go for another long walk to clear his mind, Unity became genuinely worried.

Because of his limp, taking long walks had never been her husband's habit. And now, as she listened to news reports and read the paper, it occurred to her that Fitzroy had been gone during the time that Zack Underwood was murdered.

CHAPTER 77

The carriage house on Clubhouse Road was one of several that had been converted since the days when horses and their grooms awaited their masters' pleasure, providing them with transportation and sport. At one time forty miles of bridle paths wound through the park and the Tuxedo Horse Show had been a world-class event. Over the years, cars and SUVs had replaced carriages and horse-drawn sleighs. Human beings now lived in the stables.

When they entered the front door, Eliza immediately remembered why she'd rented the place. The combination living and dining room was crowned with rough-hewn beams crisscrossing a vaulted ceiling. The floor was wide-plank antique oak partially covered with sisal rugs. Big, comfortable chairs flanked the fireplace, and an inviting sofa slipcovered in white duck cloth was positioned under the window. A round table surrounded by four ladder-back chairs filled the dining area. Sunshine streamed into the room, warming the pale taupe walls. In the kitchen, open shelves were stocked with glassware and white crockery. All the appliances were modern and of high quality.

Eliza opened the Sub-Zero refrigerator.

"Great," she said as she inspected the contents. "Mrs. Garcia has already been here."

Mack poked his head around the refrigerator door. "I'm hoping she made that chicken I love," he said.

"She did," said Eliza. "Want me to heat some up?"

"Later," said Mack as he leaned in to kiss her.

She led the way upstairs to the larger of two bedrooms. On the queen-size bed, the soft white sheets were turned down, a subtle contrast to the sand-colored comforter and matching linen that covered the head-board. A vase full of fresh flowers sat on the bedside table along with several pillar candles resting on a glass tray.

"Wait till you see the bathroom," said Eliza, taking Mack's hand.

A very deep freestanding bathtub was the focal point of the room. The tub overlooked a walled garden.

"I can't wait to fill that with bath salts and soak in water up to my chin," said Eliza.

Mack inspected the depth and width of the tub. "Good," he said. "There's room enough for the both of us."

CHAPTER 78

Wrapped in a heavy sweater against the chill late-afternoon air, Valentina sat on the carved bench, staring at the fountain. The falling water was mesmerizing to watch. It sprayed upward and then cascaded down over the backs of the bronze tortoises that sunned themselves at the edge of the marble basin.

The tortoise and the hare, thought Valentina, remembering the old fable that she'd been told as a child. The speedy, reckless rabbit was beaten by the steady, slow-moving tortoise. It was a lesson that she and Innis had tried to teach Rusty. Slow and steady won the race.

She was afraid Rusty hadn't learned the lesson well enough. He took too many risks, and that generally wasn't a good thing, especially for a young man who planned to go into the family business of politics. A foolish move, a dumb mistake, could come back to haunt you.

Valentina wondered when Rusty would be coming home this weekend. She had no desire to be one of those nagging mothers who wanted to know their offspring's every move. But she found herself feeling needy. She didn't want to be alone.

Getting up, she walked back into the house and went to the telephone.

"Oh, Eliza, hello," she said with enthusiasm when Eliza answered. "It's Valentina. Are you up here already?"

"Hi, Valentina," said Eliza. "Yes, we got here after lunch. How are you doing?"

"I'm all right. I was calling to see if you and Mack would like to come over for a drink."

Eliza hesitated, not wanting to disappoint her. "Honestly, Valentina, Mack flew in this morning, and it's already after ten at night on his body clock. Can we possibly take a rain check?"

"Of course, I understand," said Valentina. "I don't know what I was thinking. Innis and I would be exhausted when we first came home from Europe. Anyway, you two have more to do with your time than spend your first night together with an old lady. How about lunch tomorrow? Would you like to come around noon?"

"We'll be there," said Eliza.

CHAPTER 79

It could not be allowed to happen.

Aurelia could not be given the chance to realize what she had and turn the Pentimento pictures over to law enforcement. Even without having the pictures in her possession, she could remember them, so stealing them was not good enough.

If memory served, Aurelia owned a dog. And a dog had to be walked one last time before its owner slept for the night. All alone on the dark road, Aurelia would be vulnerable and unsuspecting. It would be the perfect opportunity to eliminate her as a threat.

No one would see.

The computer printout of the Instruments of the Passion that had provided the inspiration for Zack's murder now provided inspiration for how to get rid of Aurelia—almost as dramatically as Innis had gotten rid of himself.

CHAPTER 80

Aurelia slapped the side of her thigh.

"Come on, Midnight. Let's go, boy."

The border collie happily followed his mistress out the door, eager for the fresh air and exercise. He trotted in front of Aurelia, unleashed and confident about the route they would take. A noise coming from the bushes up ahead sent him bolting in pursuit of the squirrel or chipmunk he thought he would find there.

As she walked down the road, Aurelia pulled her fisherman-knit cardigan closer around her. It was time to get out her heavy winter coat, she thought. She couldn't remember if she had even picked up the winter clothes from the dry cleaner after she'd dropped them off last spring. She'd have to check when she got back to the house.

She shivered at the sound of a twig snapping. Looking behind her, she searched with her flashlight, but she saw nothing. Aurelia turned and continued walking.

"Midnight!" she called out. "Where are you, boy? Come back."

She could hear the rustling of leaves as the dog searched through the bushes for his quarry. The collie was going to emerge dirty and covered with grass and leaves. She was too tired and in no mood to give him a bath this late at night.

"I'm not kidding, Midnight!" she called. "Get back here."

Her attention focused on the dog, and the air filled with the sound of her own voice, Aurelia didn't sense the person approaching her from behind until the hammer came down on her head.

Aurelia's body was quickly dragged to the side of the road and then deep into the underbrush.

The dog finally appeared, bounding from the bushes but slowing at the sight of his mistress lying in the leaves. Approaching her body, Midnight sniffed at her hair and sweater and nudged her shoulder with his snout. When he got no response, he licked her face with his long tongue, and a moment later he stretched out next to her, placing his head on her warm, still chest.

It was a short walk to Aurelia Patterson's house. The laptop computer was sitting on the kitchen table. It didn't take long to find the digital camera in the hall closet.

The killer walked out of the house with both of them—the sole owner of the images of Pentimento.

SATURDAY
OCTOBER 10

CHAPTER 81

Slipping from bed as quietly as she could, Eliza put on her robe and went downstairs. She set a pot of coffee brewing and turned on her computer to check the news of the morning. Satisfied that nothing big had happened overnight, she poured herself a cup of coffee, opened the French doors, and went out onto the slate patio.

The morning air was bracing. Eliza inhaled deeply, reveling in the sights and scents of autumn in the country. Colorful leaves lay scattered on the ground. An old stone fence surrounded the rear of the property, cordoning off a well-tended garden. She detected the faint aroma of lavender, the vestige of the plants the owner had placed near the foundation of the carriage house.

As she sipped the hot coffee, Eliza wondered how Janie was doing with the Cohens. She was tempted to call and see, but she decided to wait until later. *Don't hover,* she told herself.

Going back inside, she heard Mack descending the stairs.

"Sleep well?" asked Eliza after they kissed.

"Like a baby," said Mack. He looked mischievously into her eyes. "I wonder why."

"I have no idea," she said with mock innocence.

She pulled away and went to pour some coffee for him. "What do you want to do today?" she asked, handing him the cup.

"More of what we've been doing would suit me just fine."

Eliza nodded, smiling. "And after that, I have a place I want to show you."

"This is great exercise," said Eliza.

"Yeah, but not nearly as good as the exercise we just had," said Mack, putting his arm around her shoulder and kissing her on the forehead.

As they walked around the road that circled Tuxedo Lake, Eliza filled Mack in on all that had been happening and the details she knew so far. "I went to the spot on West Lake Road, but there was nothing out of the ordinary," she said. "I want to go back there with you and see if I missed something."

"Another set of eyes, at your service," said Mack.

"That's Pentimento," said Eliza as they walked by the imposing Italianate mansion. "The Wheelock place."

Mack whistled softly through his teeth. "You've got to be in a pretty sad state if living in a place like that doesn't make you want to stick around."

"That's the operative word, isn't it?" said Eliza. "Innis Wheelock had to be very sad to do what he did."

"Or he just got carried away with his obsession with religion and St. Francis," said Mack.

They continued walking, past a few more massive houses until the road straightened out and there were no buildings on either side.

"This is certainly a nice long stretch where a car could gather speed," observed Mack. "If you drank too much or were distracted by a pretty woman in the car with you, it would be easy to lose control and crash into a tree."

Eliza slowed as they reached the area indicated on the map. "This is it," she said, holding out her arms.

They wandered around, kicking through leaves and vegetation, not sure what they were looking for.

After a while Eliza leaned against a large boulder. "Maybe this is a wild-goose chase," she said.

"And this might be the goose," Mack said excitedly as he squatted down at the base of a large old tree at the water's edge. "Come here and see this."

Eliza walked over to the tree that leaned slightly toward the lake. On the bottom of the trunk, at a point facing the water and not viewable from the road, a slab of brass, about an inch thick, a foot high, and a foot and a half wide was planted in the ground. It was in the shape of a pentagon, with nine slender rectangles protruding from the top of it. One of the rectangles stood tall and straight; the other eight were shorter, as if they had been broken off.

"What do you think this could be?" asked Mack.

"I've seen similar ones in antique shops. It looks like a large, old-fashioned doorstop," said Eliza. "In the shape of a house."

CHAPTER 82

Valentina answered the door herself.

"Welcome to Pentimento," she said, forcing herself to smile. "I'm so glad you could make it."

"We're so happy to be here," said Eliza as she handed a paper bag to Valentina. "These are some jars of Mrs. Garcia's spicy peach preserves."

"Oh, that's so thoughtful. Thank you." Valentina took hold of the gift with two hands and led Eliza and Mack to a small round table by one of the windows.

"I thought it would be nicer to sit here looking out at the lake rather than eating at that big table in the dining room," she said.

The table was set with colorful hand-painted Italian pottery featuring the Wheelock family crest.

"These bowls are wonderful," said Eliza.

"They were made for us in Deruta," Valentina said wistfully. "Innis actually deserves all the credit. He worked with the pottery maker, and they came up with this unique design just for us."

All three of them were quiet.

"He was such a gifted person," Valentina whispered.

"He certainly was," said Mack. "And so are you, Valentina. Anyone who has followed your career over the years knows that you two were a force to be reckoned with. You accomplished some wonderful things for the people of America."

"That's nice of you to say, Mack. But to be perfectly honest, without Innis I wouldn't have accomplished much at all. Others helped, too, of course, but Innis called the shots."

Bonnie entered the room carrying a tureen. She ladled corn chowder into the bowls and left a basket of fresh-baked bread on the table.

"Bonnie here has just been a lifesaver," said Valentina. "She's helping me until I can find a permanent replacement for Eunice—though I doubt I'll ever really be able to replace her." She nodded and smiled at Bonnie. "That will be all for now. Thank you."

"I'll be out in the aviary for a little while, Mrs. Wheelock," said Bonnie. "I'm going to feed the birds."

"Bringing that parrot some grapes?" Eliza asked, smiling. "My daughter told me all about it."

"I know," said Bonnie. "Each time I've gone out there, that bird is always squawking about grapes, but he never eats them. I don't understand."

"I wish Innis never got it in his head to build that aviary," said Valentina. "It's more trouble and money to maintain than it's worth. But he loved the aviary at the Villa Borghese in Rome and wanted one of his own. Thank goodness he didn't insist on making it as large or as grand."

They ate their lunch, deliberately limiting the conversation to light topics. But after they were finished eating, Valentina was the one who brought Innis back into the conversation.

"You know, Zack Underwood's murder has something to do with Innis's death," she said. "I'm sure of it."

"What's the connection?" asked Eliza.

"I don't know," said Valentina. "But at the lunch at the club on the afternoon he was killed, Zack told me that he thought Innis had left a message behind in a puzzle he'd planned. He told me about numbers on a pot in our greenhouse that he said led to the place where a car crash happened over two decades ago."

"The one on West Lake Road?" asked Eliza.

Valentina seemed surprised. "How did you know about that?"

"Someone else actually told me about it," said Eliza, always conscious of protecting her sources. "But Zack and I talked about it at the luncheon, too."

"We took a walk to the spot this morning," said Mack.

"You did?" asked Valentina.

"Yes, and we found something," said Eliza. "We're just not sure what it is."

"Describe it for me," said Valentina.

"Actually, we brought it with us," said Eliza. "It's in the car."

"I'll go get it," offered Mack.

"Maybe we should go outside to see it," said Eliza. "It's covered with dirt."

Valentina examined the tarnished brass object sitting on the floor of the car.

"We were thinking it resembled a house," said Mack.

"A house with a lot of chimneys," added Eliza.

Valentina straightened. "Why would Innis want to point to *that* house?" she mused softly.

"What house?" asked Mack.

"The old Heavener house," said Valentina. "Nine Chimneys."

They went back inside Pentimento. While they had coffee, Valentina told a story.

"Nine Chimneys was a beautiful, gracious old place that had been in the Heavener family since the early days of Tuxedo Park. It passed from one generation to the next, but unfortunately the family money ran out. Even more unfortunate was the fact that Fitzroy hadn't really been brought up to go out and earn a living.

"So, as the bills mounted," continued Valentina, "the Heaveners gradually had to let their servants go. Eventually things got so bad that they were living in just a few rooms and had closed the others off so they wouldn't have to pay to heat them."

"You said Nine Chimneys *was* a beautiful old place," said Eliza. "What happened to it?"

"It burned to the ground," said Valentina, putting down her coffee cup. "There was suspicion of arson, of course. But nothing was ever proven. Fitzroy and Unity moved into an apartment over the Black Tie Club and have been living off the insurance money ever since."

"If Innis is directing us to something," said Eliza, "why point to a house that's not even there anymore?"

"What are you all talking about?"

The three of them turned to see Russell Wheelock standing in the doorway.

"Oh, Rusty, you're home." Valentina rose to meet her son and kissed him warmly on the cheek. "I'm so glad you're here, dear."

Russell shook hands with Eliza and Mack. They filled him in on the replica they'd found on West Lake Road.

Eliza felt comfortable leaving Valentina now that her son was with her. "I'd like to see for myself where Nine Chimneys once stood," she said. "And see if we can't figure out what Innis is trying to tell us."

CHAPTER 83

After thanking Valentina for lunch, Eliza and Mack headed to Nine Chimneys. The road that led to the house was rutted, and the long driveway was overgrown with weeds and twigs. Majestic oak trees lined the drive, their branches and leaves reaching over to create a golden canopy.

"It once must have been quite beautiful here," said Eliza as she looked out the window.

Boulders and crumbling cement marked the circumference of the enormous foundation. The remains of several stone chimneys could be seen, their walls reduced to rubble scattered at the base. One intact chimney still stood erect.

"Just like the brass model that Innis left," said Eliza.

"We *think* Innis left it," corrected Mack.

Ivy and tall grasses had taken over, covering the ground. Eliza and Mack trudged through the growth. A brown rabbit appeared out of nowhere, startling Eliza as it hopped past.

"I don't know why I'm so jumpy," she said, shaking her head.

"You've got to admit, it feels kinda creepy up here," said Mack.

Eliza nodded as she took his hand. "You can imagine the kind of life that must have been lived here, but now it's all gone."

They walked around the foundation, finding broken glass, animal droppings, beer cans, and faded magazine pages lying in the dirt.

Mack shrugged. "I don't get it," he said. "There really isn't much to go on here. What do you think?"

"I don't know," said Eliza, pacing across the ground of the foundation. "If Innis has left some clue to his puzzle, I don't see it. Let's try to put ourselves in his mind. If you were trying to hide something here, where would you do it?"

"He could have buried something anywhere," said Mack.

"That's right. And the area is just too big for Innis to think anyone would find it," said Eliza. "He'd plant the clue somewhere unique, somewhere that would stand out yet not be easily seen."

At the same time, both of their heads turned toward the only completely unbroken chimney.

Mack bent over and twisted his head around, trying to look up into the chimney stack. He put his arm inside and reached up.

Eliza cringed. "Be careful. There could be something alive and nesting in there."

His fingers felt something smooth protruding from the rough inner wall of the chimney. Mack awkwardly grasped at the edge of the flat surface and tried to jiggle it free.

"Got it," he said as he lowered his arm.

"What is it?"

"A box of some kind." Mack slowly raised the lid. Inside, there were five wooden cubes. He held one up. The letter *C* was carved into one of the six faces of the cube. On the exact opposite face, a small raised turtle appeared.

"These look almost like children's blocks," said Mack as he took the others out of the box.

Eliza studied the cubes. There was something familiar about them, but she couldn't tell what.

"C, E, R, T, Y." She recited each of the letters on the respective cubes. "What does that mean?"

"Nothing as far as I know," said Mack.

Eliza tried other combinations, moving the blocks around. RETYC, TYCER, ERYCT. None of them meant anything.

"What about TRYCE?" asked Mack.

"What does that mean?"

"It's a card game," said Mack. "You find runs and groups and spell out words."

"Never heard of it," said Eliza. "But it sounds like the kind of thing Innis would eat up."

CHAPTER 84

They went back to the carriage house. Eliza spread the familiar-looking wooden cubes out on the pine table in the dining area. As she studied them, she realized where she had seen similar ones.

"Mack! The blocks we found in the chimney are just like the ones on the fireplace at Pentimento. The ones that spell out 'ROMA.'"

"So Innis had these all made at the same time?" Mack wondered aloud. "And used some for his house and planted the others at Nine Chimneys?"

Eliza nodded. "It looks that way," she said.

Finding scissors in the kitchen drawer, Eliza cut out four squares from a paper bag. She marked each one with a letter, then spread the squares alongside the wooden cubes.

ROMA TRYCE.

"Does that make any sense to you?" asked Eliza.

"Not really," said Mack.

She began rearranging the letters.

MARTY CEO.

"Marty CEO?" asked Mack.

"Marty was the name of the man who owned the car left at the side of West Lake Road," said Eliza.

"What about the CEO?" said Mack. "You said he was a landscaper. Was it his own business?"

"Even if he owned his business, I doubt that Innis Wheelock would call him a CEO." Eliza shrugged, moving the letters around some more. "It's got to be something else."

For the better part of an hour, Eliza and Mack played their own version of Scrabble.

"Are you thirsty?" Eliza asked.

"I can't believe I've been at this game all this time without a scotch in my hand. Do you have any?"

Eliza got up to check. She found the Dewar's on a shelf in the pantry above the case of wine. She stepped out into the kitchen and held the bottle up in triumph. "How's this for being prepared?"

"Perfect."

Eliza found ice cubes in the freezer, poured the caramel elixir into two glasses, and, taking a sip of hers, handed Mack his favorite scotch.

"Come on," said Eliza. "Let's keep at it. Other than TRYCE, the five letters in the chimney don't make much sense. Innis Wheelock could have carved any word into his fireplace, but he chose 'ROMA.' These extra four letters just *have* to fit."

Mack savored his drink as he watched Eliza move the letters around on the table. After a few two-word phrases, like MY CREATOR and RACY METRO, were considered, he suggested, "What if it's three words?"

Eliza found A MERRY COT and shot a glance at Mack, whose eyes were already twinkling.

"Ours has certainly been merry," he said.

Ignoring him with a half-suppressed smile, Eliza considered and then rejected MY ART CORE, TO MY RACER, and many other combinations.

"I'm thinking it might be just one word," she said. "There were nine numbers on the pot in the greenhouse, and now we've got nine letters."

She tried putting them in alphabetical order. "How many nine-letter words do you know, Mack?"

They both stared at the letters, almost willing them to spell something. Eliza moved the *C* to the beginning and then separated the two *R*'s. And then it hit her.

"CREMATORY!" she cried with excitement. Eliza then brought her hand to her lips and said, "My God, how awful. The letters spell 'crematory.'"

CHAPTER 85

When he heard Eliza Blake's words transmitted via the listening device he had installed in her carriage house, Clay Vitalli's face flushed and he could feel his pulse actually pounding in his ears. He wasn't sure which was worse, the reality that Innis had been disloyal to the people who had risked everything to protect him and Valentina or the likelihood that Eliza Blake would figure out that Nine Chimneys had been used to dispose of Marty O'Shaughnessy's body.

There would be time later to sort out his feelings about Innis's treachery. The man was dead now. There was no reasoning with him, and there was nothing Clay could do to change the diabolical plan Innis had already set in motion.

But Eliza Blake was very much alive. She had the potential to uncover the layers of deception that had been set in place over twenty years ago. She had to be diverted from going any further.

Clay picked up the phone and called Fitzroy Heavener.

"The situation is getting worse, Fitzroy," he said. "You'll be very interested to hear what Eliza Blake is onto now."

CHAPTER 86

Midnight stayed with his mistress all through the night. At times he snuggled beside her; at others he laid his snout and paws on her body to keep her warm. Occasionally he lifted his head and licked her face, urging her to awaken.

Every time he heard a car approaching, he would leave Aurelia's side and climb to the road, barking as the vehicles rode by. But the drivers inside thought nothing of an unleashed dog and didn't stop.

As the day wore on, the border collie heard human voices. He barked insistently as the voices got louder. It was a man and a woman, out for an afternoon walk.

"What is it, boy?" asked the man, seeing the dog's excitement. "Whose dog are you?"

Midnight barked loudly.

"He's trying to tell us something, Hank," said the woman.

"Where's your owner, boy?" asked the man. He reached out to pet the collie, but the dog darted away toward the bushes, where he continued barking frantically.

"Is there something in there you want us to see, boy?" asked the man. He began following the dog.

"Be careful, Hank," called the woman.

The man made his way through the underbrush. "Where are you taking me, boy?" he asked. The dog answered with a mournful yelp as the man saw a woman's body lying in the dead leaves.

"What's in there, Hank?"

"Stay back, Colleen. Stay back. You don't want to see this."

The woman's head was smashed in, and he doubted there was any chance she was still alive. He knelt down beside the body and put his cheek close to the women's nose and mouth, trying to detect if she was breathing. Nothing.

He went to feel for a pulse, picking up her arm. As he took her wrist between his fingers, her hand opened and a pair of dice fell to the ground.

CHAPTER 87

W hat's the matter?" asked Fitzroy. "What was so important that you needed to see us right away, Clay?"

"And why did you want to meet here, for God's sake?" asked Peter.

The three men stood in the overgrown ruins of Nine Chimneys.

"I picked this place for two reasons," said Clay. "First, because the tennis house is in full use on Saturday afternoon."

"And second?" asked Peter.

Clay looked directly at Fitzroy. "Because Eliza Blake and her boyfriend have made a connection about this place and cremation."

"How?" Peter asked urgently. "How did they figure that out?"

"It seems we have our old friend Innis to thank again," Clay explained. "He hid some blocks or something in the chimney over there." Clay gestured to the stone column. "Pentimento's fireplace had similar blocks on it. Eliza took all the letters on the blocks, and they spelled out the word 'crematory.'"

Fitzroy looked stricken. He sat on what was left of the foundation wall and held his head with his hands.

"I knew it would all come out someday," he moaned. "I knew it."

"Don't be so damned pessimistic, Fitzroy," said Peter. "We aren't at the point where it's 'all' come out. Not by a long shot."

"Easy for you to say," said Fitzroy. "*You* weren't the one who torched Marty O'Shaughnessy's body. *I* have that distinction."

"No, I wasn't," agreed Peter. "But I played my part in this thing, too. And I have as much to lose as you do if all of this becomes public knowledge."

"Peter is right," said Clay. "Each one of us has too much to lose. I staged that car accident scene. You, Fitzroy, burned the body so that it couldn't be identified, at least not by the scientific standards back then." Clay turned and pointed to Peter Nordstrut. "And you took care of things at the lake. But all of us were in on the whole cover-up. If what happened back then comes to light now, we're all going to pay for it."

CHAPTER 88

Eliza called the Cohens to see how the trip was going. Janie got on the phone and enthusiastically recounted the things she had seen and done.

"We went on the rides, and you know what, Mom? The lights on the street look like chocolate kisses!"

"I can't wait to hear all about it when you get home, sweetheart."

"Okay, Mom. I can't wait either! I'll see you tomorrow."

Eliza felt pangs of pride and relief. Janie was fine, and well enough emotionally to enjoy herself away from her mother.

As they drove out of Tuxedo Park on their way to dinner, Eliza called Annabelle and told her what she and Mack had found at Nine Chimneys and what the letters spelled when combined with the ones on the fireplace at Pentimento.

"You think the place was used to burn bodies?" Annabelle asked skeptically.

"I don't know what to think," said Eliza. "But will you see what you can find out about the fire at Nine Chimneys? There was some suspicion that it was arson, that Fitzroy Heavener might have set it to get the insurance money."

"All right," said Annabelle. "I'll see what I can dig up. But keep in mind it's Saturday night. If I can't find anything about it on the Internet, I might have to wait until Monday morning to make phone calls."

The River Palm Terrace was a fifteen-minute drive down Route 17 into New Jersey. As they sat at a table draped in crisp white linen, Mack and Eliza made a conscious effort to avoid mentioning Tuxedo Park. Ordering a bottle of pinot noir, they perused the menu. Mack ordered a New York shell steak, rare, and cottage fries while Eliza chose grilled jumbo shrimp and steamed fresh asparagus.

For the next two hours, they sat, talked, and held hands across the table. The empty bottle of wine was replaced by two brandy snifters at the end of the meal.

"Will you be all right to drive?" asked Eliza as they stood to leave. She steadied herself by holding on to the back of her chair. "Because I'm sure not."

"Don't worry," said Mack. "I'm fine."

CHAPTER 89

*T*here they were, laughing and leaning against each other.

Such a happy couple. Happy and nosy. A couple with powerful resources. A couple who wouldn't be satisfied until they figured out Innis's damnable puzzle.

He opened the door for her to get inside the Volvo and then walked around to the driver's side and got behind the wheel. As soon as the car pulled out of the restaurant parking lot, it was time to follow them.

The Volvo was traveling at a pretty stiff clip up Route 17.

The driver seemed to be in a hurry to get home. That was understandable. Just about any guy would want to be home with Eliza Blake.

The Volvo slowed as it approached the Tuxedo Park entrance gate.

Hold back.

Wait until the Volvo is admitted and begins driving up the road.

Now that it was clear Eliza Blake and her beau hadn't noticed the car following them, it was safe to glide up to the gate and be quickly waved through.

CHAPTER 90

L et's take the long way home," said Eliza, edging a bit closer
to Mack. "It's such a beautiful, clear night. Let's take a ride
around the lake."

Mack drove slowly, unfamiliar with the unlit road. "Thank goodness for the moon and headlights," he said. "It's dark as pitch up
here."

The car coasted down the incline that led to the boathouse and the
clubhouse beyond that.

"Pull in at the area next to the boathouse," urged Eliza.

Mack parked the car at the edge of the lake, pointing it at the water. He turned off the engine. "I feel like I'm in high school," he said as
he reached out and put his arm around her. "I don't know when was
the last time I made out with a girl in a car."

"Who says you're going to make out now?" Eliza asked teasingly.

"I say." Mack leaned over and kissed her, a kiss so intense that
neither one of them noticed the car that had come to a stop a hundred
yards away.

"Let's get out of here," Mack said breathlessly. "There's not enough room in this thing."

"All right," said Eliza.

He steered the car out of the lot and turned right.

"I think you should have gone left instead," said Eliza after they had driven a ways. "But to tell you the truth, I'm not really sure where the carriage house is from here."

"Great," said Mack. The dark road was curved and narrow. "I can't turn around here."

"Go a little farther," said Eliza. "There should be a driveway or someplace where the road gets wider."

She was straining to spot an opportunity to maneuver the car when suddenly the Volvo lurched forward.

"What the hell?" Mack yelled. He looked into his rearview mirror. The outline of the front of another vehicle, driving with no headlights on, was barely visible. Before Mack could decide what to do, the vehicle rammed into them again.

"It's trying to push us off the road!" cried Eliza.

"Hold on," said Mack through clenched teeth. "I'm going to speed up and try to get away from this nut."

Mack accelerated, and the Volvo gained speed.

Eliza looked out the rear window. "We're not losing it, Mack!" she cried. "It's coming right at us!"

As Mack began to answer, the car reverberated with another impact, forceful enough to send it off the road and careening over the edge, down toward the lake.

Eliza felt as if everything was taking a long, long time. The tumble down the hillside, the crash into the tree, the inflating of the air bags, the minutes spent in shock, staring straight ahead, not quite sure what exactly had happened.

Was she all right? She told her brain to move her arms and legs. They did as they were commanded. She couldn't identify anything hurt, didn't think she was bleeding.

"Mack," she called out, reaching toward the driver's side of the car. She couldn't see him in the dark and with the air bag blocking her view. "Are you all right, Mack?"

She was answered with a low groan.

"Mack, answer me. Please, Mack."

No response at all this time.

Eliza pushed at the air bags, desperate to see his face. She leaned forward into the darkness and listened. She could hear Mack breathing. *Thank God.* But the breathing was heavy and labored.

She felt around, found her purse, and took out her cell phone. She dialed 911. Nothing happened. She looked at the screen. No signal.

Eliza knew she had to get out of the car and go get help. Adrenaline pulsed through her. She struggled to undo her seat belt, opened the car door, and began to scramble up the hill.

CHAPTER 91

What if the job wasn't complete? What if Eliza and her boyfriend weren't taken care of for good?

That was a damned dangerous drop to the lake at that point in the road. Even a Volvo wouldn't ensure survival.

Still, it would be a good idea to go back and check. There was also a little calling card to leave behind.

CHAPTER 92

Eliza climbed up, grabbing hold of rocks and branches to help her. As she reached the edge of the road, she heard a car approaching. She was about to wave her arms and yell for help when the outline of the vehicle came into dim view. Its headlights were dark.

It was the car that had driven them off the road!

Looking around desperately for someplace to hide, Eliza dived behind the trunk of a tree. She crouched down, holding her breath as she heard the car come to a stop and its door open.

Her heart pounded as she listened to the footsteps on the macadam. Was whoever it was going to climb all the way down to the car and find Mack there, alone and helpless? The driver's aim had obviously been to kill them. What would happen if Mack were found alive but unconscious, unable to defend himself?

Eliza, still somewhat dazed, didn't know what to do.

CHAPTER 93

*T*he moonlight reflected off the roof of the Volvo. It was apparent that nothing was moving down there except the steam rising from the hood.

The darkness on the road was suddenly pierced by two beams of light in the distance.

A decision had to be made quickly. Stay and risk someone seeing the car and wondering what it was doing there, or leave right now and take the chance that the occupants of the Volvo were still alive.

Eliza and her boyfriend, if not dead, had to be injured. Nobody would find them tonight and maybe not tomorrow either. With a little luck, it would be too late—whenever the car was discovered.

Even if they did survive, they would be smart enough to realize they'd been warned.

Just to make certain—so there would be no doubt—silver coins were hurled into the air, and the sound of metal showering down on the Volvo's roof echoed in the eerie autumn silence.

CHAPTER 94

Crouched in the darkness, Eliza heard strange pinging sounds, metal against metal, hard objects raining down on her car. Then she heard a door slam and the vehicle drive away.

She crawled out from behind the tree and clawed her way up the rest of the hill. When she got up to the road, she began running.

SUNDAY
OCTOBER 11

CHAPTER 95

Sitting alone in the waiting room at Good Samaritan Hospital, Eliza looked down at her hands, noticing for the first time that they were covered with dried blood. She wasn't quite sure if it was Mack's blood or her own. She had cut herself while clawing her way up from the crash site, but Mack's head wound had bled profusely.

Eliza closed her eyes. Mental images of his body being dragged up the hill on a backboard filled her with dread. He had lain there so perfectly still that Eliza was sure he must be dead.

But Mack wasn't dead. He was having emergency surgery. "Internal injuries," the doctor had said.

"It's going to be a while."

At the sound of the voice, Eliza opened her eyes and saw a nurse standing in front of her.

"Can I get you anything?" the nurse asked. "Would you like to freshen up?"

Realizing that the question was really a suggestion, Eliza shuffled down the hallway, wearing the loafers given to her by the woman who'd stopped her car when she saw Eliza running down the road. In the ladies' room, she washed her hands. Looking in the mirror above the sink, she almost didn't recognize herself.

Her face was colorless except for the dirt smudged across her cheeks. Her hair was tangled and messy. But it was her eyes that were most unfamiliar. They stared back at her, the dark pupils wide, almost eclipsing any blue. There was an anxious, fearful look in them, the look of someone who was deeply frightened.

The thought that she might lose Mack now that she'd finally allowed herself to love again was more than Eliza could allow herself to fathom. She had already gone through losing John almost eight years ago. For most of the time since then, she'd focused on Janie and her career, unable to let down her guard enough to allow someone else in. It couldn't be possible that now that she had, he might be taken away from her.

But unfortunately, terribly, it *was* possible. Cruel and unfair things happened all the time.

Splashing cool water on her face, Eliza prayed. "Please God, let Mack come through this. Don't take him from me."

"My purse and cell phone were left in the car," said Eliza as she leaned over the counter of the nurses' station. "Is there a telephone I can use?"

"I can't let you use the one here on the desk," said the nurse. "But you can borrow my cell." The nurse took it from her pocket and handed it to Eliza. "The only problem is, you have to go outside to use it."

When Eliza walked out of the hospital, the sky was beginning to lighten, hinting that the sun would be rising soon. She hated to call Annabelle this early, but she really needed to talk to her friend.

"I'm on my way," said Annabelle before Eliza could finish telling her everything that had happened.

"I know it's Sunday, and I hate to impose on you like this, but—" Eliza was cut off in midsentence.

"Stop it," said Annabelle firmly. "I'll be there in about an hour, and I'll have my cell phone with me. Call me if you need to talk to me about anything before that."

"Annabelle?"

"What?"

"Thank you."

CHAPTER 96

After the sun came up, the Tuxedo Park police, led by Chief Vitalli, searched the area of the accident. Tire-tread marks were found in the dirt at the point where the Volvo was forced off the road. The car had torn an obvious swath down the hillside, coming to a violent stop when it hit the tree.

"They're lucky to be alive," said one of the officers as he inspected the crushed vehicle.

"Yeah," said another. "But somebody wanted them dead."

The policemen made observations and took notes about the condition of the car and its position.

"This is strange," one of the officers remarked, reaching out and picking up several quarters from the roof of the Volvo.

"There are more on the ground."

Altogether they found thirty coins.

CHAPTER 97

W e all wanted to come," announced Annabelle when she arrived in the waiting room with Margo and B.J. in tow.

Eliza rose and hugged each of them. "I'd say you shouldn't have, but I'm so glad you did," she whispered.

"What's the latest on Mack?" asked Margo.

"I'm not sure," said Eliza. "He's in surgery, but nobody has come out to tell me anything more."

"Let me see what I can find out," said Margo, squeezing Eliza's hand before taking off for the nurses' station.

"It's nice to have an M.D. on your side," said B.J. "Especially when you're in an unfamiliar hospital."

"When is a hospital ever familiar?" asked Annabelle.

"You know what I mean," said B.J. "If Mack were in a hospital in the city, we'd feel better about it."

Annabelle shot him an exasperated glare. "You idiot," she mouthed.

B.J. looked embarrassed.

"It's all right, Beej," said Eliza. "I know what you meant, but John was in arguably the best cancer hospital in New York—in the whole country, for that matter—and it didn't make things better. I guess when it's your time, it's your time."

Annabelle wrapped her arms around Eliza. "It's not Mack's time, Eliza. Not even close."

Margo came back to the waiting room.

"Great news," she announced "There's no brain or spinal-cord injury."

Eliza let out a deep sigh of relief. "Thank you, God."

She tried to read the expression on Margo's face. It wasn't joyful.

"What's wrong?" she asked.

"Mack's shaken up," said Margo. "He fractured some ribs, one of which punctured his lung. His spleen was torn badly enough that they had to remove it. His liver was lacerated as well, and they're working on stitching that up now."

B.J. let out a low whistle.

"Mack's going to be all right, though, isn't he, Margo?" asked Eliza.

Margo looked directly into Eliza's frightened eyes. "I'm going to be honest with you, Eliza," she said. "Mack has some very serious injuries, and the coming days are going to be hard and painful for him. But he's got youth and good health on his side. Barring complications, he should probably be fine."

Probably was not definitely, thought Eliza as she wrapped her arms around herself for comfort. How was it that Mack was so badly injured—and she had walked away practically unscathed? She was responsible for getting him involved in what had become a deadly situation.

But who was responsible for this nightmare in the first place?

"Do you want to talk about what happened, Eliza?" asked Annabelle when all four of them sat around a table in the hospital coffee shop.

Eliza shook her head in bewilderment. "I don't know," she said. "We had just come back to the park after a wonderful dinner. We stopped to look at the lake. When we started for the carriage house, we went the wrong way, but before we could turn around, this car came up behind us and started ramming us."

"What kind of car was it?" asked B.J.

"I don't know. It was pretty dark, and the car didn't have any headlights on."

"So you couldn't see the driver?" asked Annabelle.

Eliza shook her head. "Uh-uh. I could kick myself now for not getting a look at his face when he came back."

"He?" asked Margo. "You know it was a man?"

"No," said Eliza, "I don't. I'm just assuming it was."

"What do you mean, 'when he came back'?" asked Annabelle.

Eliza recounted how she had climbed up the hill to get help and had hidden when their attacker returned.

"I think he just wanted to make sure that he'd finished the job. And I wonder what he'll do when he finds out he didn't."

Annabelle went outside, ostensibly to get some fresh air. She really wanted to make a phone call but didn't want to take the chance of upsetting Eliza.

She identified herself, her affiliation with KEY News, and her friendship with Eliza Blake.

"I would like some information on the accident last night," she said.

"Wish I could help you, ma'am, but I'm not at liberty to divulge any information on an ongoing investigation."

"Give me a break, will you?" asked Annabelle. "Somebody tried to kill the host of *KEY to America* and almost succeeded in murdering another KEY News correspondent. I demand to be given information."

Even as Annabelle spoke, she realized she should have alerted Range Bullock and Linus Nazareth about what had happened. They would be furious when they learned that they hadn't been called right away.

The police officer responded to the determination in her tone. "Captain Vitalli is the only one who is able to give out the kind of information you want," he said.

"Then please let me talk to him."

"He's not here right now, but if you give me your number, he'll return your call as soon as he can."

Annabelle recited her phone number, but she knew damn well that Chief Vitalli wasn't going to call her back.

The president of KEY News answered the phone. "Bullock," he said brusquely.

Annabelle explained what had happened the night before. "Eliza's fine," she said. "But it looks like Mack has some serious injuries."

"I'm coming out there," said Range. "But the first thing I'm going to do is arrange for security details to guard Eliza and Mack."

CHAPTER 98

C lay came home to grab a cup of coffee and a shower. He was cold and dirty after tramping around the crash area.

As he watched his daughter standing in the living room, swinging her tennis racket and talking to herself, Clay felt that everything was coming apart at the seams. Innis's suicide, the murders of Zack Underwood and Aurelia Patterson, and now the deliberate attempt to kill Eliza Blake and Mack McBride had all the park's residents reeling.

The mayor was calling repeatedly and pressing for information on the investigation, and Clay's job would be in certain jeopardy if he didn't come up with some answers. The board of trustees had held an emergency session, and as a result an official message had been posted on the village Web site announcing stricter security measures in the park. Residents were reminded to take special care about their safety and were urged not to walk alone, to lock their doors, to remove keys from their parked cars, to ensure that all children were accompanied both to and from school, and to immediately report anything suspicious.

Tuxedo Park residents weren't going to stand for the threat and disruption to their sheltered world. They would find somebody else who could keep them safe if Clay didn't.

While his immediate reaction was to stonewall the press, that wasn't going to work any longer. Once it got out that Eliza Blake had been attacked, every imaginable news outlet would be demanding facts and details—demands that complicated an already escalating and tangled situation.

He simply had to release some information. Otherwise it would look like he had something to hide.

CHAPTER 99

The surgeon finally emerged.

"Mr. McBride has made it through surgery. He's in intensive care now," he announced.

"He's all right, then?" Eliza asked hopefully.

The doctor's face was devoid of expression. "When we got in there, the liver was more damaged than we thought. He's sustained some very serious injuries. He'll be carefully monitored, and we'll know better in a day or two."

"Can I see him?" asked Eliza.

The doctor hesitated. "He'll be out of it for a while."

"I still want to see him," said Eliza.

"All right," said the doctor, aware of who she was and hearing the determination in Eliza's voice. "But brace yourself. It's not going to be pretty."

After Annabelle, Margo, and B.J. watched Eliza leave the waiting room, Annabelle spoke first.

"What kind of answer is that?" she asked.

"An honest one," said Margo. "We *will* know better in a day or two. Mack is in for a rough ride."

"Mr. Personality," B.J. said under his breath. "That guy has no bedside manner at all."

"Don't be so hard on him," said Margo. "You don't want a doctor who can win a personality contest. You want one who knows what he's doing."

Eliza swayed as if struck when she saw him.

His face, so tanned and healthy-looking as they'd sat at dinner just hours before, was gray, almost white. A breathing tube protruded from his mouth. His hands lay limp and motionless against the cotton blanket beneath which his chest barely moved.

She steadied herself, grabbing hold of the bed railing.

A nurse was studying a beeping monitor. When she noticed Eliza, she smiled feebly. "Try not to worry," she said. "Sometimes it looks worse than it really is."

"Is this one of those times?" asked Eliza as she reached over to take Mack's hand.

The nurse either didn't hear or pretended she didn't, because she didn't answer Eliza's question.

![puzzle piece] CHAPTER 100

S he'd been so excited she hadn't been able to sleep all night. Still, Susannah wasn't the least bit tired when she arrived at the tennis house. She was exhilarated and hopeful.

There really was no reason for her to be there so early. The caterers weren't scheduled to arrive for at least another hour, and the volunteers Valentina had recruited wouldn't get there until another hour after that. But Susannah relished the time alone and the chance to walk around the deserted outdoor tennis courts. If things went the way she wanted them to go, soon she'd be able to play on the courts herself as a member of the Black Tie Club.

Susannah was roused from her daydream by the sound of a car pulling into the parking area adjacent to the courts. She looked over and saw a woman she recognized get out of her dark green Jaguar. The woman walked toward Susannah, a worried expression on her face.

"Hello, Marjorie."

"Hi, Susannah."

Susannah was thrilled that the woman knew her name. Marjorie was one of the park residents who usually ignored her, acting as if she didn't exist.

"Have you heard?" asked Marjorie.

"Heard what?"

"Eliza Blake and her boyfriend were run off the road near the boathouse last night."

Susannah winced. "How horrible. Are they all right?"

"I heard she's okay, but he was really hurt." Marjorie shook her head as she unzipped her jacket. "I don't know what's going on around here, but it scares me to death. First the Wheelock suicide, then his architect murdered, and then that poor woman who lives in the little ranch."

"What woman? What little ranch?" asked Susannah.

"I didn't know her, but apparently she was hammered to death when she went out to walk her dog. Can you imagine? They found her body in the bushes down the road from her house. Didn't you know? Everyone is taking about it."

Susannah averted her eyes and shook her head. "I've been so focused on this Special Olympics thing that I haven't really talked to anyone. What are the police saying?"

"They don't seem to be saying or doing a thing," said Marjorie. "I tell you, I feel like I'm going to jump out of my skin. That's why I figured I'd come down here and get some time in the exercise room. It helps me hold on to my sanity."

Susannah watched as the woman started toward the tennis house. Marjorie turned around and called back, "You know, Susannah, organizing this event was very good of you. I'll be back later to help out."

Marjorie smiled, and Susannah thought, *Good. My plan is working.*

CHAPTER 101

They think he's going to be out for quite a while," said Eliza as she rejoined the group in the waiting room.

"Why don't you go home and take a hot shower and try to get a little sleep?" suggested Margo. "I'll stay here and wait."

Eliza looked at her uncertainly. "I don't know if that's such a good idea. I want to be here when he wakes up."

"Listen to me, Eliza," said Margo, taking her friend's arm. "It doesn't make sense for you to sit here. Don't forget, you were in an accident, too. Go, get cleaned up, get something to eat, and take a rest. I truly doubt that Mack is going to wake up anytime soon."

Reluctantly, Eliza agreed. "All right," she said. "But I want to call Mack's parents in Florida first and let them know what's happened."

"We'll take you," said Annabelle, indicating B.J. "I spoke to Linus while you were in with Mack. We've got some work to do."

Eliza looked at them quizzically.

"Chief Vitalli is finally going to hold a news conference, and B.J. and I are going to cover it." Annabelle's facial expression was strained.

"There's something else, isn't there?" said Eliza.

"Yes," Annabelle answered in a somber tone. "It just crossed the wires a little while ago. There's been another murder. Aurelia Patterson is dead."

Within the next half hour, Eliza made the difficult phone call to the senior McBrides, assuring them that everything possible was being done and promising that she would keep them posted, calling as soon as Mack woke up.

While Eliza talked, Annabelle drew her a hot bath.

"Oh, that feels good." Eliza sighed as she sank into the deep tub.

"You've got to realize that you took a pretty serious tumble in that car, Eliza. Your body is going to be sore," said Annabelle. "Beej is downstairs making some tea. Then we've got to get going if we expect to make the presser. Will you be all right?"

Eliza nodded. "Yes. I feel like I should be going to the press conference with you guys. I asked Vitalli for the police report on that accident twenty years ago on West Lake Road when I spoke with him on the phone on Friday, but he put me off."

"I'll see if I can get it from him," promised Annabelle. "And don't worry about not being there yourself. We'll fill you in on whatever we find out."

Annabelle left Eliza, went downstairs, and came back up again with a tray.

"Tea and toast," she said. "Just what the doctor ordered."

"Thanks, Annabelle. Now you'd better get going."

Annabelle hesitated. "I hate to leave you, but I'm feeling a little better about it since the security guard has arrived. He's stationed outside."

"I'll be fine, don't worry," said Eliza. "But will you lock the doors downstairs? The residents of Tuxedo Park may feel all right about leaving their houses open, but I don't—even with a guard in front."

"All right," said Annabelle. "And I'm leaving my cell phone for you in case you need it."

CHAPTER 102

News that someone had tried to kill Eliza Blake and Mack McBride sent media coverage into high gear. The Tuxedo Park police station was being deluged with calls from national and international newspapers and television and radio stations demanding information, requesting that a police press conference be held, and pleading that they be permitted to enter Tuxedo Park.

Chief Vitalli had tightened security at the main gate. He had chosen to hold his press conference at the public library in town. The parking lot was filled with print and broadcast journalists and camera crews eager for information about the attack on two of their own. Satellite trucks and other news vehicles choked traffic on the main roadway, requiring police to move things along.

"Good news travels fast," said Annabelle, seeing the media. "Even Tokyo Broadcasting is here."

B.J. plugged his audio line into the mult box, joining the other network and local television and radio stations that also planned to record Chief Vitalli's statement and the answers to their questions. The din of voices and shouts of the newspeople quieted down as the tall, uniformed man with the buzz cut and craggy face stepped up to the microphone.

"Good morning. I am Clay Vitalli, chief of the Tuxedo Park Police Department. I have a statement which I will read to you, and then I'll take a few of your questions."

Vitalli cleared his throat and looked down at his notes.

"Over the last week, Tuxedo Park has been the scene of a series of violent and deadly incidents that have left our community reeling and fearful. Last Sunday the suicide of one of our most respected citizens, Innis Wheelock; on Wednesday the murder of Zachary Underwood, a talented architect who has worked on many renovations in the park; and yesterday the body of Aurelia Patterson, a park resident, was found hidden in a wooded area close to her home. And as most of you also know, last night Eliza Blake and Mack McBride of KEY News were run off the road inside the park as they drove home from dinner. Fortunately, both of them survived."

Vitalli looked out at the assemblage.

"We consider all these to be heinous and horrific acts, and we take them, and the investigation of them, very seriously. The Tuxedo Park Police Department is devoting itself to following any and all information that could possibly lead to solving the murders of Mr. Underwood and Mrs. Patterson and the attack on Ms. Blake and Mr. McBride."

"What condition are Eliza and Mack in now?" asked a reporter.

"As I understand it, Mr. McBride is in Good Samaritan Hospital. Ms. Blake was uninjured. But for the particulars on that, you'll have to consult the press information department at KEY News."

A reporter in the back shouted out, "Are you calling in outside help? You have a small department."

"We are working with the Tuxedo police on the Underwood murder, since it happened outside the park itself. But any crime committed on park grounds will remain exclusively under Tuxedo Park police jurisdiction."

"What details can you give us about Aurelia Patterson?" asked a CNN producer.

"Mrs. Patterson worked as a secretary for Mr. Underwood. She lived alone. We think she was murdered while walking her dog on Friday night. Her body was discovered by a couple who were taking a stroll on Saturday afternoon."

"How was she killed?"

"Blunt-force trauma to the head," said Chief Vitalli.

"Do you know what kind of instrument was used?"

"We suspect it was a hammer."

There was a momentary pause in the questioning as the journalists digested the information.

"Was there anything outstanding or interesting about the way the body was positioned?" Annabelle called out.

Chief Vitalli looked up sharply. He didn't answer right away.

"Beyond the fact that her head had been bashed in?" he asked sarcastically. "I'd say that was pretty outstanding."

Annabelle was undeterred. "Let me be more specific, Chief. Had the killer staged the murder scene? Had he moved the body so as to suggest that he was trying to send a message? Had he left any sort of calling card?"

"No comment," said Vitalli.

Annabelle broke away from the crowd, following Vitalli as he left the microphone.

"Chief!" she called. "Wait."

Vitalli turned and looked at her with irritation.

"I'm Annabelle Murphy, with KEY News. Eliza Blake asked you

for an old police report, the one on the West Lake Road accident. I'd like to get it from you and bring it to her."

"And I'd like to be a millionaire, but that ain't gonna happen," snapped Chief Vitalli. "Are you kidding me? My department has much more important things to work on than pulling old police reports and worrying about something that happened two decades ago. We've got life-and-death situations right now."

CHAPTER 103

Easing herself out of the bathtub, Eliza dried herself carefully. Her body ached all over. Her neck was stiff, her legs and arms felt heavy, and the palms of her hands hurt from the cuts she'd suffered climbing up the hill.

She put on a robe and lay down on the bed, noticing that Annabelle had left her cell phone on the table. Eliza picked it up and called Margo, who told her that Mack was still asleep but assured her that everything was going as well as could be expected. A security guard was posted outside Mack's room.

"You should close your eyes and try to sleep, too," said Margo.

Eliza knew she had some Advil in her purse, but she'd left that in the car. For the first time, she thought about her wallet and the credit cards and driver's license that she needed to get back. The keys to her house in Ho-Ho-Kus were also in the bag.

Worried and vulnerable, Eliza got up and went back into the bathroom, where she found a bottle of aspirin in the medicine cabinet. She took three. But deep and satisfying sleep wouldn't come as she lay down again on the bed. She kept drifting in and out of wakefulness.

Images of the accident ran through her mind. The terror of being pushed over the hillside, the fear of losing Mack, her flight to get help, hiding from the person who had attacked them so viciously, crouching in the darkness unsure of what to do, the sound of metal raining down against metal. *What was that noise?*

Then the visions switched. Innis with the stigmata wounds and Zack, strangled and sitting in a chair, holding a reed scepter like royalty. There was something that connected them. But what?

A sharp knocking on the door downstairs startled Eliza. She got up and slowly descended the staircase. Before opening the front door, she looked out the window. Valentina Wheelock was standing outside with the security guard.

"I heard about what happened, and I've been trying to reach you, but there's been no answer," said Valentina, frowning.

"That's because I left my phone at the scene of the accident. It wasn't getting any reception there."

Valentina shook her head in disgust. "We *have* to have something done about that. Cell service is so spotty up here. Maybe now that there's been an accident where people's lives were at stake, we can demand better service." Valentina's voice softened as she asked, "Are you all right?"

"I'm fine," said Eliza, opening the door wide for her to enter. "It's Mack we have to worry about."

Eliza gave Valentina details. "Valentina, all of this is connected with Innis's death. I'm sure of it," she said. "When we left your house after lunch yesterday, Mack and I went to Nine Chimneys. We found five carved wooden blocks inside the only standing chimney." She nodded toward the table where the cubes still sat. "The blocks are just like the ones on your fireplace."

"The ones that spell 'ROMA'?"

"Yes," said Eliza, "and look at this."

Valentina followed her over to the table. Eliza arranged the wooden cubes and cutout paper squares to spell "crematory."

Valentina held her hand to her chest. "My God. Was Innis telling us that Nine Chimneys was used as a crematorium? That someone was . . . cremated there?"

"I don't know," said Eliza. "Try to think back, Valentina. Can you remember when Nine Chimneys burned down? Was it before or after Marty O'Shaughnessy's car was deserted on West Lake Road?"

The older woman's face had turned ashen. "It was several *years* before," she said slowly. "Let me see," she said, her brows furrowing as she searched her memory. "Yes, I remember that I was pregnant with Rusty when the car was found, and Fitzroy and Unity had already been living in the apartment over the clubhouse for several years by then."

"Well, that's a relief," said Eliza.

Valentina glanced at her watch. "I'm sorry, dear, but I have to get going to that Special Olympics thing."

Eliza closed her yes. "Oh, I completely forgot about it."

"And understandably so," said Valentina.

"If you can wait for a few minutes, I'll go upstairs and throw something on," said Eliza, starting for the stairs.

Valentina took hold of her arm. "No one expects you to come, dear," she said. "We couldn't have known all that would happen when you committed to it. Everyone will understand."

"I'll just go for a little while," said Eliza. "People are expecting me, and I don't want to disappoint them. I had said I would go, and I will, if only for a little while."

CHAPTER 104

Blue and white balloons decorated the fences surrounding the tennis courts while people watched the matches being played. Even the weakest serves and the shortest volleys elicited rousing cheers as the spectators rooted enthusiastically for the challenged yet determined athletes.

Eliza smiled, shook hands, and made conversation. As she walked through the crowd, accompanied by the security guard, she was aware of the stares and whispers that followed her. Most people came right out and asked her how she was and told her how worried and upset they were about her accident and all the other dreadful things that had been happening.

An attractive yet frantic-looking woman approached. "I'm Susannah Lansing," she said, extending her hand. "And I want to thank you so much for coming today, especially after what you've just been through."

"I'm glad I was able to make it," said Eliza. "You're the person who organized all this, aren't you?"

"Yes," said Susannah. "I'm flattered you knew that."

"Valentina told me," said Eliza. "She spoke quite highly of you."

"She did?" Susannah asked with surprise.

"Yes." Eliza nodded and gestured toward the tennis courts. "And I can see why."

"You have no idea how much I appreciate hearing that," said Susannah.

The cell phone she was carrying in the pocket of her jacket vibrated. It was Annabelle.

"What did you get at the press conference?" asked Eliza.

"Not that much," said Annabelle. "They think Aurelia Patterson was killed with a hammer; besides that, the chief didn't really divulge anything we hadn't already suspected. Although when I asked him if there was anything particularly strange at Aurelia Patterson's murder scene, he wouldn't comment. But I got the distinct impression that he was holding back on something."

"He doesn't know that Aurelia told us about the staging of Zack Underwood's body," said Eliza.

"Right," said Annabelle. "And neither does CBS, ABC, NBC, or any of the others, as far as I can tell. B.J. and I have to put together a piece on all this for the show tonight. A satellite truck is on its way so we can feed from here."

"Where are you now?" asked Eliza.

"At the gate. The guard won't let us back in again."

"Put him on the phone," said Eliza. "And when he lets you in, ask him how to get to the tennis house. I'll be waiting."

CHAPTER 105

Cleo Vitalli finished her tennis game, a broad grin on her face, and applauded along with the spectators who clapped for her. Her big blue eyes searched from behind thick glasses, eager to find her father in the crowd and bask in his approval. But she couldn't see him anywhere.

One of the policemen who worked for her dad had picked her up at home and driven her to the game. He'd said her father would be there in time to see her play and that he would take her home afterward. Not finding her father, Cleo was confused.

"Hey, Cleo. Nice game."

Cleo turned in the direction of the voice. She smiled when she saw Rusty. When they were little, she and Rusty had played together, but when they got bigger, Rusty had other things to do and couldn't play with her anymore. She still liked him. She missed him and wished she saw him more.

"Hi, Rusty," she said shyly.

"You did a great job out there, Cleo."

"Thank you." She cast her eyes downward.

"Where's your father?" asked Russell.

"I don't know," she said. "He's supposed to be here."

"Let's see if we can find him." Russell held out his hand, and Cleo eagerly took it.

CHAPTER 106

Eliza was tired, sore, and having a hard time keeping a pleasant smile on her face. She couldn't wait for Annabelle and B.J. to arrive so they could take her back to the hospital to be with Mack. When yet two more people approached her, it was all she could do to stop herself from running away.

"Hello, Ms. Blake, my name is Colleen D'Alessandro, and this is my husband, Hank."

Eliza shook their hands.

"It's so good of you to come today," said Colleen.

"Especially after what happened to you last night," said Hank.

Eliza nodded, too exhausted to talk.

"We almost didn't come today ourselves," said Colleen. "We were so upset by what happened yesterday."

"We were the ones who found Aurelia Patterson's body," said Hank.

Eliza felt a surge of energy.

"We were out for our walk, and that poor border collie was barking and barking. I knew he was trying to tell us something," said Colleen.

"I followed the dog into the woods, and there she was, her head beaten in, lying on the ground." Hank shuddered. "It was awful."

"Tell her about the dice, Hank."

"Yeah, I can't figure this," said Hank. "The woman had a pair of dice in her hand, like she was ready to roll 'em. What do you think that was all about?"

CHAPTER 107

Chief Vitalli got out of the police vehicle and headed for the tennis courts. He looked for his daughter but didn't see her. Checking with one of the volunteers, he learned that Cleo had finished her game half an hour earlier.

He felt downhearted at the thought that he not only missed seeing Cleo play but hadn't been there to greet her and celebrate when she walked off the court. Cleo didn't get all that many opportunities to shine. He didn't get all that many opportunities to rejoice.

Damn that news conference.

As he searched the area for his daughter, Clay was stopped by residents wanting to question him about what was going on. He put them off, saying that commenting could jeopardize the ongoing investigation. Most of them seemed satisfied with his response; some of them were angry.

Maybe Cleo went into the tennis house.

Clay went inside to look for his daughter. She wasn't in the trophy room or the exercise room. She wasn't on the real tennis court. As he went deeper down the hallway, Clay began calling out her name.

Where is she?

When he reached the back of the building, Clay started to panic. What if Cleo had wandered away? What if someone had lured her to go off with him? She was so trusting. No matter how many times she'd been taught otherwise, Clay continued to suspect that anyone could talk Cleo into doing anything, because she wanted to please. For Clay, it was a source of continuing anxiety and the reason for many sleepless nights.

He approached the door to the racket court where he and Fitzroy and Peter had met a few nights before, the dark, closed-in space with thick concrete walls and no windows. A perfect place to do something you didn't want anyone else to see.

Trying not to make any noise as he opened the door, Clay saw Cleo standing on the cement floor—and Russell Wheelock close beside her.

CHAPTER 108

As soon as she saw the car drive up, Eliza hurried to meet it.

"Guess what I just heard," she said as she got into the backseat. Without waiting for Annabelle or B.J. to answer, Eliza continued. "Aurelia Patterson was found with dice clasped in her hand."

"Dice?" asked B.J. as he maneuvered the car out of the parking area, with the security vehicle close behind. "As in gambling?"

"Yeah, or game playing," said Eliza. "In either case, I doubt that Aurelia was carrying a pair of dice while she was walking her dog."

"So Zack was strangled with some sort of leather strap and then positioned on his throne with a reed scepter," mused Annabelle. "And Aurelia was hammered to death and then dice were put in her hand?"

"What are we supposed to make out of that?" asked B.J.

"The only connections I see are, one, both victims knew each other and worked together and, two, the murderer is staging his crime scenes."

The three of them were quiet as they considered what they knew so far.

"Think we should include this in tonight's piece?" asked Annabelle, finally breaking the silence.

"No doubt about it, we should," said Eliza. "The police didn't ask that we refrain from reporting it. They didn't even give us this information. We uncovered it ourselves, from eyewitnesses, and we have every reason to report it. It's news."

CHAPTER 109

Clay reached out and grabbed Russell by the collar of his shirt.

"What the hell do you think you're doing? If you touched her, I swear to God, Rusty, I'm gonna make you wish you'd never been born."

Russell's face was beet red. "Calm down, Clay. Calm down. It's not what you think."

"What is it, then?"

"Cleo and I came in here to practice. Didn't we, Cleo?"

Clay looked at his daughter. Her blue eyes were open wide. Her cheeks were flushed. Her sweat suit was rumpled.

"We were practicing hitting with the rackets," Russell continued. "Weren't we, Cleo?"

Cleo said nothing, her mouth agape.

"See, Clay? The rackets and the balls are right there." Russell pointed to the sports equipment. "Cleo asked me if I would play with her."

"Did you, Cleo?" asked Clay.

Her eyes filled with tears at the angry tone of her father's voice. Her lips quivered, and she started to cry.

Clay knew better than to push his daughter any further. Continuing to confront Russell in front of Cleo would be a big mistake, only making her inconsolable.

He hadn't actually seen Russell touching Cleo, but Clay worried he might have.

There'll be another time and place to take care of Russell.

As he escorted his daughter out of the tennis house, Chief Clay Vitalli did wish that Russell Wheelock had never been born. The young man's existence had wreaked havoc with his life and so many others.

CHAPTER 110

W hile we're in here, we really should get some shots of the pertinent locations," said B.J. "Like exteriors of Pentimento, of Aurelia Patterson's house, of your wrecked car, Eliza."

Annabelle agreed. "And let's get shots of that old accident site on West Lake Road and Nine Chimneys."

"That will take too long," said Eliza.

"No it won't," said B.J. "I'll work fast, not only because I know you want to get to the hospital but because we aren't supposed to be taking pictures to begin with. We don't want to get caught."

In just over half an hour, B.J. had gotten the video they wanted.

"On the way out, let's make a quick stop at the police station," said Eliza. "I want to see about getting my purse back."

"I'll go in with you," said B.J. as he parked the car. The security guard pulled into the space behind theirs.

"Good," said Annabelle. "I'm going to stay out here and work on my script."

The officer staffing the front desk looked up and recognized Eliza immediately.

"Good to see you, ma'am. How are you doing?" he asked politely.

"I'm okay," said Eliza. "But my friend isn't. He was very badly hurt. We're on our way to see him in the hospital now."

The policeman nodded. "It's a miracle that you walked away," he said. "I've seen some accidents in my time, but that one was a doozy."

"Oh, you saw the car?" asked Eliza.

"Yes, ma'am."

"I was out there this morning. I'm glad you're all right."

"Thank you," she said. "I left my purse and cell phone in the car, and I was wondering how I can get them back."

"We have them here," said the police officer. "If you wait a minute, I'll go get them."

"That's a relief," Eliza said to B.J. while they waited. "I hated the thought of having to replace all that stuff."

As the officer returned and handed her the purse, he smiled. "May I ask you a question?"

"Sure," said Eliza.

"Why do you carry so much change?"

"I'm sorry?"

"All those quarters," said the policeman. "My partner and I were pretty sure you didn't need them for a Laundromat."

"I don't know what you mean," said Eliza.

"We found thirty quarters scattered over the area. Some on the roof, more on the ground."

Eliza and B.J. looked at each another.

Thirty quarters, thirty pieces of silver.

"Oh, good. You got it," said Annabelle when Eliza got back into the car with her recovered purse.

"We've got more than that," said B.J., turning the key in the ignition.

They told Annabelle about the quarters.

"That was the sound I heard as I was hiding," said Eliza. "Whoever tried to kill Mack and me threw quarters on the roof of the car."

"I don't get it," said Annabelle. "What does that mean?"

"There were thirty quarters, Annabelle," said B.J. "What does that make you think of?"

Annabelle thought. "Thirty quarters," she said aloud.

"Thirty pieces of *silver*," B.J. said impatiently.

"Like what Judas betrayed Jesus for?" asked Annabelle.

"Exactly," said B.J.

"And think about it, Annabelle," said Eliza excitedly. "Remember that Jesus was whipped with some kind of leather scourge on the way to Calvary, and the people who mocked him put a reed in his hand as a scepter because he claimed to be King of the Jews?"

"And that the soldiers who guarded him threw dice for his robes?" asked B.J.

"And a hammer was used to pound in the nails at the crucifixion?" added Eliza.

"My God," said Annabelle. "Not only did we have a suicide by stigmata, now we have murders using the instruments of Christ's death."

CHAPTER 111

As they drove out the front gate, they passed the news crews and satellite trucks stranded outside, unable to get into the park.

"God," said B.J. "Can you imagine how frustrated those guys are?"

"We lucked out when I rented that carriage house," said Eliza.

B.J. drove slowly and carefully through the crowded area. Eliza looked out the window and saw a reporter pointing to their car. Suddenly a gaggle of camerapeople rushed forward, starved for video and determined to get a picture.

"Should I get out and say something?" Eliza wondered aloud.

"No way," said Annabelle.

Riding to the hospital, Eliza checked the messages on her recovered phone. Range Bullock, Linus Nazareth, Harry Granger, and Paige Tintle had been trying to get in touch with her, unaware that she'd been without her cell. There was also a message from Susan Cohen saying that they would be back from Hershey with Janie at about 8:00 P.M.

"Now, you're sure you don't need me to record that track?" asked Eliza as Annabelle and B.J. dropped her off at the entrance.

"No, Bruce Harley came out with the truck. He'll do the narration, and we'll shoot a stand-up of him at the park gates or someplace more creative, if we can come up with one." ·

"Maybe we should go into the Catholic church in Tuxedo and see if we can have Harley stand under a crucifix—the more graphic the depiction of Christ's crucifixion, the better," suggested B.J.

"You are a sick man," said Annabelle. "Truly and deeply sick."

B.J. smirked. "Nowhere near as sick as our murderer."

More newspeople were staked out in front of the hospital. Eliza forced her way through the crowd.

KEY News president Range Bullock was sitting with Margo when Eliza walked into the waiting room. He stood up and hugged her.

"Thank God you're all right," he said.

"I'm fine," said Eliza. "Sore, but fine." She immediately turned to Margo. "How is Mack?" she asked.

"Stable, but still out of it," said Margo. "The doctor was just in there a little while ago and checked him."

"Thanks a million for staying here with him," said Eliza. "You don't know how much I appreciate that."

"We've organized a chain, people who'll take turns being here, at least until Mack gets out of intensive care," said Range. "I'm taking the next shift. After you go in and visit him, Margo will give you a lift home."

Eliza straightened. "Clearly you have it all planned."

"We do," said Range. "What sense does it make for you to wear yourself out waiting here round the clock?"

Eliza looked at Margo.

"Do you really think that your standing vigil at Mack's bedside is going to make him wake up any sooner?" asked Margo.

If Janie hadn't been coming home in a few hours, Eliza was certain she would have put up a bigger fight. But she longed to see Janie, hug her, talk to her. If Mack came to, Eliza could be back at the hospital in less than half an hour.

"Maybe you're right," she said. "We're not sure when Mack will wake up, and I could use a night in my own bed before doing the show in the morning."

Range looked surprised. "I just assumed that you'd take a day or two off," he said.

Eliza shook her head. "When I let you in on what's been happening with the Tuxedo Park murders, you'll understand why I want to tell the *KTA* audience about it myself."

CHAPTER 112

*T*he leather strap used to kill Zack Underwood represented the scourging Jesus received just before he was condemned by Pontius Pilate. And the reed scepter positioned in his hand was similar to the one given to Jesus as he was mocked by the Roman guards for claiming to be king of the Jews.

The hammer pounded into Aurelia's skull symbolized the one that had fastened Christ to the cross. The pair of dice placed in her hand was a reminder of the soldiers gambling for Jesus's robe.

It had all gone according to a hastily devised plan—a plan of which the very inventive Innis Wheelock himself would have been proud.

The one glitch had been Eliza Blake and Mack McBride. Trying to kill them with a car, instead of something from the ancient list, had been a mistake. Throwing the thirty quarters on the Volvo, while in keeping with the grisly symbolism, didn't provide any real satisfaction—since they had both lived.

So far, all of it was done to make sure that the Pentimento puzzle would never be solved and that the threat of exposure would remain just that—a threat. So far, only the old accident on West Lake Road and a murky role for Nine Chimneys had been uncovered as a result of that damned puzzle, but *none of the details of what had actually happened so long ago were apparent. Everything else was still a secret.*

Only Father Gehry—because of the confessional—knew the whole story. And Eliza Blake was probably still determined to unravel the puzzle at all costs.

The next kill would stick to the original plan.

CHAPTER 113

S unday was always a long day for Father Gehry, and today was no different.

He'd said three of the four Masses in the morning, and while the twelve-fifteen Latin Mass was being celebrated by a visiting priest, he'd met with the parents of the First Communion class in the parish hall, answering questions about white dresses and blue suits and whether flashbulbs could be used during the ceremony. He skipped lunch because he'd promised to check in on the sister of the parish organist who was in a nursing home, and after praying with her he'd sped to the hospital to visit five of his parishioners. On the way home, he remembered to stop at a convenience store, buying a quart of milk for his coffee in the morning.

Pulling into the rectory driveway, Father Gehry knew he didn't have time for that nap he'd promised himself. The entire month of October was dedicated to the Blessed Virgin, and the eleventh was the church's old feast of the Divine Motherhood of Mary. Some parishioners would be praying their beads tonight.

With quiet resignation he walked over to the church, leaving the carton of milk on the front seat.

After slowly reciting fifty Hail Marys and giving a brief impromptu meditation on Mary's virtue, Father Gehry said his farewells to the pious men and women as quickly as they let him. He then fetched the green velvet sack from the sacristy and walked back into the church to collect the candle money and empty the poor box of its meager contents.

Rehearsing in his head the list of everything he had to do the next day, he suddenly sensed someone behind him. He turned.

"Hello, Father."

Father Gehry nodded. "Were you at the rosary tonight? I didn't see you."

"No, Father. I just got here."

"Do you need something?"

"Yes, I do, Father. I'm sorry to bother you, but I really need to talk to you."

His first impulse was to explain how long a day he'd had and suggest meeting tomorrow morning, but the priest thought better of it. "All right," he said. "Why don't we sit right over here?"

He chose one of the pews opposite the poor box.

"What is it you want to talk about?"

"I think you know, Father."

"You'll have to tell me what it is. Say it out loud. You'll feel better for it, I promise you. It will be a relief to get it out in the open."

"It can never be out in the open, Father. You know that. My life would be ruined."

He struggled a few moments for a way to respond. "Then let's pray together," said Father Gehry. "St. Raymond is the patron saint of secrets, so let's ask for his special intercession." He knelt down and bowed his head. "We come before you, St. Raymond, with many secrets locked in our hearts. So many innocent people have been hurt.

We humbly beg for the assistance of your prayers from heaven. Watch over us, we pray, and keep us safe. Through Christ our Lord."

While Father Gehry had his head still bowed, waiting silently for an "Amen" that didn't come, a knife was shoved deep into the left side of his chest.

On the right wall of the sanctuary was the ambry and, inside, three bottles filled with the church's holy oils.

It was too late for the Oil of the Sick. And what the hell was the Oil of Catechumens?

The third bottle, with the words SACRED CHRISM etched into its surface, was filled with a thick liquid, a warm yellow instead of the cool olive green in the other two.

This is it.

Sacred chrism, which had been rubbed into Father Gehry's palms on the day of his ordination, was poured over the dead priest's head, just as Jesus had been anointed with fragrant myrrh before he was wrapped in a shroud and laid in the tomb.

MONDAY
OCTOBER 12

CHAPTER 114

earing noise coming from the other twin bed, Unity rolled
over and switched on the light. She squinted as she read the
numbers on the clock.

"It's after midnight, Fitz," she said. "Why are you still awake?"

"Don't worry about me, Unity. Go back to sleep."

"Are you crying?" she asked incredulously. She took her glasses
from the bedside table, put them on, and leaned closer to see his face.
"You are. You're crying. What's *wrong*?"

He ran his fingers through his white hair. "I don't know how long
before it's going to be exposed—before *I'm* going to be exposed," Fitzroy answered, his voice cracking.

Unity closed her eyes as she decided how to respond. "Let me tell
you something, Fitz," she finally answered. "There isn't anyone around
here who doesn't know that you burned down Nine Chimneys for the
insurance money. I've never asked you about it, and you've never told
me, but believe me, everybody knows. I never mention it you, they
never mention it to us, but everybody *knows*. So don't worry about being exposed now."

"That's not it," said Fitzroy.

"What then? What else could it be that has you so upset?"

His words came pouring out. "After Nine Chimneys burned, several years after, after the insurance company completed its investigation without proving any wrongdoing, I did something wrong, much worse than setting fire to a house." His shoulders shook as he began to sob.

Unity threw back the blanket and got out of bed. She joined Fitzroy on his bed and sat next to him. "What?" she asked softly. "What did you do?"

"I've got to get it out, Unity. I've got to tell somebody about it." Tears ran down his cheeks. Unity couldn't ever remember seeing such a tortured expression on her husband's face.

"All right. Tell me, then," she said, putting her hand on his arm.

"I set fire to a man," he blurted.

She stiffened. "I don't understand."

"I set fire to a human being, Unity."

"You set fire to him while he was alive?" Unity asked with horror.

"No, he was dead. I set fire to his body so he couldn't be identified. And later we buried what was left of him at Nine Chimneys."

"Who was it, Fitz? And why?" Questions flowed from Unity. "And who are the 'we' who buried him?"

"Marty O'Shaughnessy," answered Fitzroy. "It was Marty O'Shaughnessy I burned."

Unity's eyes widened. "You were involved in all that back then? The car accident, his disappearance?"

Fitzroy hung his head.

"But then you knew he didn't run off and go to Ireland or somewhere," said Unity. "You knew he was dead?"

Fitzroy nodded and rubbed his eyes with his pajama sleeve.

"Why didn't you go to the police?" asked Unity.

"Believe me, the police knew," Fitzroy said sarcastically. "Clay Vitalli knew all about it."

"Clay was in on it?"

"Absolutely," said Fitzroy. "And so was Peter Nordstrut. We were all in on it, to protect Valentina and Innis. The three of us were incredibly devoted to them. We were the ones they could trust to do anything that needed doing. We were determined to win that gubernatorial campaign."

"I don't understand," said Unity. "Protect them from what?"

Fitzroy shook his head. "No. I've already said too much. It's just that I'm trying to rack my brain for ways to make sure that the whole truth doesn't come out. Yet I think part of me would actually be relieved to finally have everything out in the open. It's been horrible to have all this on my conscience for so long and to live in fear of it all coming to light."

Unity digested the information. "Well, how in God's name is anyone going to find about all that now? It happened so long ago."

"As I said, Unity, I've told you too much. I don't want to get you involved in all this and make you some sort of accessory or something."

Unity stood up and went back to her own bed. As they lay in the dark, trying to fall asleep, she had a thought. "Fitzroy, you could talk to Father Gehry about this, you know. He might be able to help you, make you feel better. You could unburden yourself."

Fitzroy rolled over and pulled the blanket close to his chin. "Forget it, Unity," he said. "That's not an option."

CHAPTER 115

Confronting him with the information about the staged murder scenes and the religious symbolism used in the attacks, Annabelle was able to persuade Tuxedo Park police chief Clay Vitalli to appear exclusively on *KEY to America* Monday morning. She suggested that KEY News send out a transmission truck and do the interview in Tuxedo Park, but Vitalli refused. He would come to the broadcast center in New York City.

Linus Nazareth himself went over all the questions Annabelle had prepared in advance. A video package, narrated by Eliza Blake and scheduled to run in *KTA*'s first half hour, would lead to the live interview with Vitalli.

Annabelle was called when Vitalli arrived. She went to meet him in the lobby and escort him to the *KTA* studio. As they walked to the elevator, Annabelle informed him of the plan.

"We have time to stop in hair and makeup," she said.

"If you haven't noticed, I have a crew cut," Chief Vitalli said gruffly. "And I don't want any makeup."

A battery pack was clipped to Vitalli's belt, and the wire, running to the microphone attached to his lapel, was hidden. He took his seat in the chair Annabelle indicated and listened while Eliza Blake, at the news desk, introduced the packaged report.

"Tuxedo Park, New York, a historic, wealthy, and exceedingly private enclave about forty miles north of Manhattan, has had more attention in the last week than it perhaps has ever had, beginning with the bizarre suicide of Innis Wheelock, husband of Valentina Wheelock, former governor of New York and United States ambassador to Italy. Wheelock killed himself by stigmata, stabbing himself in the five places where Jesus Christ's body was pierced at the crucifixion. Two murders have followed, and on Saturday night fellow KEY News correspondent Mack McBride and I were forced off the road in Tuxedo Park, our car sent tumbling down a steep hill. Mack was seriously injured but is in stable condition."

Vitalli watched a monitor at the side of the studio as the picture switched from Eliza at the news desk to a shot of the exterior of Zack Underwood's office. Eliza was no longer speaking live. The story and her narration were now on tape.

"Zack Underwood, the award-winning architect of the Wheelock estate's renovation, was strangled in his office last Wednesday evening."

The shot changed to show the front of the Patterson home as Eliza continued speaking. "Aurelia Patterson, Underwood's assistant, was bludgeoned to death as she walked her dog on Friday night. KEY News has learned that each murder scene was manipulated, as if the killer were leaving a message or signature."

The police chief's jaw clenched as he saw the surreptitiously obtained video. Next, on the screen, pretaped video appeared of Eliza in front of a blown-up aerial map of Tuxedo Park and the area immediately surrounding it. As she talked, she indicated the places where the murders had occurred.

"In the Underwood case, the body was positioned in a chair and the dead man's hand wrapped around a long reed. Mrs. Patterson was found with a pair of dice clasped in her hand."

Now Eliza pointed to the spot on the map where her Volvo had been forced off the road.

"When our car left the road here, it tumbled down the hillside and came to rest at the bottom, near the lake. With no cell-phone service, I had to leave Mack alone while I went for help. As I got up to the road, the vehicle that had rammed us returned. I kept out of sight of the attacker, whom I did not see. I did hear a metallic sound, but I wasn't able to identify it. Then the attacker drove away, and I ran to summon help."

Pictures of the badly damaged Volvo appeared on the monitor.

"In the investigation at the crash site, police officers found quarters strewn on the car's roof and scattered on the ground around the car. Altogether, thirty quarters were counted."

Finally a graphic appeared, showing illustrations Annabelle had found on a religious site on the Internet to illustrate the story. The first third of the screen showed an image of Jesus Christ scourged and holding a reed in his hand while being mocked by his tormentors, the middle third showed an image of Roman soldiers gambling for Christ's garments, and the last third showed Judas Iscariot and his change purse filled with thirty pieces of silver.

Clay Vitalli observed the graphic while Eliza left the news desk and took her place in the chair across from his. He looked angry now as the last lines of narration were heard.

"The manner of each of the attacks has a clear association with the suffering and crucifixion of Jesus Christ. While Innis Wheelock's death was suicide by stigmata, Tuxedo Park is being brought to its knees by someone inflicting violence and death of a grotesquely blasphemous sort."

The taped piece ended. A two-shot of Eliza and Clay appeared on the screen.

"Clay Vitalli, chief of the Tuxedo Park Police Department, is with us this morning," said Eliza. "Thank you for coming in, Chief."

Clay nodded curtly.

"What is the latest news on the investigations, Chief Vitalli?" she asked.

"I really must say, I think the story you just showed was an irresponsible piece of work," said Clay.

"Really?" asked Eliza. "In what way?"

"I don't know where you're getting your information. Those details were not released by our department."

"Are you saying they aren't true?" she asked.

"I'm saying that you have no right scaring the public, in particular the residents of Tuxedo Park, without official corroboration."

"There are other channels of information, Chief Vitalli," said Eliza. "And in fact we did get some of the information from one of your own officers."

Clay's eyebrows rose. "Name him," he said.

"You know I'm not going to do that, Chief," Eliza admonished. "But let's move on, if we can. Do you have any suspects yet?"

"I really can't say. It could jeopardize the investigation."

"Well, what do you make of this seeming connection between Innis Wheelock's suicide and the manner in which these crimes are being committed?"

"It's too soon to know—if there even *is* a connection," said Clay.

"Come now," said Eliza. "This can't be a coincidence."

"Look," said Clay, "I'm not even confirming that everything in your report is true."

Eliza looked down at her notes. "At your news conference yesterday, you said you had no plans to call for help from other investigative officials. Do you think that's wise, Chief?"

"I feel confident that our police department can handle what's going on."

"Two murders in less than a week and what was certainly a murder attempt on Mack McBride and me would seem to be too much for such a small police force," said Eliza. "Why not call in help from outside?"

"Because we don't need it," said Clay as he reached for his microphone. "Now, you'll have to excuse me. I have work to get back to."

CHAPTER 116

Ever since the maintenance man retired some four years earlier, seventy-two-year-old Mary Meehan had volunteered to open the church for the morning weekday Mass. Driving into the empty Mount Carmel parking lot, she chose the space closest to the sacristy.

As she walked the few steps from her car to the sacristy door, Mary realized that she practically lived in the church these days. It had been only twelve hours since she'd finished praying the rosary. She loved everything she did at her beloved Mount Carmel, and she felt especially privileged to open the church each morning.

There was no need to rush, as she had a full hour to fill the cruets with water and wine, select the chalice and fresh linens, move the ribbons in the sacred books, and set out the celebrant's alb, chasuble, and stole before Father Gehry would come shuffling in to vest. He always said, "Thank you, Mary," just before he rang the bell to signal the start of Mass, and Mary couldn't imagine a nicer start to the day.

The liturgical calendar indicated that it was a simple Monday in Ordinary Time, but the civil calendar marked today as Columbus Day. Mary wondered what that would mean: Would there be more people at the eight A.M. Mass or fewer? She counted out twenty Communion wafers and placed them on the paten, along with the priest's host, hoping there wouldn't be an unexpected crowd.

Mary walked to the light panel on the sacristy wall and flipped the "Daily Mass" switches, illuminating the nave, side aisles, and sanctuary with "just enough" light, as Father Gehry always said—not too much and not too little, but "just enough" for all the worshippers to see what they needed to see, walk where they needed to walk, and read what they needed to read.

She had to get to the front doors of the church and unlock them for her fellow parishioners. Walking down the side aisle, she stopped at the first candle stand. She wanted to light one for her husband, who had gone to God over ten years earlier. Though she was certain that George would ultimately make it to heaven, she thought the candle each day, and the prayer she said when lighting it, was a good insurance policy.

Aware of a fragrance she hadn't noticed last night, Mary made the sign of the cross as she finished her prayer, and as she turned around, her gaze fell upon the pew in front of her.

The church keys jangled obscenely as they fell to the floor, and, frozen where she stood, Mary let out a tiny scream when she saw Father Gehry's body.

CHAPTER 117

With minutes to go before the broadcast concluded, the story crossed the AP wire. Father Michael Gehry had been killed.

Eliza could hear the voice of Linus Nazareth in her earpiece, reciting the basic information in the wire story and instructing her to ad-lib.

"We've just received word that the priest who presided over a Catholic church in Tuxedo, New York, has been murdered. Father Michael Gehry's body was found this morning by a female parishioner of Our Lady of Mount Carmel Church. Father Gehry, the priest who presided at Innis Wheelock's funeral Mass last Wednesday, had been stabbed.

"This makes the third murder in the Tuxedo Park area in the last week. Of course, we'll be following this story. More news tonight on the *KEY Evening Headlines* and, tomorrow morning, here on *KTA*."

As soon as the stage manager signaled they were off the air, Eliza quickly got up from the news desk.

"I want to go out there with Annabelle and B.J.," she told Linus as he emerged from the control room.

"Great," said Linus. "And I'm going to spring for a helicopter to get aerials. We'll get a bird's-eye view of that walled-in utopia coming apart at the seams."

CHAPTER 118

Valentina knocked softly on the door of her son's room. Hearing no response from within, she knocked harder.

"Rusty," she called. "It's me. Can I come in?"

A low groan came from behind the door. "It's Columbus Day, and I don't have classes. Let me sleep."

She turned the doorknob anyway and entered the darkened room.

"Rusty, the most terrible thing has happened," said Valentina as she walked to the side of the bed.

Russell's eyes snapped open, and he felt his body tense. "Listen, Mother, don't pay attention to anything Clay Vitalli tells you," he said. "I can explain."

"Explain what?" asked Valentina. "I'm not talking about Clay."

He breathed out with relief.

"I'm talking about Father Gehry, Rusty. He's been murdered."

Wearing a T-shirt stretched over his muscular frame, Russell sat upright. "What?"

"I just heard it on the news. Father Gehry was stabbed to death. His body was found in the church this morning."

"My God," said Russell. "That's awful." He got out of the bed, drew back the curtains, and opened the window.

"It feels like everyone attached to us is doomed," said Valentina.

"Hold on a minute, Mother," Russell said as he turned from the window. "This is a terrible thing, but don't be melodramatic."

"The very priest who just said your father's funeral Mass, the architect and his assistant who worked on this house," said Valentina. "They're all linked to us in some way. And I still have a feeling that Eunice's death was no accident. We're all living in some kind of nightmare."

"Stop it, Mother," he said, walking toward her. "Father Gehry knew hundreds of people around here. So did Zack Underwood and Aurelia Patterson. We're not the only people they were connected to." Russell put both his hands on his mother's shoulders and kissed the top of her head. "I tell you what. Let's go down and have some breakfast."

As Russell pulled on his robe, Valentina leaned forward to get a closer look at his face.

"What are those scratches?" she asked.

"Oh, they're nothing," Russell said dismissively.

"How did you get them?"

"Playing basketball the other night."

"Really?" asked Valentina. "Tell me the truth. Did you get in trouble with another girl?"

"Nothing happened, Mother."

She studied her son, wondering if she should push it further with him but not having the energy or heart to do so. That had been Innis's department. With Russell's father gone, she supposed she should step up, but not now.

"All right," she said finally. "Let's go have breakfast. When we're finished, I have to run over to the travel agency and pick up some documents."

"Good," said Russell. "And I'll be able to go back to bed."

CHAPTER 119

Eliza, Annabelle, and B.J. made a stop at Good Samaritan Hospital. Paige Tintle, who had volunteered to cover the early-morning vigil in the waiting room, reported that Mack still had not wakened. After going in to see him, Eliza spoke to the duty nurse, who assured her that Mack's vital signs were stable.

"I have to leave again, but I'll be back later this afternoon," Eliza told the nurse. "Please call me if he wakes up."

From the hospital they went to Our Lady of Mount Carmel Church. B.J. took pictures of the building and the police tape that was festooned across the front door.

Parishioners and others arriving to pray for Father Gehry were told by the police that the church was closed until the crime-scene investigation was concluded.

A group of those turned away had gathered around the fountain in front of the rectory. B.J. shot video while Annabelle and Eliza talked to some of the devastated congregants.

"I just can't believe this has happened," said one woman tearfully. "Father Gehry was such a good and holy man. Everybody loved him."

"Not everybody," said Annabelle as she and Eliza walked closer to the fountain. While B.J. finished getting his video, Eliza gazed at the gushing and falling water. Her thoughts shifted to the conversation with Innis at the Pentimento fountain on the night he killed himself. He'd been so insistent, so certain that she wouldn't let him down.

I'm doing my best, Innis. But I still don't understand what you wanted. Where is your puzzle leading? What did you mean as we sat and talked by the fountain that night?

The fountain at Pentimento.

The *turtle* fountain.

Suddenly Eliza thought she knew the meaning of the carvings on the backs of the wooden letter blocks they'd found at Nine Chimneys.

CHAPTER 120

S usannah couldn't be happier about the way things had gone the day before. So many people had come up and congratulated her, thanking her for running the event. One woman had even asked her if she played paddle tennis and talked about the need for additional players on her team. Susannah interpreted it as a signal that the woman wanted her to be a Black Tie Club member.

Susannah showered and dressed. She wanted to take some flowers to Valentina to thank her for making the club's tennis facilities available.

Susannah wanted to keep the good feelings alive. Sending Bonnie to fill in for Eunice had been a help. Further ingratiating herself with Valentina couldn't hurt.

CHAPTER 121

G ood morning, Bonnie," said Eliza as she stood at the front
door of Pentimento. "Is Mrs. Wheelock available?"

"I'm sorry, Ms. Blake, but Mrs. Wheelock left just a little
while ago."

"Will she be back soon?"

"I'm not sure," said Bonnie, adjusting her apron. "She said she had
several stops to make."

Eliza looked at her watch. "As usual, my colleagues and I are
pressed for time. I was going to ask Mrs. Wheelock if we could take a
look at the fountain in the garden."

"I don't think Mrs. Wheelock would mind if you did that," said
Bonnie. "Tell them to come in."

"Thanks, Bonnie," said Eliza. "But we can just go around to the
side of the house."

Eliza walked over to the continually present security car and
asked the guard if he would mind going to the carriage house and
seeing if everything was secure there.

"I'll be fine," she said. "I'm not alone here."

Eliza signaled for Annabelle and B.J. to get out of the car and led them to the garden. The replica of Bernini's well-known fountain was the focal point of the space.

"How delightful is that?" asked Annabelle, smiling at the bronze turtles caught climbing into the fountain's bowl. "I remember reading that the one in Rome was recently restored. I'd defy anyone to tell the difference between this one and the original."

"Let's dispense with the art-appreciation class," said B.J., "and get to the point." He walked around the fountain, studying it, looking for a clue of some sort.

"I hope you see something," said Eliza, "because I don't."

"Me neither," said Annabelle.

"Hold on," said B.J. "Hold on. Did you expect Innis Wheelock to leave a clue out in the open where it would be easily found?"

They continued to examine the fountain, inspecting the base, the spout where the water sprayed out, and the basin that caught it. They looked about the garden immediately surrounding the fountain, but they found nothing that could be interpreted as a clue.

"A turtle was carved into each of the letter blocks," said B.J. "Not a fountain. Maybe we should concentrate on the turtles."

He reached out and touched one of the bronze turtles. The shell on the turtle's back moved.

"Look at this!" he called excitedly.

CHAPTER 122

It was a glorious Indian-summer day, clear and warm.

Susannah's arms were filled with the flowers she'd brought for Valentina. She had to put them down so she could use the heavy door knocker. Then she picked them up again, imagining the impression she would make when the door was opened. Lady Bountiful with her beautiful bouquet.

When Bonnie told her that Mrs. Wheelock was out, Susannah was disappointed as she handed the flowers to her maid. Susannah hadn't really expected Valentina to answer the door, but she was hoping that Valentina would at least be home. She wanted to talk more with Valentina about her impressions of Sunday afternoon's event, but she also just wanted to have the opportunity to talk to her. Period.

Walking away, Susannah heard voices coming from the side of the house, and a horrible thought crossed her mind. Bonnie wouldn't lie, would she? What if Valentina really *was* home? *What if she's home but avoiding me?*

Susannah didn't recognize the dark sedan parked in the driveway. It was not one of the Wheelocks' cars. She was sure of that. Was Valentina entertaining some of her club friends and didn't want Susannah bothering them?

Feeling compelled, Susannah walked toward the voices.

CHAPTER 123

Eliza and Annabelle gathered around B.J. as he manipulated the bronze shell hinged to the body of the turtle. With minimal effort, B.J. lifted it. On the underside of the shell, there were markings.

"What are those?" asked Eliza.

"Dots and dashes," said B.J.

"Like Morse code?" asked Annabelle.

"Exactly," said B.J. He went to the next turtle and the next and the next. Each of the four opened, and each one had a different series of dots and dashes etched into the underside of its shell.

"I recognize this one," said B.J. "Three dots, then three dashes, then three more dots. S-O-S."

Eliza looked at the other turtles. "Then the markings in these could spell out something as well."

"Too bad I don't remember more of my Morse code from Boy Scouts," said B.J.

"Somehow I can't imagine you starting a fire by rubbing two sticks together," said Annabelle. She held up her BlackBerry. "Lucky for us, we've got the Internet at our disposal."

They worked as a team. Eliza called out the series of dots and dashes from the undersides of the turtle shells. Annabelle, straining to see the Web site with the directory of Morse code that she'd pulled up on the tiny screen of her handheld, called out the corresponding letter. And B.J. transcribed the code, letter by letter, in his reporter's notebook.

"It's absolutely amazing that assigning dots and dashes to letters and numbers can create an entire language," said Annabelle.

Together they worked until they'd figured out the clue hiding inside each turtle.

The first shell contained the message S-O-S.

The dots and dashes under the second shell spelled out G-U-V.

The third set gave up the word D-O-C-K.

The last one, P-I-X.

As they called out each discovery, they were unaware that someone else was listening to everything they said.

CHAPTER 124

From Pentimento, Eliza, Annabelle, and B.J. drove to the rented carriage house to eat something, talk about the clues on the turtle shells, and decide how to proceed. Eliza opened the refrigerator, took out cold cuts, and started heating up some tomato soup on the stove.

"'SOS,' 'guv,' 'dock,' and 'pix,'" said B.J. "What did Innis mean by these?"

"Well, 'SOS' is obviously the code for help," said Annabelle. "'Guv' could refer to Valentina, couldn't it? Because she was governor of New York."

"All right. That makes sense," said Eliza as she stirred the soup. "And 'pix' is short for pictures."

"Do you think 'dock' refers to the dock on Tuxedo Lake?" asked Annabelle.

"That's as good a place as any to start," said Eliza.

"'SOS,' 'guv,' 'dock,' and 'pix,'" B.J. repeated. "We don't know if there's any particular order for these, a way in which Innis wanted them to be read."

Eliza carried over the mugs of soup and placed them on the table.

"True," she said, "but 'SOS' tells me that Innis either wanted help or was signaling that someone else needed help. And of all the clues, the only one that actually indicates a place where we can go to investigate anything is 'dock.' I say we should start with that."

They hastily finished eating. Annabelle and Eliza cleared the table while B.J. sat still.

"Hey, chauvinist," said Annabelle. "We're not your slaves. It would be nice if you helped."

"What the hell?" B.J. said as he looked up.

The others followed his gaze.

B.J. held his index finger to his mouth and gestured with his other hand toward the beamed ceiling. He rose to get a closer look, his jaw dropping at what he saw. A thin black wire protruded from the side of the wrought-iron chandelier. He motioned silently to Eliza and Annabelle to keep talking naturally. "Well, I guess we'd better get going," he said. "C'mon. We've got work to do."

Once outside, B.J. said, "Somebody could hear everything we were talking about."

"I wonder how long it's been there," said Eliza. She thought back. "If the bug was there when Mack and I discussed the 'crematory' clue, that could help explain why we were run off the road on Saturday night."

"Yeah," said Annabelle. "And it means that whoever is listening knows we're on our way to the dock right now."

"We should have the entire place swept for bugs," said B.J.

"All right," said Eliza. "But let's leave whatever is there in place. We don't want whoever is listening to know we're onto him."

CHAPTER 125

Columbus Day was a big campaigning day. There were parades to attend, crowds to greet, hands to shake. Peter Nordstrut followed the candidate he was being paid to guide through his first congressional race.

A high school band played "Born in the U.S.A." as the would-be congressman marched behind, waving and smiling. The guy was a natural, thought Peter. He actually seemed to be enjoying himself, and the spectators were responding to his energy. He had performed well in the town-hall meetings and nursing-home events and diner stops that Peter had insisted he make to court voters. Only three weeks remained until election day, and Peter was feeling confident that his man would be going to Washington, D.C., in January.

Halfway down the parade route, Peter felt his phone vibrate. He broke off from the marchers and answered.

"Hello!" he shouted over the din.

"It's Clay, Peter."

"What's up?"

"Eliza Blake and her friends are on their way to the dock. Innis, damn him, left another clue. It's going to lead them to your part in all this."

"They'd have to dredge Tuxedo Lake, Clay. Even then, it's been so long that I don't think they could prove anything."

"Don't be so cavalier, Peter. We all played our part. We're all in this together. If one of us goes down, we all go down."

CHAPTER 126

There were several boats floating in the water at the dock maintained by the Black Tie Club. B.J. steered the KEY News car into the parking area, and Eliza's ever-present security pulled in to a nearby spot. Annabelle and Eliza walked toward the water's edge while B.J. took his camera out of the trunk.

"Try to be inconspicuous with that thing, will you?" suggested Annabelle.

"Look around," answered B.J. "We have the place to ourselves." He began recording video of the area.

Eliza was studying the scene. There were three sailboats and four pontoons, flat-bottomed and tethered by electrical cords to charging stations on the shore.

"I remember Valentina telling me that no gas motors are allowed on the lake," said Eliza. "Too noisy."

"And look at this," said Annabelle as she leaned in to look inside one of the pontoons. "They left the keys in the ignition."

They walked to the wooden boathouse, which was long, low, and painted a dark green. Inside, single sculls and rowboats were stored on racks. Stuffed wildlife specimens—caught, shot, or trapped by club members—hung on the walls, and beneath the carefully preserved animals and fish were pictures of the hunters and fishermen who had snagged them.

"I abhor taxidermy." Annabelle shuddered. "Look at the poor, beautiful red fox. I hope he never knew what hit him."

"Hey, get a load of this," said B.J., stopping in front of one of the photographs.

"Bingo!" Annabelle yelled as she studied the photograph and read the brass plaque affixed to the wall just beneath it. A young Innis and Valentina Wheelock were standing on the deck of a large sailboat. Innis was smiling and holding up a fish he'd caught. The name inscribed on the stern of the boat was GUV.

"Guv," whispered Eliza. "They named their boat for their dream of Valentina's becoming governor." She squinted to read the shiny plaque beneath the photograph.

" 'Sunken Dreams,' " she said. "But why would the caption for this picture be 'sunken' dreams? Their dream came true."

B.J. looked more closely. "This is a new plaque," he said. "It's replaced an older one. See? You can tell it's slightly smaller than the one that was originally there."

"You're right," said Annabelle.

Eliza moved to look at the fish mounted on the wall above the photograph of the Wheelocks. It was on the small side, with spiny fins. The brass plaque beneath it was also shiny and new. It was inscribed FEATHERED PERCH.

"I've heard of freshwater perch," said B.J., "not feathered perch. That makes no sense."

"Let's look at our clues from the turtle fountain again," said Eliza. " 'SOS.' "

"Help," answered Annabelle.

" 'Guv,' " said Eliza.

"The name of the Wheelocks' boat," answered B.J.

"'Pix,'" said Eliza.

"That would be the pictures on the wall here," said Annabelle. "Innis wanted us to see this particular photo and notice the perch he caught, too, because he replaced that plaque as well."

"And 'dock,'" said Eliza, "is the clue that brought us here in the first place."

"But where is it all taking us?" asked B.J.

"'Sunken dreams,' 'feathered perch,'" mused Eliza. "We've got to figure out what Innis meant by that."

"What's our next step?" asked Annabelle.

Eliza considered their options for a moment. "In all the craziness of the weekend," she remembered, "I never did get a chance to go over and talk to Bill O'Shaughnessy. Since he's the brother of the man who seems to be at the center of Innis's puzzle, maybe he can help us figure it out."

CHAPTER 127

Directory assistance provided the number for William O'Shaughnessy. He answered on the second ring. Eliza identified herself and asked if she could talk with him in person.

"About what?" he asked.

"Your brother Marty," said Eliza.

"I don't think that's such a good idea," said Bill. "He's been gone a long time, and there's no sense dredging all that up again."

"Whether we like it or not, Bill, 'all that' *is* being dredged up again. And we suspect that the three murders in the last week are somehow related to what happened back then. Anyone who knows anything that could help has a responsibility to stand up before anyone else gets hurt."

There was a pause on the phone. "All right," Bill said finally. "But let's talk outside the park, at my house. I have to work later, so now's a good time for you to come over."

The clapboard bungalow was just off Route 17, on a road with a dozen similar ones. Most of them had peeling paint and overgrown yards, but O'Shaughnessy's was well maintained. A big green shamrock was painted on the mailbox.

Bill was waiting at the door and welcomed them in. The living room was neat, with space for only a sofa, two chairs, and a coffee table. There was a small fireplace, a wedding picture hanging above it.

"Is Mrs. O'Shaughnessy here, too?" asked Eliza, glancing toward the back of the house where she supposed the kitchen would be.

"My wife is dead," said Bill.

"Oh, I'm *so* sorry," said Eliza. "Forgive me."

"Nothing to forgive," said Bill. "She's at peace now."

He gestured for everyone to take a seat. Once they were all settled, Eliza got right to the point.

"When you and I talked on the day of Innis Wheelock's funeral, you told me about the accident on West Lake Road all those years ago, but you didn't mention that it was your brother's car."

Eliza looked expectantly at Bill, waiting for him to explain.

"I just don't like to talk about what happened to Marty," said Bill. "I never have."

"I can understand that," said Eliza. "But what happened to your brother is influencing what's happening today. We believe that Innis Wheelock devised a puzzle before he died, and the first clue led to West Lake Road—and therefore to your brother. But somebody doesn't like the idea that the pieces of the puzzle are being put together."

"Have *you* figured out any more of the puzzle?" asked Bill.

Eliza thought quickly. Perhaps she had to give some information to get some.

"Well, we found something at West Lake Road that led us to the old Heavener place," said Eliza.

"Nine Chimneys," added Annabelle.

Bill nodded. "I remember the place," he said. "It was beautiful before it burned down."

"It was at Nine Chimneys that we found another clue," said Eliza.

"Some lettered blocks that when put together with similar ones at Pentimento spelled out the word 'crematory.'"

Bill's head fell forward. "Oh, dear God, no," he said softly. "Don't tell me that bastard burned my brother."

Annabelle went into the kitchen and returned with a glass of water. Bill's hand trembled as he took it from her.

"Can you continue, Bill?" asked Eliza.

"Yes," he said, shaking his head in disbelief. "That miserable, evil bastard."

"Who?" asked Eliza.

"Clay Vitalli," said Bill. "The great protector of the people, that son of a bitch. And I'm no better. In fact, I'm worse. I let him get away with it."

"What do you mean?"

"I mean that I didn't raise a ruckus back then, didn't scream bloody murder to find out what happened. I should have fought for my brother, but I didn't. I just kept my mouth shut when Marty went missing, like Clay Vitalli told me to."

"There must have been a reason you did that," said Eliza.

"Clay told me if I didn't drop the whole thing with Marty, something might just happen to Moira." Bill looked beseechingly at Eliza. "You have to understand. Even then Clay was very connected. There was no telling what he could make happen. I really believed he might hurt my Moira—or worse."

"It must have been horrible for you," said Eliza.

"It was," said Bill. "But you can rationalize a lot when you want to. I came to realize that Marty had no one but himself to blame."

"How so?" asked Eliza.

Bill got up and walked out of the room. When he came back, he held a snapshot in his hand. He turned it over to Eliza.

"He was good-looking, wasn't he?" asked Bill.

Eliza nodded as she looked at the red-haired man standing shirtless with one hand on his hip and the other propped up on a shovel. She passed the picture to Annabelle.

"And he knew it," said Bill. "Marty was a player. Handsome, great build, and a real way with the ladies. He had established his own landscaping business, and it gave him access to well-off women who lived in the big houses. You dip your pen into somebody else's inkwell enough times and you're bound to get caught."

"You think somebody's husband found out that his wife was fooling around with your brother?"

"Maybe," said Bill.

"And that Marty was killed for it?"

"Put it this way," said Bill. "His car was found crashed and empty. He was never seen or heard from again."

"It said in the old newspaper accounts that it was thought he'd gone to Ireland," said Annabelle.

"If that was the case, don't you think we would have heard from him again after all this time?" asked Bill. "No, Marty is dead. I'm certain of that."

Everyone sat quietly for a moment.

"Perhaps you'll allow me one last question," Eliza said eventually. "Can you think of any reason that *Innis* sent us to West Lake Road?"

Bill fidgeted in his seat, uncomfortable with saying more but knowing that the truth had to come out.

"Because," he finally answered, "Marty had an affair with Innis Wheelock's wife."

CHAPTER 128

A walk along the water's edge, a close examination of the boats, a slow and purposeful stroll through the boathouse—all of it was necessary in order to figure out what Innis had meant with his clue about the dock.

Had Eliza Blake and her cohorts figured it out?

"Sunken Dreams" below the picture of Innis and Valentina aboard the *Guv* was a very fitting caption. When the boat sank—or, more correctly, was sunk—it took a dream along with it. The dream of the perfect union of Innis and Valentina Wheelock, the coming-together of a man and woman, united in purpose and exclusive to each other, was dead.

Though there was little doubt that Innis had loved Valentina to his dying day, he must have known he could no longer trust his wife. Once unfaithful, she would be forever suspect in his mind.

Who could blame him?

Perhaps even worse was the fact that Innis had been forced, or at least had chosen, to cover up her indiscretion. With a political campaign under *way for the governorship, a scandal like that would ruin everything for which they'd all worked so hard.*

So Innis had swallowed it.

There was no way in the world that should have been an option. When a woman did something like that, it could never be forgotten—or forgiven.

CHAPTER 129

Eliza, Annabelle, and B.J. kept interested but dispassionate expressions on their faces as the conversation with Bill O'Shaughnessy continued.

"What can you tell us about their relationship?" asked Eliza.

Bill shrugged. "What can I say? I know he was with her for a couple of months."

"This would have been before she was governor, right?" asked Annabelle, thinking back to the date of the newspaper articles on Marty's disappearance. They'd been dating prior to Valentina's move to Albany.

"Yes," said Bill.

"Was the relationship with Valentina still going on when your brother disappeared?" asked Eliza.

"I think so," said Bill. "But Marty never gave me too many details about any of the women he snagged. He could be a dog, but he wasn't a big mouth. He didn't brag about his conquests."

"Did Marty ever say that he thought Innis knew about his wife's affair?" asked Eliza.

"Not to me he didn't," answered Bill.

"Let's switch gears for a minute," said Eliza as she consulted her notebook. "Let's look at the places Innis has pointed us to so far. First, West Lake Road, the site where Marty's car was found abandoned. Second, he sent us to Nine Chimneys and the letter blocks that spelled out 'crematory.'"

Bill winced as she said the word.

"I'm sorry," Eliza apologized, "but the carvings on the blocks also led us to the turtle fountain at Pentimento, which led us to the club's boathouse."

"Find anything there?" asked Bill.

"A picture of Innis and Valentina together on their boat along with a stuffed fish that Innis was seen holding in the picture. The name of the boat was *Guv*, but we didn't see it moored out by the dock."

"And you won't," said Bill. "The boat disappeared a long time ago."

Eliza, Annabelle, and B.J. glanced at one another. "Disappeared?" asked B.J.

"Maybe it sank," said Bill. "Maybe it didn't. All I know is that suddenly it wasn't moored there anymore. You see, I paid attention to that boat. I'd look for it every time I drove past the dock on my way to work, because I knew that it was Marty and Mrs. Wheelock's little love nest."

CHAPTER 130

As they left Bill O'Shaughnessy's house, Eliza's phone sounded. The hospital was calling to say that Mack had regained consciousness.

Eliza closed her eyes, "Thank God," she said, and told Annabelle and B.J. the good news. "Let's get to the hospital."

On the drive to Good Samaritan, they discussed what Bill had told them.

"That was a bombshell, huh?" said Annabelle.

"Yeah, America's sweetheart is a fallen woman," said B.J.

"It happens," said Annabelle. "The question is, do we report it?"

"My feeling is we don't," said Eliza. "At least not yet. Unless it turns out that the affair had something to do with Marty O'Shaughnessy's disappearance and death."

"We've got to talk to her, you know," said Annabelle.

Eliza nodded. "And we will. I'll call her later and ask if I can come to Pentimento and speak with her. But now all I want to do is get to Mack."

Eliza entered the hospital room, walked over to the bed, and kissed Mack on the forehead.

"Mack," she said softly. "It's me, sweetheart. It's Eliza."

He slowly opened his lids. His eyes were dull and cloudy but brightened a bit when he recognized her. He raised his hand to his throat as he tried to speak.

"Don't try to talk, darling. You can't with the breathing tube," said Eliza, taking his hand. She felt him feebly squeeze hers.

"Oh, Mack, I've been so worried about you."

She looked into his eyes, and he gazed back at her. Eliza detected frustration even in his weakened state and knew he wanted to say something.

"How about you blink once for yes, twice for no?" she suggested.

Mack blinked once.

"Great," said Eliza. "There's more than one way to communicate, isn't there?"

She brought his hand up to her lips and kissed it. There was so much she wanted to tell him, but all she could do was hang on to him and pray he was through the worst of it.

Pale and helpless as he lay in the hospital bed, Mack tried to stay awake.

"Go ahead, sweetheart," she said. "You have to rest. Let yourself fall asleep."

He blinked once and closed his eyes.

When she felt confident he was going to be out for a while, Eliza stepped out and spoke to one of the nurses. The nurse told her there was no predicting how long Mack would sleep and that even when he awoke, it was best that he rest quietly.

"Can the breathing tube be removed?" asked Eliza.

"Not yet," said the nurse. "The doctor wants to leave it in for a while. He's not out of the woods quite yet."

CHAPTER 131

After she left the hospital, Eliza called Mack's parents and gave them an update. Then she called Valentina and asked if she could come and talk to her about something. They agreed that Eliza would come to Pentimento tomorrow morning, after she signed off on *KTA*.

Eliza, Annabelle, and B.J. conferred and agreed they would hold off on reporting their discoveries at the fountain and in the boathouse until the meanings were clearer. They also agreed not to tell anyone about Valentina Wheelock's affair—at least not until Eliza had a chance to talk with her.

"All right," said Eliza as she got into the security car. "We're all on the same page. *We* won't be reporting any of this on the show tomorrow morning."

"Got it, boss," said B.J.

"Me, too," said Annabelle.

When Eliza got home, Janie burst from the front door and ran down the driveway to meet her.

"Mommy, I missed you!" she said, wrapping her arms around her mother. "I thought you were going to come home early since I had no school today."

"Well, I'm home now, Monkey," she said as she hugged her child back. "The rest of the day is just for us."

Janie stretched and twisted along with Eliza as she did her yoga exercises. They played Scrabble Junior and multiple hands of Go Fish before dinner. While Janie took her bath, Eliza called the hospital. Mack was asleep and resting comfortably.

"What do you want to read tonight?" asked Eliza as Janie got ready for bed.

"My St. Francis books," said Janie.

"Good idea," said Eliza. "And let's see if we can come up with some plans for your Halloween costume from the pictures."

They snuggled beside each other and read about the poor man of Assisi, the man who wanted his life to be a perfect imitation of Christ's. They read about his vow of poverty and aid to the poor, his caring for the lepers, his love of nature, his sermon to the birds, his taming of the wolf, his prayer, his fasting, his manual labor.

"I don't think I could ever be as good as St. Francis," said Janie, her eyelids growing heavy.

"He was a saint, Janie," said Eliza. "Not many people grow up to be saints, but you can just try to be the best person you can be."

When they got to the end of the second book, Janie insisted that Eliza read her the Canticle of the Sun. By the fifth stanza, Janie was nodding, and by the tenth the child was asleep. Eliza read the last stanzas out loud anyway.

She closed the book, wondering not why Innis Wheelock had chosen St. Francis's beautiful song for his prayer card but rather why he had chosen only four of the fourteen stanzas.

Quietly Eliza slipped out of Janie's bed, switched off the lights, and tiptoed from the room, carrying the book with her. She went down the hall to her own bedroom and retrieved Innis's prayer card from her purse. She read the stanzas and compared them to the ones in Janie's book. Not only had specific stanzas been selected, but they were not listed in the same order as in the original Canticle of the Sun.

> ALL PRAISE BE YOURS, MY LORD, THROUGH OUR
> SISTER EARTH, OUR MOTHER, WHO FEEDS US IN
> HER SOVEREIGNTY AND RULES US, AND PRODUCES
> VARIOUS FRUITS WITH COLORED FLOWERS AND
> HERBS.

Had Innis been pointing to his first clue, dying in the greenhouse with a clump of earth grasped in his hand, next to a pot that led them to an earthen ditch on West Lake Road?

> ALL PRAISE BE YOURS, MY LORD, THROUGH BROTHER
> FIRE, THROUGH WHOM YOU BRIGHTEN UP THE
> NIGHT. HOW BEAUTIFUL HE IS, HOW GAY! FULL OF
> POWER AND STRENGTH.

Could "Brother Fire" refer to Nine Chimneys? A beautiful home set afire and possibly used as a crematory?

> ALL PRAISE BE YOURS, MY LORD, THROUGH SISTER
> WATER; SO USEFUL, LOWLY, PRECIOUS, AND PURE.

Did "Sister Water" point the way to Tuxedo Lake and the dock and the boathouse?

Were these the messages Innis was trying to send by selecting these verses?

Earth, fire, water. Innis had chosen three of the four elements when planning the pieces of his puzzle.

Eliza looked at the prayer card and read the fourth and final stanza.

> ALL PRAISE BE YOURS, MY LORD, THROUGH BROTHERS
> WIND AND AIR, AND FAIR AND STORMY, AND ALL
> THE WEATHER'S MOODS, BY WHICH YOU CHERISH
> ALL THAT YOU HAVE MADE.

Air, the last element.

She turned the card over and examined the Giotto fresco of St. Francis preaching to the birds. In the center the medieval artist had captured a white bird flying through the air toward the saint.

Birds fly through the air!

"Feathered perch" wasn't the name of the species of fish hanging on the wall at the boathouse. It was Innis's clue leading to the aviary at Pentimento!

TUESDAY
OCTOBER 13

CHAPTER 132

All of the morning shows did pieces on the "stigmata murders," as they were invariably being called, leading their stories with information about the newest victim, Father Michael Gehry. But KEY News had by far the best pictures, exclusive video taken inside Tuxedo Park that no other network could obtain. Linus Nazareth was thrilled, and he let B.J. and Annabelle know it in the staff meeting right after the broadcast.

"As your reward, you two can cover the police presser at one o'clock," said Linus. "Go up and see what Chief Buzz Cut has to say today."

After the meeting, Eliza took Annabelle and B.J. aside. "I'll try to make it to the news conference, too," she said. "I should be able to get there after my meeting with Valentina at noon. But first I want to tell you what occurred to me last night."

Eliza explained that she thought the prayer card at Innis's funeral laid out the essential elements featured in his puzzle clues. She passed the card to them.

"If the last element is air and our last clue is the plaque that reads

'Feathered Perch,' Innis had *birds* in mind, so I'm thinking the aviary at Pentimento is the place to look."

"How are we going to do that?" asked B.J. "Sneak in there tonight?"

Eliza shook her head. "No, we'll get permission from Valentina, and we'll explore in broad daylight. But if our killer is studying the clues, too, and resorting to murder because he doesn't want Innis's puzzle solved, he's not going to want us poking around in the aviary. I think we should trick our killer into exposing himself, and I have an idea of how to do it."

CHAPTER 133

The KEY News car pulled up in front of the carriage house, with the security car close behind.

"Now, remember," said Eliza to Annabelle and B.J. before they got out. "Our aim is to get the killer to come into the open."

They went inside, sat around the dining-room table, and began discussing what they'd found in the boathouse and why it was leading them to the Pentimento aviary.

The listening device in the wrought-iron chandelier picked up every single word.

CHAPTER 134

Fitzroy Heavener finally answered the phone on the fifth ring. "Hello?"

"It's Clay, and I've got Peter on the line, too."

Every muscle in Fitzroy's body tightened. "I don't know if I can bear much more," he said.

"Well, there's more to tell, and you've got to hear it," said Clay, sternly enough to get both Peter and Fitzroy listening intently. "Eliza Blake has stumbled upon one more clue of Innis's damned puzzle. If he wasn't already dead, I'd kill that sanctimonious bastard with my bare hands."

"What has she figured out now?" asked Peter quietly.

"I don't know," Clay admitted. "But she says that Innis has left a clue in that folly of an aviary he built on his property."

"Well, what can we do about it at this point?" asked Fitzroy.

"*Do?* You're asking me what we should *do*?" he asked with contempt. "You didn't have to ask that question twenty years ago! We've got to stop her—*that's* what we've got to do!"

"I don't have the stomach for this anymore, Clay," said Fitzroy. "Twenty years ago I was younger. And stronger."

"All I know is," Clay said with menace, "I haven't kept quiet for twenty years just to let a dead man give everything away. We've got to get to Eliza Blake before she learns anything else."

CHAPTER 135

Susannah stood on her balcony, looking down at Pentimento. She'd been hoping that Valentina would have called to acknowledge the flowers.

But the call hadn't come.

She really wanted to speak with her face-to-face and gauge her feelings. Had the event on Sunday redeemed Susannah in Valentina's eyes? Would she use her influence to help the Lansings gain admittance to the Black Tie Club?

As she watched two dark sedans pull into Pentimento's driveway below, Susannah wondered.

Did she dare go to Valentina's house again?

CHAPTER 136

A re you sure you're going to be all right?" asked Annabelle as they rolled into the driveway at Pentimento. "I don't feel good about leaving you here."

"I'm just going to talk to Valentina about the affair with Marty," said Eliza. "That's something I have to do on my own. Don't worry. The security guard will be right here."

"Promise you won't go to the aviary without us?" asked B.J.

"Promise," said Eliza as she got out of the car. "I'll try to meet up with you at the police press conference later."

Valentina answered the door. She looked tired and drawn. Her hair, usually so perfectly coiffed, was slightly disheveled.

"I've been waiting for you to get here, Eliza," she said. "I didn't sleep much with all that's been happening, and I was wondering what you wanted to talk about. It's such a beautiful, warm day, one of the last ones, I suspect. I thought Bonnie could serve us a little something in the garden and we can chat there."

Bonnie brought them tea and little chicken-salad sandwiches with the crusts cut off. Once she was sure the woman was out of earshot, Eliza gently introduced the motive for her visit.

"I'm really here for two reasons, Valentina. The first is very delicate and difficult to bring up."

Valentina waited for her to continue.

"Yesterday I spoke with Bill O'Shaughnessy and—"

Before Eliza could speak another word, Valentina put up her hand to stop her.

"You don't have to go any further, Eliza," she said. "I know what you're going to say."

"Well? Is it true?" Eliza asked quietly. "Did you have an affair with his brother?"

Valentina wrung her hands. "I knew it would come out someday," she said. "It's a miracle it didn't happen sooner. So I suppose in some ways it's a relief. I've lived with the secret for so many years. But let's face it, my political career is over, and with how things are today, an affair in somebody's background doesn't seem like such a big deal. At my age it could actually make me seem more interesting and glamorous."

"Did Innis come to feel that way?" asked Eliza. "That it wasn't such a big deal?"

"No," she said softly. "It bothered him, always. In fact, I've been thinking that maybe the affair was the reason Innis committed suicide."

"Your relationship with Marty O'Shaughnessy happened two decades ago, Valentina. Your marriage went on, your life together was successful and productive. Why would Innis wait until now to kill himself?"

"Because he couldn't live with what happened as a result."

CHAPTER 137

*I*t was a lesson learned long ago.

It was so simple to eavesdrop when the parties you were listening to were concentrating on their own conversation. Valentina and Eliza were so engrossed in what they were saying that they didn't suspect that their every word could be heard.

Was Valentina going to tell Eliza Blake everything?

Would she reveal why and how the affair ended? Would she tell what everyone else had had to do to clean up the mess? Would Valentina come clean about the fact that it was she who was with Marty O'Shaughnessy when he died?

She wouldn't be that stupid, would she?

CHAPTER 138

What did happen as a result of the affair?" asked Eliza.

"Oh, so many things happened, Eliza. I don't even know where to start." Valentina put down her teacup, leaned back in her wicker chair, and changed the subject. "You said you had two reasons for coming here today. What was the other one?"

"I wanted to ask your permission for my colleagues and me to look inside your aviary. One of our clues leads there. We have reason to think it's the final clue, Valentina, and hope it will make clear everything Innis wanted us to know."

Valentina stood up. "Why don't we go down there right now?" she asked.

Eliza thought of her promise to Annabelle and B.J. that she wouldn't go into the aviary without them. But Valentina Wheelock wasn't a threat, and Eliza couldn't wait to see what she could find in the aviary.

CHAPTER 139

Scores of newspeople waiting in the church parking lot received a five-minute warning from a young female police officer. Annabelle craned her neck to see if she could find Eliza. She was going to miss the start of the press conference.

Annabelle took out her BlackBerry, hit a button, and waited for Eliza to answer her cell phone. But the rings led to Eliza's voice mail. Annabelle was about to leave a message when a uniformed officer in his late forties strode to the microphones to begin answering questions.

It was *not* Chief Clay Vitalli.

CHAPTER 140

The birds chirped and chattered as the door to the aviary opened.

"Oh," said Eliza. "It takes my breath away in here."

"Yes," said Valentina, looking up and around. "Even though I was against the place being built, Zack and Innis did a great job."

The roomy rectangular structure had Italian stone walls and windows inset with a fine wire mesh instead of glass. A large bell-shaped dome was spacious enough for birds to fly up into it. A solid foundation and stone floors ensured that snakes, raccoons, and other wild animals would not be able to gain entrance.

The place was filled with exotic plants, flowers, and trees, and with paths for people to walk among them. Birdbaths were stationed throughout the aviary, and at various spots there were elaborate cages. But by far the building's most impressive aspect was the floor-to-ceiling fresco on a stretch of wall in between the mesh windows.

The painting was a reproduction of the Giotto fresco that had been featured on the front of Innis's prayer card. The image was familiar to Eliza by now, but as she stared at the painting on the wall, she sensed there was something slightly different about this version. She wished she could compare the two right now, but she'd left her bag back on the patio. She'd look at the holy card again later.

"Grapes!"

Eliza jumped as she heard the screeching sound.

"Grapes!"

It dawned on her that it was the parrot that Janie told her about, the one who'd been taught to say the things he liked.

"Sun! Air! Grapes!"

"That damned bird drives me crazy," said Valentina. "And to think Innis spent a lot of money and countless hours with a trainer trying to teach that parrot to talk. What a waste that was. Those are the only words I've ever heard him say."

Eliza and Valentina had been in the aviary for fifteen minutes, walking around but finding nothing that stood out to them as a clue, when Bonnie found them on one of the paths.

"Excuse me, Mrs. Wheelock," she said, "but Mrs. Lansing is here again."

Valentina closed her eyes. "Oh, I have to go speak with her. She came with flowers yesterday when I wasn't here. I should have called and thanked her, but I didn't get around to it. I can't send her away again." She looked at Eliza. "Will you be all right for a little while by yourself? This shouldn't take long."

"I'll be fine," said Eliza. "Take your time."

CHAPTER 141

*W*here was the clue? Where was it?

Eliza walked along the aviary path, stopping to watch the birds flitting around in the wire cupola and alighting in the trees. She spotted finches and parakeets and a couple of cockatoos, but there were many birds she didn't recognize at all.

She checked every single perch she could find, in birdcages and out, but nothing of any significance popped out at her. Maybe "feathered perch" was only meant to get her to the aviary, not to the actual clue.

There has to be something more.

She looked up again at the fresco of St. Francis preaching to the birds and uttered a silent prayer. *Help me see what's here. Help me learn what Innis wanted me to know.*

As she stared at the fresco, it dawned on Eliza what was different from the image on the prayer card. St. Francis had a white halo around his head in both versions, but in the one on the wall there were words, in a beautiful medieval script, written along the inside rim of the saint's halo.

She stretched to read.

SI TROVA TUTTO NEL TAVOLO GRANDE.

Eliza cursed herself for not speaking Italian. But she did know that *grande* meant "big" or "large," and she was pretty sure that *tavolo* meant "table."

Big table.

She had noticed a beautifully carved wooden table at the back of the aviary, had even noted that it was similar to one she'd seen next to Innis Wheelock's bloody body in the greenhouse. *Could the key to Innis's puzzle be in the big table?*

She started to walk toward the back of the aviary, the sound of the creaking entry door masked by the mad chirping of all the birds.

CHAPTER 142

The police officer had fielded an onslaught of reporters' questions for almost an hour. He'd obviously been adequately briefed beforehand and had been able to describe the heightened security measures in the park, Mack McBride's improved condition, and what was known about the victims.

As the press conference came to a close, Annabelle asked herself why the police chief wasn't there to face the media himself.

CHAPTER 143

The table was covered with sacks of seed, pellets, and powdered nectar and a jumble of plastic toys for the birds. Eliza picked through the collection but saw nothing that might be construed as a clue.

There was a large drawer running the entire width of the table. She opened it and found more toys and some manuals on the care and feeding of birds.

Maybe there's something behind it.

Eliza tried to tug the table away from the wall, but it hardly budged. She repositioned her grasp and pulled again, harder this time. It moved a bit more at the same time Eliza heard the man's voice behind her.

"Can I help you with that?"

CHAPTER 144

While the newspeople packed up their gear and filtered away from the press conference, Annabelle ended another frustrating attempt to reach Eliza.

"It's still going to her voice mail, Beej," she said. "I don't like it."

"All right," said B.J. as he slid the camera into the backseat of the crew car. "Let's get back to Pentimento."

CHAPTER 145

Eliza swung around at the sound of the voice but relaxed when she saw who it was.

"Oh, Russell," she said, holding a hand to her chest. "You scared me."

"I'm sorry. I didn't mean to."

"What are you doing home? Don't you have classes today?"

"Nope. Only on Mondays, Wednesdays, and Fridays."

"Nice schedule," said Eliza.

"It works for me." Russell nodded toward the table. "What are you doing?"

"I'm looking for something, a clue to the puzzle that your father left," said Eliza. "I think it's somewhere in or around this table."

"Stand back," said Russell. "I'll pull it out from the wall."

The table made a scraping sound as he moved it. Eliza leaned around to see the rear side of it. With no drawers, it was flat and smooth.

"I don't understand," said Eliza. "Something's got to be here."

She went around to the front of the table again, got down on her knees, and stretched beneath it. Groping along the underside of the tabletop, her hand felt a protrusion. A small object was affixed to the wood.

"There's something here, but I can't get it loose," said Eliza as she pulled at it.

"Let me try," said Russell.

They changed positions. With a little effort, he was able to snap the object away from the wood.

"Got it," he said as he stood upright again.

Eliza looked at what was in his hand. "It's a pocket video camera!" she said excitedly.

"Yes," said Russell.

"Well, this is wonderful," she said. "Hit the 'play' button and we can view what's on it."

"We don't need to view it," said Russell. "I recognize it. It's my father's. And I already know exactly what we'll see."

CHAPTER 146

The guard at the front gate was having none of it. He wouldn't let Annabelle and B.J. enter the park.

"We were in here just this morning," said B.J. "We've been coming in and out with Eliza Blake for the last few days."

"Well, Eliza Blake isn't with you now," said the guard. "And she didn't leave your names on the list."

CHAPTER 147

I don't quite understand," said Eliza, fearing that she did. "What do you mean, you already know what's on the tape?"

"Because I know that Innis surreptitiously taped a conversation we had in his study," said Russell as he moved closer. "If I'd known I was being recorded, I never would have admitted to all that I did."

He reached out and touched her face. "You are very pretty, do you know that?" asked Russell.

Eliza backed away.

"Don't be afraid," said Russell as he took hold of her arm. "I won't hurt you—unless you give me a good reason."

Eliza broke free of his grasp and started running for the entrance. She could hear the parrot squawking excitedly, and the realization came to her.

The bird isn't saying "Sun, air, grapes." It's saying "Son, heir, rapes!"

CHAPTER 148

Annabelle leaned over from the passenger seat to speak with the security guard at the front gate.

"Ms. Blake isn't answering her phone," she said. "But we think she's at Pentimento. Would you mind calling there?"

CHAPTER 149

Eliza's heart pounded as she ran through the aviary. She could hear Russell's footfalls on the path behind her, feel that he was gaining on her. She was panic-stricken at the thought that Innis's parrot had been trained to say that the Wheelock son and heir was a rapist.

She was reaching for the door handle when Russell grabbed her from behind and pushed her to the floor. Looking up at him, Eliza saw that his eyes were wild with rage.

Think. Think. You have to think.

Rape was not about sex. It was about power—and anger.

As he came down on top of her, Eliza pushed back, but Russell was stronger. She felt his hand pulling up her skirt.

"Russell, *please.* Stop. Please *stop,*" she said, her voice breaking. "You've got to think what this will mean. Think what this will do to your mother. Your father's dead. You're all she has left."

"I don't want to think about my mother," he sneered. "I don't want to think about either of them. Innis Wheelock wasn't my father. And Valentina is a slut."

Eliza couldn't believe what she was hearing.

"I've known since I was seven years old, though neither of them suspected I did. I overheard them talking about it one night when they thought I was in bed asleep. My real father is Marty O'Shaughnessy, a townie my mother was banging on the boat while Innis, the weakling, was busy busting his butt trying to make her governor."

Keep him talking. Keep him talking.

"It had to be terrible for you," she said. "Horrible to know all that."

"That wasn't the half of it," Russell said through gritted teeth. "How'd you like to know that your *real* old man wanted to be paid off in cash to keep the whole thing quiet? Or worse—that your own mother killed him?"

"Valentina killed Marty O'Shaughnessy?" asked Eliza incredulously.

"Yeah, she said it was an accident, but who knows whether the whore was telling the truth? But once again Innis took care of everything for her, getting his friends to cover the whole thing up. They sank the blood-drenched boat, got rid of the body at Nine Chimneys, and crashed O'Shaughnessy's car on West Lake Road so that it would look like an accident and that he'd run away."

"But the puzzle Innis designed reveals the story of something that happened before you were even born," said Eliza. "You had nothing to do with that."

"Right—except for what's on the videotape," said Russell. "When Innis found out that I'd been having, shall we say, 'power struggles' with certain young women, he decided that he was going to make it impossible for me to have any kind of political future. He tricked me into incriminating myself on the videotape. Nice *father*, huh?"

"Does your mother know about all this?" Eliza asked.

"She knows about the business with the girls. She and Innis would fight over what to do about it. He wanted to face it all head-on; she didn't. I doubt very much that she knew he made the tape."

He pulled back and looked into her eyes, his facial expression turning darker as he realized what she'd been doing.

"You've been playing me, haven't you? Trying to buy yourself some time. Well, time's up, Eliza, and just so you know, I don't shoot blanks the way Innis did."

CHAPTER 150

Valentina and Susannah stopped talking when Bonnie entered the living room.

"Mrs. Wheelock, two colleagues of Ms. Blake's are at the gate," said Bonnie. "They want to talk to you about getting into the park so they can come and pick her up."

"Bonnie, kindly explain to them that I can't come to the phone just now. But tell them that Eliza has a security guard here with a car to take her where she wants to go."

Valentina turned to look at Susannah again. "Now, where were we?" she asked.

CHAPTER 151

Russell held her arms against the stone floor as Eliza writhed underneath him, trying to kick her way free.

"Stop fighting me, Eliza," he said angrily. "It'll be easier for you if you don't fight." He pressed down harder. "I'm so much bigger than you are. There's no way you can beat me."

She finally forced her body to begin to relax beneath his.

"Thatta girl," he said. "I knew you were a smart one."

He let go of one of her arms and reached to unbuckle his belt.

"Don't you dare try anything," he threatened. "I swear to God, I'll kill you if you try anything."

And he'll probably end up killing me even if I don't try anything. He knows I know about the tape. He's told me too much. He isn't going to let me live.

Quickly and with as much strength as she could muster, Eliza brought her free arm down and aimed her fingers for Russell's eyes while bringing her knee into his groin. He uttered a loud, anguished cry, squeezing his eyes shut. He pulled back, his body coiling into a self-protective position.

Eliza tried to wriggle free, but the weight of his lower extremities kept her tethered. Able now to use her other arm, she reached over and dug into Russell's face with her fingernails. He screamed with pain, even as he regrouped and pinned her down again.

Oh, God, this can't be happening to me.

She knew she should keep fighting, but he was too big, too heavy, too strong. He was going to force himself on her, and there was nothing else she could do about it. Eliza closed her eyes to wait for the inevitable.

"Get off her, you animal!"

Eliza heard the man's booming voice.

"Get off her or I'll kill you."

Russell looked up at the man standing in the aviary doorway.

"You won't do that, Clay," he said.

"Just watch me," said Chief Vitalli, pulling his gun out of its holster. "I've caught you in the act this time. My days of protecting you are over. The years of covering for you and your family are over, too—even if it means I have to pay for what I've done. I've had enough."

Russell climbed off Eliza and stood up.

Clay looked down at her. "Are you all right, Ms. Blake?" he asked.

"Yes." Eliza nodded as she fixed her skirt. "Yes, I'm all right," she said. "You got here before he could finish what he started."

As Clay offered his hand to help Eliza get up, Russell sprang for the police chief. With split-second reflexes, Chief Vitalli pulled the gun's trigger. Russell Wheelock fell to the floor.

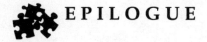 EPILOGUE

Eliza tapped on the sliding glass door of B.J.'s editing room.

"Ready?" she asked.

"It was a bear trying to keep it under two minutes, and I didn't include anything on the attack on you and Mack, thinking that you and Harry can discuss that on camera after the piece runs," said Annabelle as she handed the script to Eliza. "See what you think."

While B.J. fiddled with audio dials on the control panel in preparation for recording the narration, Eliza read the script to herself.

TRACK:

> IT'S A CASE THAT SPANS TWO DECADES, INVOLVING A BIZARRE
> SUICIDE, THE WEALTHY AND EXCLUSIVE COMMUNITY OF TUXEDO
> PARK, NEW YORK, AND AN INGENIOUS ARCHITECTURAL PUZZLE
> THAT THE ALLEGED KILLER DIDN'T WANT SOLVED. TWENTY-
> YEAR-OLD RUSSELL WHEELOCK, THE ONLY SON OF VALENTINA
> WHEELOCK, FORMER GOVERNOR OF NEW YORK AND AMBASSA-
> DOR TO ITALY, IS CHARGED WITH COMMITTING FOUR MURDERS.

THE MOTIVE? TO MAKE SURE THAT HIS REPUTATION REMAINED UNTARNISHED SO HE COULD FULFILL HIS DREAM OF A POLITICAL CAREER.

AN AWARD-WINNING ARCHITECT, THE WOMAN WHO WORKED AS HIS ASSISTANT, AND A ROMAN CATHOLIC PRIEST WERE KILLED, EACH IN DIFFERENT WAYS MIMICKING ASPECTS OF THE PASSION OF JESUS CHRIST. IN ADDITION, AN AUTOPSY REVEALED THAT VALENTINA WHEELOCK'S MAID DID NOT DIE FROM FALLING DOWN A FLIGHT OF STAIRS AS ORIGINALLY HAD BEEN THOUGHT. SHE WAS DELIBERATELY SUFFOCATED.

SINCE THE MURDER CHARGES WERE ANNOUNCED, SEVERAL YOUNG WOMEN HAVE COME FORWARD ACCUSING WHEELOCK OF RAPE.

SOUND BITE:

Dr. Margo Gonzalez, KEY News Consultant/Psychiatrist:

Rape is not about sex, it's about power, taking control and dominating another person. It's rooted in fear, disrespect, and anger toward women.

RUSSELL WHEELOCK'S DEFENSE TEAM CONTENDS HE HAD GOOD REASON TO BE ANGRY. HIS BIOLOGICAL FATHER WAS KILLED BY HIS MOTHER, A FACT THAT WHEELOCK SAYS HE DISCOVERED WHILE EAVESDROPPING AS A CHILD BUT WAS NEVER REVEALED BY EITHER OF THE PARENTS WHO RAISED HIM. THE DEFENSE IS ARGUING THAT WHEELOCK WAS DEEPLY AND IRREPARABLY SCARRED PSYCHOLOGICALLY AND DEVELOPED AN INTENSE, UNCONTROLLABLE HATRED OF WOMEN, WHICH LED TO THE RAPES. AT THE SAME TIME, BROUGHT UP TO BELIEVE THAT A CAREER IN POLITICS WAS HIS DESTINY, HE WAS DESPERATE THAT NO ONE FIND OUT ABOUT THE CRIMES HE'D COMMITTED.

VALENTINA WHEELOCK HAS ADMITTED THAT OVER TWENTY YEARS AGO SHE ACCIDENTALLY KILLED HER LOVER, MARTIN O'SHAUGHNESSY, WHILE THEY WERE ON THE WHEELOCKS' SAILBOAT. THREE ASSOCIATES HAVE ADMITTED COVERING UP THE MURDER BY STAGING THE CRASH OF O'SHAUGHNESSY'S CAR, SINKING THE BOAT, AND BURNING THE BODY BEFORE BURYING IT, ENSURING THAT IT WOULD NOT BE LINKED TO THE WHEELOCKS IF THE BOAT WAS EVER DISCOVERED. VALENTINA WHEELOCK IS FACING TRIAL, THOUGH THE PERPETRATORS OF THE COVER-UP ARE NOT, SAVED BY THE FIVE-YEAR STATUTE OF LIMITATIONS FOR OBSTRUCTION OF JUSTICE.

SOUND BITE:

William O'Shaughnessy/victim's brother:

It's horrible to imagine what he went through, but it's a relief to finally know what happened to Marty.

A KEY PIECE OF EVIDENCE IS A SECRETLY RECORDED VIDEO-TAPE, IN WHICH RUSSELL ADMITS TO RAPING THREE YOUNG WOMEN. THE TAPE WAS THE FINAL PIECE OF AN INTRICATE PUZZLE CREATED BY INNIS WHEELOCK BEFORE HE COMMITTED SUICIDE BY STIGMATA.

AT COMPETENCY HEARINGS, RUSSELL WHEELOCK'S ATTOR-NEYS HAVE ARGUED THAT THEIR CLIENT WAS SO MENTALLY DIS-TURBED THAT HE LACKED THE MENTAL CAPACITY TO COMMIT A CRIME. PROSECUTORS CONTEND THAT WHEELOCK KNEW EX-ACTLY WHAT HE WAS DOING. TODAY THE JUDGE WILL ANNOUNCE HER DECISION ON WHETHER WHEELOCK IS FIT TO STAND TRIAL.

"Nice script," said Eliza after she finished reading. "But there's no way this will run under two minutes," said Eliza.

Annabelle smiled sheepishly. "I know, but I was hoping that you'd see we need the time to tell it properly."

"You mean it'll be easier to convince Linus if I've already agreed?" asked Eliza.

"Exactly."

"Go for it," said Eliza.

As Annabelle called the executive producer to make her case for more time, Eliza reflected on what had happened. Innis had taken his life, four people had lost theirs, several others would never be the same again. So much pain had been inflicted, with more to come.

But the truth had been revealed. There was satisfaction in that, and in knowing she'd followed through for Innis, just as he'd predicted she would the night they sat beside the turtle fountain at Pentimento.

"Want to go out to lunch today?" asked Annabelle when Eliza finished recording the narration.

"No thanks," said Eliza. "I'm going straight home after the show. This is my last weekend with Mack before he goes back to London, and I need to savor every minute with him. This afternoon we're going to the Halloween parade at Janie's school. Despite everything that's happened, I want to see my own little St. Francis."

AUTHOR'S NOTE

There is no Black Tie Club in Tuxedo Park. In describing the fictitious Black Tie Club, I took certain liberties, inspired by the private club that does exist there and by other exclusive social clubs where prospective members yearn to gain admittance and sometimes never know exactly why they are denied.

St. Francis of Assisi's Canticle of the Sun was written in the thirteenth century. Translations from the medieval Italian vary.

"*Si trova tutto nel tavolo grande,*" the message in St. Francis's halo in the aviary fresco, means "All can be found in the large table."

ACKNOWLEDGMENTS

Puzzles are tangled and twisted and take time to solve. For me, at least, the writing process is like that. The ideas don't come in a straight line. Things that happened many years ago can come to the fore, finding expression in the present.

Growing up near Tuxedo Park, I was fascinated whenever we drove past the guarded entrance and wondered about the secret world beyond the gates. As an adult, I've had the chance to go inside and discover that what truly exists there is even more majestic and magical than the version conjured by my youthful imagination. I became haunted by the thought of evil lurking in this protected and idyllic place.

Tina McEvoy and Pam Graetzer shared their understanding of Tuxedo Park, showing me around and revealing one curious and marvelous location after another. It was with them that the story began to really come alive as I began to imagine my characters moving through that unique world. Many thanks as well to Jim Jospe, who very generously lent me his extensive collection of books about Tuxedo Park.

ACKNOWLEDGMENTS

Inspiration also came from the other side of the Atlantic Ocean. Trips to Italy aroused an interest in the life and death of St. Francis of Assisi along with an appreciation of all things Italian. While I was viewing the magnificent architecture, sculptures, frescoes, and ceramics in that fabulous country, the puzzle began to loosely take shape.

In brainstorming sessions, Father Paul Holmes shared his passion for Italy and extensive knowledge of religious history. Initially, the idea of suicide by stigmata took his breath away, but he seized on it with enthusiasm. If not for his reaction, I don't know if I would have felt secure enough to continue with the concept. Throughout the writing of this book, he offered wonderfully creative ideas, exacting research, and unflagging encouragement. *Tante, tante grazie*, Paolo, for all that you do.

Criminal defense attorney Joseph Hayden graciously answered some last-minute questions about the legal ramifications of my characters' dastardly deeds. I owe you and Katharine a dinner, Joe.

Fortunately, Carrie Feron is my editor. She did an expert job of trimming, tightening, and making the manuscript better. The story is stronger and more suspenseful because of her considerable talent and skill. Once again, Carrie and her trusted assistant, Tessa Woodward, carefully shepherded the book through all its stages. Their professionalism is greatly appreciated.

Maureen Sugden copyedited with exacting care. Her notes were a joy to read and consider. Thanks to Mary Schuck and Richard Aquan for designing an enticing cover. I'm very grateful for the support of everyone at William Morrow, including Liate Stehlik, Lynn Grady, Sharyn Rosenblum, Nicole Chismar, Bobby Brinson, and Virginia Stanley.

Beth Tindall designs and runs maryjaneclark.com, while Colleen Kenny produces the much-commented-on "movie trailers." Thanks to them for making it possible for me to enjoy the benefits of all their hard work.

Jennifer Rudolph Walsh and Joni Evans are still guiding my writing career. Between them, they offer the best of everything: experience, business acumen, pragmatism, wisdom, and sage editorial advice. It is an invaluable asset to be able to call on them.

And finally, my boundless thanks to Peggy Gould. She knows why.